A Senseless Killing

A Detective Inspector Benedict Paige Novel:
Book 6

Joshua Black

Rathbone Publishing

Copyright © 2023 Joshua Black

All rights reserved.
ISBN- 9781739573829

All rights reserved.

No part of this publication may be reproduced, distributed, or transmitted in any form or by any means, including photocopying, recording, or other electronic or mechanical methods, without the prior written permission from the author except for the use of quotations in a book review.

This is a work of fiction. Names, characters, and incidents portrayed in this production are fictitious. Any resemblance to actual persons (living or deceased), or actual events is purely coincidental.

Joshua Black

Joshua Black is the pen name of Rupert Colley.

Rupert is the author of ten historical novels, all set during the 20th century.

The Love and War Series
The Lost Daughter
Song of Sorrow
The White Venus
The Woman on the Train
My Brother the Enemy
The Black Maria
Anastasia
Elena
The Mist Before Our Eyes
The Darkness We Leave Behind

The Searight Saga
This Time Tomorrow
The Unforgiving Sea
The Red Oak

rupertcolley.com

A Senseless Killing

R
Rathbone
Publishing

rupertcolley.com/joshua-black/

Prologue
Today

He knew exactly what to do and where to go. He'd been fully briefed. The man of the house would be out; he went out every Tuesday evening. His daughter would be over to babysit but she always had her boyfriend in; she'd be too distracted to notice.

He slipped on his gloves and inserted the key into the backdoor. It yielded with ease, not a sound escaping to betray his presence. He crept in, his haversack slung over his shoulder. He was told he'd find himself in a boot room. Sure enough, it had a tiled floor and plenty of hooks and racks for hanging coats, hats, scarves and bags. He removed his trainers with the utmost care, as if any sudden movement would awaken the house itself, and found the staircase. Yes, he could hear music and voices coming from a room nearby, a man and a woman having what sounded like an earnest conversation. He spotted the faint thread of light seeping beneath the door. He puffed out his cheeks, his breath hitching in his throat. It only needed for one of them to come out now and he'd be done for.

He crept up the stairs, avoiding the fourth step, as told, the dimness of the house adding to its sinister aura.

Second door on the left. He eased the door open and stepped in. Yes, she was there, lying in her bed, a carved wooden bed frame, her hands on the quilted bedspread. A side lamp cast a feeble, wavering glow, revealing her long, sallow face, etched with deep lines, her lips thin and grey, as if touched by the spectre of death itself.

She was awake, perfectly tranquil. Her eyes fixed on him with an unsettling intensity. If she was surprised to see him, she didn't show it. He whispered a hello and flashed her an apologetic smile. She didn't respond, but her eyes followed him as he moved through the room. He approached the dresser, its mirror framed with ornate details, a collection of delicate porcelain figurines adorning its surface.

He was told there'd be a tiny key in the small drawer beneath the mirror. Yes, it was there. The key opened the bottom drawer on the right. He slid the drawer open to reveal a trove of jewellery boxes. He didn't have time to check their contents. Instead, he stuffed them into his haversack.

He had to leave. The old woman was still watching him but still not a sound came from her. He noticed her hand grip the bedspread. He felt an unsettling pity for her, depriving her of her cherished possessions. But still, she wasn't long for this world. It's not as if you can take it with you. He relocked the drawer and returned the key to its place. A sudden series of thumps made him jump. He spun around – the woman had a walking stick in her hand and was slamming it against the floor. His heart pounding, he dashed out, closing the bedroom door behind him. He heard the door downstairs open, the clear echo of voices. His heart somersaulted. Footsteps on the stairs. He darted into the nearest room, quickly closing the door behind him. He found himself in a bathroom. He slid the lock closed.

He heard footsteps trotting up the stairs and going into the old woman's bedroom; he heard the woman, presumably the daughter, asking her if the old woman was alright and something about taking her medicine. Please don't come to the bathroom, he thought, his skin clammy with sweat. The woman seemed to be taking an age. Everything had gone quiet. What was she doing in there? He urged her to hurry.

Finally, finally, he heard the woman close the bedroom door, wishing her mother a good night, a whispered promise of care. This was it, the moment of reckoning. He held onto his breath, his heart pounding. Luckily, she returned downstairs. Oh, the relief.

The music downstairs was turned up a couple of notches, some dreadful tune by Ed Sheeran.

That was OK, it meant he could slip out of the house unnoticed, like a malevolent shadow retreating into the darkness, leaving behind the unscrupulous remnants of his intrusion, and he'd be several thousand pounds richer, the tainted spoils of his nefarious mission.

Chapter 1: Susan
An hour earlier

Susan couldn't wait for her father to leave the house. He said he was meeting a friend and wouldn't be back until late. The implication here was that this was just a friend, a male friend, but Susan suspected it was, in fact, a woman. But she held her tongue; this was not a discussion she wanted right now. She just wanted him to leave so she could get on with her evening, an evening she'd been dreading but had to face up to. Her father had dressed up for his evening out – collar and tie, a dark green jacket she hadn't seen before. He reeked of aftershave. 'You've put in a lot of effort for your friend,' she said. 'Have I met him, your friend? What's his name?'

'Patrick. You've met him a couple of times, I think.'

'Patrick? Scottish guy, big beard.'

'That's the one.'

'Didn't know you were such good friends.'

'Susan, have you seen my phone? Can you ring it? No, wait, here it is.'

He hadn't mislaid his phone, he was simply trying to

change the subject. He patted his pockets. 'Right, now are you sure you'll be OK?'

'Don't worry. All's cool.'

'Main thing is you don't forget her medicine. I've left instructions.'

'I know, Daddy, I know. You've told me a hundred times.'

'Don't exaggerate. I've told you a million times.'

'Very funny.'

'Right, I'll be off. Any problems with Mum, just give me a ring.'

He kissed her goodbye. 'Have fun,' she said.

He hesitated, picking up on her tone. 'Yeah. Thanks. Don't wait up.'

At last, Susan had the house to herself. She wondered who her father was really meeting. There was no way he was meeting Patrick. She'd long suspected he was seeing someone. He'd been behaving differently recently, more cheerful, a spring in his step. In some ways, she didn't blame him; it'd been a long time since he had a 'proper' wife. But it didn't make it right; Mum was still here, still living at home. It wasn't her fault she was so poorly.

She checked on her mother, knocking on the bedroom door before entering. 'Hi, Mum, you OK?'

Her mother gazed at her with that faraway look she always had. Her bedspread had slipped to one side, leaving her partially exposed. She rearranged the covers, making her comfortable. 'There you are,' she said. 'That's better, isn't it?' She patted her mother's hand. 'Daddy's meeting a friend tonight. That's nice for him, isn't it? Do you remember him? A Scotsman. Patrick. So, I'll just be downstairs watching the telly. I'm not going anywhere.'

Her mother showed no sign of response.

Returning downstairs, Susan texted Robbie: *Coast clear. Come over now if you can.*

The response was immediate: *On my way.*

She rushed back upstairs to her room, passing her parent's bedroom. She got changed quickly, swapping her old shirt for something more alluring, tighter around the chest. She brushed her hair and applied a hint of makeup, not too much. She wanted to look nice for her lover but not come across as if she'd put too much effort into how she looked. She applied her favourite perfume, a Christmas present from Robbie.

She was dying for a drink, a nice glass of red wine, but she hadn't touched a drop since she found out. How was Robbie going to take it? The news had come as a shock; they'd always been so careful. She still wasn't sure what to think of it. It would certainly make things more complicated, especially for Robbie. But, on the whole, she welcomed it. She wasn't getting any younger. And it would force Robbie's hand. He was stuck in his loveless marriage but too fearful to actually do something about it. Well, now, one way or the other, he had to. She hadn't seen him for a few days so hadn't had a chance to tell him. Tonight was the night. She wasn't relishing the prospect. She was a good five years older than her boyfriend; she was heading for thirty-five. She needed to keep this baby.

She heard his knock on the front door. She rushed downstairs, buoyed by the thought of seeing him again. He breezed in, his hair tousled, his face flushed. 'You look nice,' he said, kissing her on the cheek. 'So, how long have we got?'

'Hours and hours.'

'Fantastic.' He hugged her. 'Got any wine on the go?'

'Sure.'

He fell onto the settee. 'Bloody hell, what a day.'

'Anything wrong?' asked Susan, as she opened the wine.

'You could say that. Hellish day at work. The shit hit the fan today. Tucker was testing a car and the stupid bastard scraped it against a bollard. You can imagine what the customer said. Aren't you drinking?' he asked.

'No, don't feel like it.'

'Really? Bloody hell, never thought I'd hear you say that.'

Susan shouted at her Alexis speaker, asking for the best of Elton John. Robbie proceeded to tell her about his 'hellish' day. He worked as a mechanic and Tucker was one of his colleagues. Susan, only half-listening, handed him his wine. Sitting on the settee next to him, she sympathised as he related his tale.

'Anyway,' she said once he'd finished his tale of woe. 'You're here now.'

'Yeah.' He put his wine down. 'So, you've got rid of the old man. How is he?'

Robbie hadn't met her father but he was asking as if they were familiar with each other. She was not prepared to tell him that she suspected her father was meeting another woman. Instead, she answered banally.

'And how's your mum?'

'I ought to go check on her. Daddy's worried. He doesn't trust me.'

'What could go wrong? She spends all her life asleep anyway.'

That hurt. Robbie had no right to speak of her like that. She hadn't always been like this, ravaged by this cruel disease; she'd once been a happy, confident, lovely woman. But Robbie hadn't known her then. To him, she was just an old woman who had no choice but to spend most of her life in bed.

'I've missed you.' He put his arm around her. She nestled into him. 'I've been thinking about you.'

'Oh yes? In what way?'

'Naked.'

'Oh, Robbie, stop it.'

'So, er…' He brushed his lips across her cheek. 'We've got plenty of time then?' His hand crept up towards her breasts.

'Robbie.' She knew he'd want sex, they usually ended up in bed, but not this time. 'We need to speak first.'

'Speak about what? We can talk later.' He kissed her again. 'I've missed you, baby.'

She pulled away from him.

'Hey? What's up?'

She stood. 'Look, we don't have to have sex every time you come around.'

He looked puzzled. 'Why not?'

'We can just…'

'What? What do you want to do?'

'I don't know. We can talk, watch telly.'

'God.'

'What?'

'That's so dull. That's what I do with Margot. So, what do you want to talk about? What's been happening on the news?'

'How is Margot?'

'I don't want to talk about her.'

'No. You never do.' And this, thought Susan, was the problem. They had no one in common. None of their respective friends knew the other existed. Theirs was a relationship in the vacuum and once you took away the sex, it didn't leave much.

'Come on, Susie, sit down. You know you want to.'

'No, Robbie, I don't. Not tonight.'

'I don't want to watch the bloody TV.'

'We'll talk then.'

'Christ.' Robbie drank his wine.

'Actually, there is something…'

The loud thud on the ceiling took them both by surprise.

'What the hell was that?' asked Robbie, his eyes staring upwards.

'Oh God, I'd better go and check.' Susan ran upstairs. That was one loud thud. Maybe Mum had fallen out of bed. It had happened before. Christ, let her be OK. She barged into the bedroom. 'Mum? Mum, are you OK?'

Her mother was in bed, wide awake, sitting up, but she seemed alright. 'Did you fall out of bed, Mum?'

'They were here,' she said in her shaky voice. Her eyes were wide with fright.

'Who? Who was here?'

She pointed towards the window. 'They were here.'

'Who, Mum?' She clearly looked agitated. Something or someone had spooked her. She checked the window behind the curtains. They were locked. 'There we are,' she said, returning to her mother's bed. 'The window's locked. You must be imagining things, Mum.'

Suddenly, reaching over, her mother gripped her daughter's arm with both her hands with surprising strength. 'Don't leave me, Susie. Don't leave me.'

'It's OK, Mum. It's OK.' She sat on the side of the bed, holding her mother's hand. 'There's nothing to worry about. Just a bad dream.' Yes, that was all it was, a dream.

'Don't leave me.'

'I won't leave you.'

Susan looked at the time on her mother's digital clock. Ten thirty. She sat there, on her mother's bed, holding her hand, conscious that Robbie was in the living room, waiting for her. The minutes ticked by, the red numbers flipping over. Her mother was drifting off, her breathing slower and deeper, but as soon as Susan tried to move, Mum's grip on her hand tightened. She wondered what her mother had meant. Had it just been a dream? Of course, what other explanation was there? Several more minutes passed. And as she sat there, holding her mother's hand, waiting for her to fall asleep, the cruel realisation seeped into her – Robbie didn't love her, he didn't see a future with her. To him, their relationship was just about sex. Nothing more than that.

Her mother's hand slipped away. She was asleep now. Susan was about to kiss her mother goodnight when her mobile pinged. A text from Robbie: *Sorry gotta go. Something's come up. See u soon.*

Well, that just confirmed it. The bastard.

Chapter 2: Tammy
Annecy, France, ten years ago

Tamsin Fournier was still flushed with shame that she'd spent half an hour the night before going through her husband's phone trying to find evidence that he was seeing another woman. The signs were there – he was spending longer at the office, he'd brought some new clothes, which in itself was a definite red flag in her book, he took more care of his appearance, keeping his beard trim. Last night, he did get in from work at the usual time but, he said, he was tired. They ate and watched the old war film with Jack Hawkins, *Bridge Over the River Kwai*, on TV with English subtitles. Eric liked a war film. Tammy was French and although her English was good, she would have struggled with the film if it hadn't been for the subtitles. As soon as the film was over, Eric went to bed. It was still only ten o'clock, unusually early.

'Are you OK, Eric?' she asked in French.

'Absolutely fine,' he snapped. 'Why shouldn't I be?'

'Oh, I don't know,' she said, adopting a light tone. 'You seem a little…'

'A little what?'

'Distracted of late.'

'Me? No. You're imagining things, *mon petit chou-fleur.*' My little cauliflower. It sounded ridiculous in English but somehow, in French, it worked. Nonetheless, it didn't fool her for a minute.

Tammy waited downstairs, half watching a documentary until she was sure her husband would be properly asleep. Creeping into the bedroom, she stole his mobile from his bedside table and took it downstairs. She knew his passcode as indeed, he knew hers. She braced herself, convinced she'd find something. She started off by checking his text messages. Nothing unusual, no names she didn't know or at least recognise. There were a couple of unknown telephone numbers which she wrote down on a scrap of paper. Nothing suspicious on his camera roll, no shots of any young beauties, just lots of photos of their girls and holiday snaps. She checked his Facebook account. He rarely used it and there was nothing untoward there. Eric only did Facebook, he didn't understand Instagram or any of the others. Having concluded there was no evidence of infidelity on her husband's phone, Tammy didn't know whether to be relieved or disappointed. She returned the mobile to the bedside table and smiled down at her sleeping husband.

Now, waking up in the cold light of day, Tammy felt rather foolish. Eric was in the ensuite, having a shower and singing *Raindrops Keep Fallin' On My Head* rather tunelessly. Eric never used to sing. No, stop, she told herself, this was stupid.

'Oh, I'm afraid I've got another meeting tonight,' he said, coming out of the shower, a towel wrapped around his midriff.

'Oh really? Eric?'

'I know, I'm sorry. Don't worry about dinner; I'll grab something at work. But I'm telling you, if we get this contract, it'll be worth it.'

'And if you don't?'

'That's the risk we take. But, like they say, you've got to be in it to win it. Now, what do you think, which tie? The red or the green.'

'Green. Always green.'

He smiled.

Eric was a partner at a firm of architects and had always done well but not so much recently. They'd lost a couple of contracts and although it wasn't affecting them personally, there was always fear that one day, it might.

'What are your plans today?'

'I'll do a bit of housework and then I'm meeting Olivia for coffee.'

'Lovely. Lovely.'

Tammy worked as a chemistry teacher but being early August, she was enjoying her long summer holidays, at least she would have been if she wasn't so knotted up about her husband.

Why is it, Tammy wondered, that housework is always harder and more tedious when you've got plenty of time to do it? They lived in a fine townhouse in Annecy, an Alpine town in eastern France, only 35 kilometres from Geneva.

She and Eric had been married for almost twenty-eight years; it'd soon be their silver wedding anniversary. He was still a dashing man, his greying hair, neatly combed and slightly receding at the temples, added to his distinguished appearance. He often sported designer glasses and had a deep, resonant voice that carried authority and charisma. She loved him and she knew he loved her. She had no doubts about that but ultimately, Eric was a man, a good-looking man who invariably caught the eye of his younger, female colleagues and clients. And for that, Tammy was worried. Very worried.

*

Tammy and Olivia were meeting in a pleasant, upmarket café in *Centreville*, a place Tammy frequented often and where the staff, dressed in black and white, knew her by her surname. Olivia hadn't turned up yet but Tammy was early. She sat outside, lit a cigarette and wondered whether it was wise to voice her concerns about Eric to her friend. After all, Olivia had enough issues of her own, having recently split up from her husband, Yves. But equally, it meant Olivia was well qualified to offer advice and sympathy. Actually, the split hadn't been recent; it had been two years, maybe three, but, to Tammy, it still felt recent. She and Eric liked Yves and they hadn't seen him since, and frankly, they missed him. There was a simplicity about Yves, the sort of man who was easy to like while Olivia could be hard work and at times dreadfully vain, a vanity that took a massive knock when her husband walked out on her.

And here she was, looking slightly flustered under the glare of the hot August sun. Tammy stood and the two women kissed. Though she showed signs of weariness from her struggles, Olivia's face retained an undeniable allure. Her chestnut brown hair, once lustrous, now had a hint of silver, adding to her dignified aura.

They ordered their coffees, but nothing to eat, and talked, catching up on news, namely their daughters. Tammy had two daughters – Susan and Elizabeth or, as she preferred, Lizzie, both in their mid-twenties now, while Olivia had the one girl, a seventeen-year-old called Francine. Francine was due to start at a new six-form college come September and she was not looking forward to it one bit.

The women were onto their second cups of coffee when Tammy nervously brought up the subject. 'Olivia, you've spoken to Eric recently, tell me, have you noticed anything?'

'What do you mean?'

Tammy took a while to answer, choosing her words carefully. 'Something's wrong and I can't put my finger on it.'

'What do you mean wrong?' She knew already, simply from her deeper tone of voice, the narrowing of her eyes.

'It's probably nothing but—'

'You think he's having an affair, don't you?'

Tammy didn't mean to cry and hadn't expected to but it was hearing the 'A' word that set her off.

Olivia reached across the table and took her hand. 'What makes you so sure?'

Had she said she was sure? No, she hadn't, so why did her friend immediately assume the worst? Because she'd been through it, of course. 'He's been acting differently of recent. I'm sure of it. No, not sure but…'

'Oh, my poor darling, Eric wouldn't cheat on you. Surely.'

Tammy hated the way she'd added that final word, somehow it implied the very opposite. 'I just don't know what to think.'

'What makes you think he's cheating on you?'

Tammy proceeded to describe what were to her the tell-tale signs. Olivia listened, nodding. When Tammy had finished, Olivia said, 'Have you checked his phone?'

'Yes but there was nothing on it, nothing at all.'

'Maybe you've got it wrong.'

Tammy shook her head. 'I don't think so. You know when

you feel it in your gut.'

'Oh yes, I remember that feeling all too well.'

'What do I do?'

'Have it out with him. Ask him straight. He'll deny it, of course, but it's the *way* he denies it – you'll know within a nanosecond.'

'You think so?'

'I know so.'

'I don't think I could bear it.'

'You think it'd be worse than what you're suffering now? No, best to know. Then you know what you're dealing with.'

'And if he is?'

'You chuck him out or he leaves of his own accord or you start again. It can be done, you know, my darling. It's not impossible. And if all that fails…'

'Yes?'

'You kill the bitch.'

Chapter 3: Eric
Today

This was the only moment in his life that Eric missed smoking – that delicious, post-coital fag. He lay on the bed, his hands behind his head and imagined lighting a cigarette and relishing that initial hit of nicotine.

'A penny for your thoughts,' said Angela.

'Oh, nothing really. Just enjoying the moment.'

Lying on her side, she rested her hand on his chest. 'It's lovely, isn't it? You have a lot of stamina for an old man.'

'Hey, you, less of the old.'

She laughed. 'Listen, Eric, I've got tickets for the Lucien Freud exhibition tomorrow at the Tate. Me and my sister. But something's come up and she can't make it now. Would you like to come?' She patted his chest. 'Go on, say yes, Eric. Make me happy.'

'No, I'm sorry, Ang. No can do. I've got to take Tammy for one of her appointments.'

'OK, short notice, I know. It was just on the off chance. No matter. But I've got something special planned which is why I'm giving you lots of notice.'

He was dreading this. He really didn't like being dragged around London. 'What exactly?'

'Madam Butterfly at the ENO next month. There might be some tickets left. What do you say?'

He could do without this. He hated the opera. 'I'm not sure,' he said, desperately trying to think of a plausible excuse. 'I'd have to check my calendar.'

'Oh, Eric, honestly. There's always something.' Angela rolled out of bed, standing stark naked. 'You do that, Eric. You check your calendar. I'm going to have a shower.' He watched as she padded over to the ensuite.

Eric groaned. She deserved better, he knew that, but he'd got to that age now where all he wanted to do was put his feet up in the evening and watch the telly. He didn't want to go gallivanting around town, going to art exhibitions and the theatre and especially not the opera. He could hear the shower coming on. He was tempted to join her but he was in her bad books now, so much for the warm afterglow of sex.

Angela, ten years younger, needed her social life. Nothing she liked better than documenting her life on Facebook, showing the world what a culture vulture she was. Angela was always doing something – she belonged to a book group, she volunteered at the local library and did a stint each week at a charity shop. She was forever going into town and doing things. She had her sister and she had her friends, lots of them, so why did she need him to tag along? Tammy was always his excuse and she never questioned that, but once Tammy was gone…

Angela emerged from the shower, combing her wet hair, a towel around her. 'So, how is she?' she asked clearly still disgruntled.

'She? *She* has a name, you know.'

'How is your darling wife?'

'Much the same. No better. Susan's keeping an eye on her tonight.'

'Well, that's great.' She continued combing her hair sitting at her dresser. 'That means you could stay the night,' she said via the dresser mirror.

'The whole night? No, I… I can't.' He got out of bed and looked for his underpants and socks.

She rolled her eyes. 'So, you're just going to bugger off again.'

They'd had this conversation before. 'Oh, come on, Angela, you know I can't stay. As much as I'd like to.' Which wasn't exactly true; he never wanted to stay, preferring to sleep by himself in his own bed.

'Look, just phone your daughter, tell her you won't be back tonight, no need to give a reason, and tell her she has to stay. It's not as if she's got anything at home, is there?'

Sitting on the bed in his underwear, Eric said, 'Look, it's not just that. I've said before, it's…'

'I know, I know. You don't want to stay the night while Tammy is still alive; that it would feel wrong. And yet, you're happy to pop over and fuck me every week, but no, apparently sleeping the night is a different matter, a different kettle of fish.'

Eric got dressed quickly. 'I'm sorry.' He needed to get out quickly now before Angela lost her temper with him. He kissed the top of her head. 'You know, I rather like the idea of Madame Butterfly.'

'You do?' She perked up. 'Oh, great, OK. I'll try and get some tickets if it isn't too late. I'll let you know.'

'I'd better go.'

'Do you have to? Stay with me, have a glass of wine.'

'I can't, Ang. It's late and I need to relieve Susan from her duties.'

'Why can't you just put her in a home?'

'Susan? I don't—'

'Don't be silly, Eric. You could afford it.'

'You think so? Have you seen the prices of those places? It's mad. I mean, OK, I know I'll have to one day soon but while I can put it off, while I can keep her at home, why spend all that money?'

'Because you'd be free of the burden?'

Didn't she realise how mercenary she was sounding? 'I can't. Not until I have to.'

'OK, OK, you go home to her then like the dutiful carer you are.'

'Dutiful husband, Ang.'

'Yes, right, if that's how you see yourself, fine, so be it.'

He kissed her head again. 'I'll see you soon, love.' She twisted her head away a fraction, a small but definite sign that she hadn't forgiven him yet.

It was only a five-minute drive back home. Usually, he walked it, enjoying the fresh air. And why, he asked himself as he drove, had he said he liked Madam Butterfly? Now, if she managed to get a couple of tickets, he'd have no excuse. But right then, in her bedroom, he was on the ropes and he needed something to distract her from her resentment of him going home every time they had sex. He'd been moments from a major character assassination. Madam Butterfly had, in effect, saved him.

He parked the car on the gravelled drive in front of the house next to Susan's Volvo V40. He and Tammy had lived in this large, 1920s detached house some ten years now, ever since they moved to London from France. It was a fine house. He still liked it here and had no intention of ever moving out. But it almost happened. For years, Tammy had said she was bored with London life and wanted to move to the country. She wanted fresh air, she said, walks in the countryside, a slower way of life. They fought over it to the point she almost got her way. If she hadn't got Alzheimer's, they'd be living in some cottage now, quaint but dull. Eric may shun London's cultural life but he did not want to be living at the arse-end of nowhere, miles from civilisation, thank you very much. He knew people around here; the neighbours were decent and he was within easy reach of at least one of his daughters. And, what's more, he loved his house, it contained too many memories simply to sell up and start afresh elsewhere.

He walked into the house surprised by how quiet everything seemed. He expected the television to be on, at least, or the radio. Susan didn't like silence, so where was she, what was she doing? Eric crept into the living room and found his daughter fast asleep on the settee, her mouth wide open, one arm draped down, her mobile on her stomach. He hoped she had remembered to give her mother her bedtime medicine.

He spied something beneath the settee. Creeping over, not wanting to wake Susan, he picked up a flat cap. It was a man's cap, the sort of farmer would wear, so the question was – whose was it? Had Susan invited a man over? She better have not. He left the cap on the armrest.

He was about to wake her up when her phone flashed silently with a notification – a text message. *Maybe next week*, it said. He tried to see who it was from but the screen blacked out. He should wake her up and tell her she could go home now but first, he thought, he'd go check on Tammy.

Tammy would be fast asleep now. She slept in their bedroom still. Eric had moved into the spare bedroom soon after her diagnosis. He decided it was for the best, Tammy needed space. Also, since her diagnosis, she'd sometimes wake up in the middle of the night and disorientated would lash out at him.

He knocked on the door – he always did, and entered. She was asleep, just as he expected. Fast asleep. He crept towards the bed despite knowing she'd never wake up. Her dreams might wake her up but not noise, not once she'd had her medicine. He gazed down at her. She looked pale, she didn't look well at all. Even in her sleep, she looked tormented. The carefree, hippy-ish wife he'd known and loved for so long was no longer. Someone else had taken her place, had hollowed her out from within. Alzheimer's was a cruel, merciless disease.

Eric had been looking at Tammy for a whole minute, lost in thought, before he realised that she wasn't breathing. 'Shit.' He touched her hand. Cold. 'Oh, shit, no, no, no.' Picking up her limp arm, he tried to find a pulse. There wasn't one. 'Oh, God. Tammy.' He shook her, gently at first, then more vigorously. 'Tammy? Tammy, please, wake up. Tammy, oh God, wake up, will you? Tammy? Tammy! TAMMY!'

Chapter 4: Eric
Today

Sitting on the bed beside his wife, Eric found it difficult to control his shaking hands as he called for an ambulance. He wasn't sure why he was bothering. He knew Tammy was dead. Dead while he was out cavorting with his 'other woman'. God, he should have stayed at home. He wasn't there for her when she breathed her last. He'd go to Hell for this.

He could hear Susan downstairs. She was awake. She called up the stairs, 'Dad? Is that you? Are you back?'

Why had she been asleep? Who'd been here with her? He patted Tammy's hand. 'I'm sorry, Tam,' he said quietly. 'I should've been here for you. I'm so sorry,' He joined Susan downstairs. 'She's dead.'

'What?'

'Your mother, Susan. While you were having a nap down here, your poor mother has died.'

Susan paled. 'Are you... No. No, that can't be.'

'Go and check if you like.'

Her eyes shot up the stairs.

'You think I've got it wrong? I'm many things, Susan, but I'm not stupid.'

'Why are you talking to me like that?'

'Because you should have been looking after her instead of–'

'Instead of what? It's hardly my fault, is it? Be nice to me, Dad.'

'Oh, do shut up, Susan. You're hardly my concern right now.'

'We should call for an ambulance, a doctor–'

'I already have. They're on their way. I need a drink.' Going to the drinks trolley, he poured himself a hefty measure of whisky. Susan hovered at the bottom of the stairs, looking up. 'Go on, go see her.'

'I'm not sure–'

'You should. You have to. Don't worry, she doesn't look any different. Go on, go say goodbye to your mother.'

He watched as she slowly ascended the stairs. He went to the kitchen, needing water for his whisky. There, on the kitchen island, a half bottle of red wine and, in the sink, a dirty wine glass. He shook his head.

Returning to the living room, he paced over to the window, drawing back the drapes. He looked out over the garden and spied a fox which looked up, concerned by the sudden infusion of light. It slunk away. Tammy was dead. It didn't seem real. The world seemed to have stopped turning. Sipping his whisky, he wondered why Tammy had died. He could only assume she'd suffered a heart attack. But then, she'd never had any problems with her heart and it wasn't as if she had a family history of heart problems. Yes, she had Alzheimer's but it wasn't that bad, not as yet.

He could hear Susan upstairs weeping. He shouldn't have taken it out of her; like she said, this wasn't her fault. No one could have predicted this and it could have happened at any time. He'd have to ring Elizabeth, Susan's older sister, not that she ever got on with her mother, or him. He hadn't seen Lizzie for a couple of years and hadn't spoken to her either. She had a business down in Bournemouth. She rarely kept in touch. In fact, there'd always been a distance between himself, his wife and their two daughters. They'd never been a close-knit family. They had a family WhatsApp group that hadn't been touched in months.

He received a text from Angela, hoping he'd got back OK and saying she'd enjoyed the evening. He started to text back, *Me too but Tammy's dead and…* No, he couldn't send that. Even by his standards, it came across as too mercenary. He deleted it.

Susan joined him in the living room. Her eyes were red. 'I can't believe it. What did she die of?'

'How in the hell should I know?'

'I'm only asking, Dad. I'm only asking.' She blew her nose. 'She looks…'

'What?'

'I don't know. Frightened, almost. Dad, she said someone had been there. She pointed towards the window and I checked but the window was locked.'

'Someone? Who?'

'I don't know. She didn't say except that *they*'d been there. I asked her who she meant but she didn't say.'

'Yes, exactly, no one was there to look after her at the end. She had to face it by herself.'

'I wasn't to know. Stop making it sound as if it was my fault.'

'You didn't hear anything?'

'Like what?'

'A cry or something.'

'No.' She sat on the armchair. They both pricked up their ears on hearing the distant sound of a siren.

'So, who was here then?' he asked.

Her eyes darted to one side. 'What do you mean?'

'Don't play me for a fool, Susan.'

She noticed the cap on the settee armrest and realised she'd been rumbled. She sighed. 'A friend.'

'Oh? And does she have a name, this friend?'

'You wouldn't know her.'

'Try me.'

'It doesn't matter, right?'

'She?'

'Yes.'

Pointedly, he looked at the cap, the man's cap. The ambulance drew up outside. 'So no doubt, you and your friend were drinking and playing loud music so even if your mother had–'

'No! No, Dad. We didn't play music, we just talked. I would have heard.'

'Did you remember to give Mum her medicine?'

'Yes, of course I did.'

Finishing his drink, he went to open the front door. The two paramedics, one man, one woman, greeted him. He escorted them up the stairs. 'She's through here.'

They thanked him. He waited at the bedroom door as they approached the bed. The woman took Tammy's hand and, feeling her wrist, shook her head. Her colleague nudged her. They noticed Eric standing there, watching them. They glanced at each other. The man approached, 'Sir, do you mind if we have a quiet chat between ourselves for a moment?'

'Really. Is there–'

'Maybe you could wait downstairs. We won't be long.'

'Is something wrong?'

'We just need to discuss something. Sir, please…'

He wasn't happy about this but didn't feel as if he could refuse, so reluctantly he returned to the living room where he found Susan drawing the drapes.

He knew he'd been too sharp with his daughter, after all, she'd lost her mother here, but she was lying to him, and he didn't like that. She was up to something.

'Will they take her away?'

'Not sure. I think you need a doctor's say-so before they can do that. They'll tell us in a moment.'

'I can't believe she's gone.'

'She left us a long time ago, Susan.'

'I know but still.'

He could see the pain in her eyes, the incomprehension of why he was being so off with her. 'Why is there only one glass in the sink then?' he asked.

'What do you mean?'

'Did your friend not want a drink?'

'She did. It was me, Dad. I didn't drink.'

'You?' He didn't believe that. He'd always considered his youngest daughter to be a borderline alcoholic. 'Blimey, that must be a first.'

'I didn't feel like it,' she said defiantly. She brushed off a bit of fluff from her jumper. 'Anyway, I wanted to remain alert, you know, in case Mum needed me.'

'Oh, really? Well, that went well.'

That stung, he could tell. She didn't know how to respond

but she looked close to tears.

'It was a man, wasn't it?'

'No,' she shrieked. 'Anyway, it's none of your business, Dad.'

'On account, you're in my house, I'd suggest it's very much my business.'

'It wasn't a man.'

'What was her name then?'

'No one you know.'

'Try me.'

'Shirley, if you must know. Any the wiser? No.'

The two paramedics came into the living room, exchanging muted hellos with Susan. They looked worried about something. The woman walked right up to him, almost causing Eric to step back. 'Can we have a word, sir?'

'Is there anything wrong?'

'Can we sit down for a moment?'

'Yes, sure.' He invited her to sit on the settee. He sat next to her, slightly conscious that they were very close to one another. 'What is it you wanted to say?'

'I'm not sure how to break this to you, sir.'

OK, he was truly worried now but surely the worst that could happen had already happened. 'Is there anything wrong?'

The woman took a deep breath and glanced up at her colleague. 'Sir, we don't believe your wife died of natural causes.'

His heart stopped. 'What do you mean?'

'Sir, I'm sorry to have to tell you this but at this stage, we believe your wife was suffocated.'

Chapter 5: Eric
Annecy, France, ten years ago

Eric sat in the restaurant, sipping water, waiting for Olivia. She was usually late but not *this* late. This was their usual meeting place, *Le Petit Bouchon*, a delightful, tucked away place that exuded a rustic and inviting ambience, with exposed wooden beams, chequered tablecloths, and vintage décor. Soft, warm lighting created an intimate setting perfect for a romantic dinner. He'd been here with Tammy as well but not for a while; it'd become the place for him and Olivia. He and Olivia should never have happened and if her husband hadn't walked out of their marriage, it wouldn't. He always liked Yves but he hadn't seen him since the split. Olivia had a daughter, Francine, and he hadn't seen for some time. Olivia liked to keep him at arm's length. She had her life; he had his. That was fine by him; he had no desire to become a pseudo-father to, by all accounts, a now sullen, angry young girl. Olivia was a headmistress in a local secondary school and two years ago, she and a school governor approached Eric's architectural firm about expanding their premises. Three days later, they bumped into each other in a dry cleaner, not the most romantic of meetings but that's where it all started. He didn't love Olivia he only loved Tammy, but Olivia made him feel good about himself and he liked that, what man wouldn't, and she was warm and witty. But there was no way he would ever contemplate leaving his wife for her. And he didn't think Olivia expected him to. They were happy with how things were; why upset the apple cart?

The restaurant was almost full, even on a midweek evening, the place was always popular. In the corner, a tuxedo-wearing man was playing the piano adding to the genteel atmosphere.

A whole twenty minutes late, Olivia finally turned up. He stood on seeing her; she liked his old-fashioned courtesy. She looked stylish, as always, wearing a crisp white blouse and slim-fitting trousers. He smiled as she approached, a smile that died on his lips on seeing her expression. 'Are you OK?' he asked, aware of the slight tremor in his voice because he knew something was wrong here.

She sat, took a deep breath and said simply, 'She knows.'

It took Eric a moment to grasp what she was saying and then it hit him like a sledgehammer. 'Fuck. How?' He returned to his seat, his eyes fixed on her. 'How?' he repeated.

'She told me.'

'She told you? But-but… what do you mean? She just came out with it?'

Olivia leaned across the table. 'She doesn't know it's me but she knows you're up to something.'

'But…'

'We met earlier. Had a coffee and she came out with it. She said you'd been acting differently.'

'What did you say?'

'I said oh, Eric wouldn't cheat on you. Imagine how I felt saying that. I told her to kill the bitch.'

'Why did you say that for?'

'I don't know. It just came out. I think I'd stopped thinking of myself as the other woman, and gone back to when Yves left me, when I was the scorned woman.'

'Shit.'

A waiter appeared at the table. 'Good evening, sir, madam. Are you ready to order?'

'No,' snapped Eric. 'Another five minutes.' He didn't want to eat now; his appetite had been shot at.

'Lucky you've got that other phone,' said Olivia.

'Why?'

'She went through your phone, checking it for, you know, evidence.'

'Oh Jesus, I could do without this.'

'Well, it didn't exactly brighten my day having my friend confiding in me. Imagine how I feel. She's bound to question you so I'd be prepared if I was you.'

'Yes.' He rubbed his chin. 'Yes, you're right. Forewarned is forearmed and all that.'

'She'll be wondering where you are now, Eric. You should go home. The later it gets, the worse it'll look.'

'Yes. Pity. I was looking forward to tonight.'

'I know. Me too, my darling.'

Eric reached over the table and took Olivia's hand. She smiled, reassured perhaps by his touch. 'We'd better quit while we're ahead.'

'For a while, yes.'

He let go of her hand. 'No, I mean…'

'What do you mean? Surely, you don't mean for good.'

'Well…'

'We just have to be more careful, darling. Perhaps not meet up so often. Be more discreet.'

'No, if she knows, she'll be watching me like a hawk. No, darling, we can't go on. Surely, you can see that?'

Olivia's usual composure was fading fast. 'No, I don't. You can't desert me now.'

'It's not a case of deserting you, darling, but what choice do we have?'

'All we have to do is to cool it for a couple of months. You play the loving husband and then we can pick up from where we left off.'

Eric looked at her. Was she being serious? He needed to be assertive here. 'I can't see how a couple of months will make any difference.'

'I *need* you, Eric.'

'And Tammy needs me.'

'I need you more. Leave her.'

'You what?'

'Are we ready to order now, sir?'

'What? Go away, will you? I'll shout for you when we're ready.'

The red-faced waiter slunk away.

Eric was beginning to panic now. 'I can't just *leave* her, Olivia.'

'Why not? Yves left me. She'll get used to the idea, just like I had to. It'll be hard, yes, but–'

'I can't. What about the girls?'

'I have a daughter too in case you forget.'

'Yes, exactly, and from what you've told me, she's still fucked up about it.'

'It's made her a strong young woman.'

OK, this conversation was veering too far out of Eric's comfort zone here. There was something in Olivia's expression he hadn't seen before, an almost feral look of panic. He needed to tread carefully before things spiralled out of control. 'Look, darling, this has all come as a shock. Let's not rush into anything. Let's keep a distance for a while and think things through and then…'

'And then what, Eric?'

'Reassess the situation. Talk about it with clear heads.'

'You're not at work now, Eric. Next, you'll be saying we need to do some blue sky thinking or some crap.'

'No, but you know what I mean.'

She seemed to deflate but he could tell he'd got his point across; he'd placated her for now and that was the main thing, simply to get out of here unscathed, damage limitation.

'Have you got your phone on you?' she asked.

She meant his second phone. He removed it from his jacket pocket and held it up.

'Good,' she said. 'I might give you a call later.'

He'd rather she didn't. 'I'll keep an eye on it. I ought to put it back on silent.' He could see the waiter loitering, ready to pounce. 'We should go.'

Olivia nodded. She rose from the table looking tired. Eric avoided the waiter's eyes as he took Olivia's arm and gently guided her outside.

The evening was still incredibly warm and Eric wished he'd brought a lighter jacket. The outdoor tables were full, people milling about looking at the display menus, couples wandering by. He used his mobile to call a taxi. 'Five minutes,' he said.

Without warning, Olivia flung her arms around his neck.

'You won't leave me, Eric, will you? Promise me you won't leave me.'

'Olivia, Olivia, please, everyone's looking.'

'Promise me, Eric.'

He managed to disentangle himself. 'Let's see how the land lies, eh?'

'No, I need more than that.'

'We'll work something out.'

'Yves left me. If you leave me too, I don't know what I'll do to myself…'

Chapter 6: Benedict
Today

Detective Inspector Benedict Paige was still in the shower trying to recapture a strange dream he had which involved a trip to London Zoo he had as a kid. The dream was based on fact. He always remembered the day with great fondness, his father making chimpanzee noises too loudly in a café afterwards, scaring a toddler in a buggy. In the dream, however, the day went wrong when all the snakes escaped and started attacking people but he couldn't remember how the dream ended and for some reason, this was bothering him. Did it have a happy ending, did they escape the snakes? Just as he thought he was about to remember, he heard in the distance the familiar ring of his work mobile. 'Could you get that?' he shouted through to his wife.

This, he thought, was bound to be bad news. No one rang him on his work mobile at this time of the morning unless *something somewhere* had unfolded. 'That was your DS, darling,' called Sonia, stepping into the ensuite.

'Hey, privacy.'

'I am your wife, Ben.'

'What did she want?'

'She didn't say but you're to phone her back asap.'

'Blast. Hey, Sonia, what's the difference between a snake and a lawyer?'

'I don't know, Ben.'

'Snakes don't wear watches.' He chortled to himself.

Five minutes later, Benedict phoned Jessica. 'DS Gardiner, what's up?'

'Sorry to bother you so early but we have a suspicious death on our hands, boss. An elderly woman called Tamsin Fournier. She was found dead by her husband late last night. They live in Highgate. I'll text you over the address. I'm heading there now.'

'OK, thanks, Jessica. I'll see you soon.'

*

It may have been summer but the day was blanketed by grey skies. The house in Highgate was a grand affair, a double-fronted detached house with extensive gardens in a quiet, leafy cul-de-sac, a Range Rover and a Volvo parked on the gravelled drive. The house was already taped off, a uniformed officer at the front door. Wishing the young man a good morning, Benedict walked in and made his way to the living room where he found DS Gardiner and Michelle Garvey, the Family Liaison Officer, comforting a grey-haired man in a polo shirt and linen jacket. Jessica approached him and ushered Benedict back into the hallway. 'That's the husband, Eric Fournier. I said you'd want to speak to him but do you want to go upstairs first? DS Collins and the pathologist are already here.'

'After you, DS Gardiner.'

The bedroom was filled with officers in white overalls conducting the initial forensics. The room was enormous, wooden floor, Turkish rug at the foot of the bed, white furniture with gold handles, spotlights in the ceiling and an acoustic guitar propped up on a wicker chair. DS Collins smiled on seeing Benedict. 'Hello, sir.'

'Adrian. So, what have we here?'

They approached the bed. The bedspread had been pulled up to her chin, her grey hair sprayed out neatly across the pillow beneath her, her eyes still open, an anguished look about them.

'Tamsin Fournier, known as Tammy, aged seventy-two. She'd been suffering from dementia. Her husband found her last night and dialled 999. The paramedics who attended were immediately suspicious. The bloodshot eyes and the discoloration around her face.'

Yes, thought Benedict, one could see it around her nostrils and mouth.

'Dick's already been and gone. He confirmed the cause of death – definitely suffocation.'

'Anything of interest around the house?'

Collins laughed. 'It's a big house, sir, give us a chance. But so far, no. Nothing of interest. But, like I say, early days.' He shook his head. 'Why anyone would want to suffocate an old person with dementia beats me. Unless of course…'

He didn't finish the sentence. Benedict caught Jessica's eye. They were all thinking the same – was this a mercy killing? 'Let's go and speak to Mr Fournier.'

They found Mr Fournier with a younger woman, dressed in a green gilet as if she was about to go for a country walk, both of them sitting on the settee but with a wide space between them. Michelle Garvey offered to make a round of tea that no one wanted so she sat down. Benedict introduced himself. 'I'm very sorry for your loss, Mr Fournier. It must be a terrible shock for you.'

He shook his head while looking out of the window.

Turning to the woman, Benedict asked, 'Can I ask who—'

'Oh, I'm Susan. Mr Fournier's daughter.'

'Mr Fournier, I appreciate this won't be the best time but would you be strong enough to answer a few questions?'

'If I must,' he mumbled.

'Thank you. Can you describe the events of last night?'

He sighed. 'I went out. I met a friend. Susan was here to look after Tammy...' He shot her a look. 'I came back about... what time, Susie?'

'Just after half eleven.'

'I went upstairs to check on Tammy and...' Susan reached for his hand but he swiped it away. 'Well, she was dead. I called 999 and that's when they said her death looked suspicious.'

'Unfortunately, it looks that way.'

'That's what I can't understand. She'd been poorly for a while. We knew she didn't have long for this world and, you know, had she died as God intended, well, I c-could cope with that. But this... no, this is beyond upsetting.'

'Susan,' said Benedict. 'Did you check on your mother during the course of the evening?'

'Yes, of course.'

'And what time was that?'

'Oh, a couple of times. I guess, the last time would have been about half ten. She, er, did say something that concerned me.' Susan described how her mother had thought someone had been there and pointed towards the window. 'But it was locked, I checked.'

'Did you see anything that looked out of place?'

'No. I mean, I didn't really look but I'd have noticed if anything was different.'

'And your mother didn't say who?' asked Jessica.

'No. I thought she'd been having a dream.'

'To be fair to Susan,' said Eric. 'That has happened before. She did have dreams that would wake her. After Susan told me, I checked all the doors and windows and nothing's been touched as far as I can see.'

'Did you hear anything, Susan?'

'No, nothing.'

'Were you alone?'

She glanced nervously at her father. 'Actually, I did have a friend around.'

'Being?'

She sighed. 'His name is Robbie–'

'Ha, knew it!' said Eric. 'Shirley, my foot.'

'We will have to speak to this Robbie,' said Jessica.

'I'd rather you didn't.' She blushed as soon as she said it. 'I suppose you must.'

'Were you playing music?'

'I… Yes, I suppose we were. But not loudly. Just a bit.'

'Who were you with last night, Mr Fournier?'

'Why are you asking me that? Surely, you can't suspect *me* of murdering my own wife in her bed.'

'We have to ask, sir.'

'If you must know, I was out with a friend called Patrick. Patrick Dunt. I went to his house for a catch-up.'

'Apart from yourself, sir, who has a key to this house?'

'Well, it's just me and Susan. Oh, and my cleaner.'

'Oh?'

'Alina. I don't know her surname. She's from Poland. I can

give you her number if you want. She comes just once a week. She's very good if you're looking for a cleaner, Inspector.'

'One last question,' said Benedict. 'Can you think of anyone who might want to harm your wife, Mr Fournier?'

'What sort of question is that? No, of course not. She was a seventy-two-year-old woman with dementia, for God's sake.'

'I mean, from her past. Your past.'

'We lived ordinary lives, Inspector. Comfortable but ordinary. There's no reason on God's earth why *anyone* would want to kill my wife.'

But *someone* did, thought Benedict. Someone did.

Chapter 7: Susan
Today

A good couple of hours after the detectives had left, there were still several forensic people around, sinister looking in their white suits, silently working, looking for clues, taking photographs and dusting every door handle and surface. Susan and her father had been confined to the living room. The Family Liaison Officer, Michelle Garvey, pottered around, making them rounds of tea and ham sandwiches for lunch. Neither Susan nor her father were hungry. At one point, men in white carried Mum's body out of the house. Susan and her father stood at the living room window as they stretchered Mum into the back of an ambulance. It seemed so inappropriate somehow, thought Susan, as if her removal deserved greater dignity. She put her hand over her father's shoulder and she could feel him tense up; he didn't like it, didn't want her touch. As soon as he could, he stepped away.

Dad tried to leave the living room but Garvey apologetically forbade it. Susan feared he was going to make a fuss but instead, he plonked down on an armchair and closed his eyes. What was he thinking about, she wondered. *Who* was he thinking about? Where had he really been last night, the night his wife died? She had met this Patrick once, briefly, he lived nearby although Susan didn't know exactly where. A scruffy individual who swore a lot and had his opinions influenced by the tabloids. There was no way Dad had dressed up and doused himself in aftershave to meet this man. He was up to something but now wasn't the time to ask him.

And it wasn't as if her conscience was clear anyway – she was pregnant with a married man's child. She still had to shake herself and ask how in the hell did that happen? Did she love Robbie? More to the point, did Robbie love her? She hated the way he'd bailed out on her last night. He didn't even bother waiting for her to come back downstairs. No, just a hasty text saying something had 'come up' and then buggered off without saying goodbye. She walked into the living room to find that he had indeed gone and something deflated inside her, staggered by his rudeness. She'd been dreading telling him about her pregnancy while at the same time desperate to share the burden. She'd had so many different scenarios on how he'd take the news and until his arrival last night, she'd convinced herself that he'd be pleased, more than pleased – he'd be delighted. He needed to get out of his marriage; he'd said so enough times but Robbie lacked the balls to actually do it. This, Susan was convinced, would provide the spur. But he'd denied her the chance to tell him. And so she had to carry on and wait for the next opportunity. Part of her was tempted just to text him – *Hi Robbie, thought you might like to know – I'm pregnant*, and sign it off with several kisses. But no, this was not the time for frivolity. But when would she get a chance to see Robbie again? He always dictated when they could meet and where and for how long. She never had a say. Susan had had enough of playing second fiddle to Margot, his wife, she was sick of keeping her pregnancy a secret. Her mother had died without ever knowing she was soon to be a grandmother for the first time, and that hurt. Susan looked over at her father, lost in his own world.

She couldn't wrap her head around the fact that someone had killed her mother. It made no sense whatsoever. She was bedbound, for goodness' sake, her intellect eroded by that horrible condition. What threat did she pose to anyone? What harm could she do? A nicer, kinder, lovely woman, one couldn't hope to meet.

And who did she see in her bedroom last night? Susan had dismissed it and now she was hating herself for it. 'Don't leave me, Susie. Don't leave me,' she'd said. And what did Susan do? Dismiss it as a bad dream. And then she left her, too distracted by Robbie bailing out on her. She knew she'd be forever haunted by her mother's final words.

Garvey sat in a chair in the corner of the room scrolling on her phone.

Dad stretched. 'I ought to phone your sister.'

'Do you want me to do it?' Susan asked.

'No. This needs to come from me.' He paced to the window and made the call. Susan heard him talking into the phone and knew straight away he was leaving a message telling Lizzie he'd try again later.

He sat down. Garvey asked if he needed anything but he waved her away without looking at her or saying thank you.

'Dad, I need to tell you something.'

'Can't it wait?'

Could it wait? Yes, she'd waited this long, another day or two wouldn't make any difference but she needed to let it out of the bag, this silence was killing her now. 'I'm pregnant, Daddy.'

'Oh God.' His hand went to his heart. 'Are you? But...'

'But what?' she said lightly.

'But you don't even have a boyfriend. How can you be pregnant?'

She tried to laugh, to make light of it. 'Well, I am.'

Dad's mobile rang. 'I'd better get that. It could be your sister.'

It was. Typical Lizzie, thought Susan, always hugging everyone's attention, even when she wasn't there. Garvey smiled sympathetically at her while Dad told Lizzie the bad news. Susan wondered how her sister would take it. Would she shed a tear? Unlikely. And then it hit her – she hadn't yet shed a tear, too wrapped up with her pregnancy, too worried about how Robbie would take it.

Dad finished the call. 'How much longer are they going to be?' he shouted at Garvey.

'Not too long now, sir.'

'Huh. That's what you said two hours ago. I'm a bloody prisoner in my own home.'

'Dad, they have to do their job. Don't you want them to find Mum's killer?'

He didn't answer.

'You didn't tell Lizzie how Mum died.'

'No. I didn't feel as if it was something I could say over the phone. She'll be here in a day or two. I'll tell her then.'

'Anyway, Dad, as I was saying...'

'You're pregnant.'

'Yes.' He didn't sound overjoyed; he didn't sound pleased

in the slightest. Why? Why didn't he sound pleased about his first grandchild?

'So, who is he then?'

'The father? You don't know him.'

'No? When shall I meet him?'

'It's complicated.'

'Complicated? How? Oh God, oh no…' His face paled in front of her. 'He's married, isn't he?'

'Well, yes, but–'

'Oh good God, Susan. Just when I thought this day couldn't get any worse. Why now? Why did you have to tell me now?'

'Because…' She so did not want to cry but the relief of saying the words out loud for the first time and her father's horrible reaction reduced her. 'Because I thought you'd be pleased.'

'Pleased? My daughter is carrying a bastard child and you expect me to be pleased?'

Susan turned her back on him, clamping her hand against her mouth as the tears came.

Chapter 8: Tammy
Annecy, France, ten years ago

Kill the bitch. Olivia's advice kept ringing in Tammy's mind. Kill the bitch. Well, if she ever found out who it was, she might not kill her but she'd certainly come close to it and do something she might come to regret. But that was what love and jealousy did to a person; it stripped them of rational thought, made them dream up impossible scenarios of violence and revenge. There was no way she could harm another human being but if faced with the woman who was sleeping with her husband, then God knows what she'd be capable of. The thought both consoled and frightened her.

Tammy sat at home watching the local news on TV but she couldn't concentrate and kept glancing up at the living room clock wondering what time Eric might come home tonight. It was still only seven. He had said he had another meeting and that was the problem – there'd been a lot of meetings recently. She didn't believe him for a moment.

She was pleased she'd spoken to Olivia; she was a good friend. She'd been through the same torment; she knew what

Tammy was going through. It hadn't provided any solutions but it was good to get it off her chest. Although Olivia had advised asking Eric outright. She'd thought of it herself, of course, but was too worried to do so but Olivia was right – she had to. This not knowing was torturous; she'd rather know where she stood. *You'll know within a nanosecond*, she'd said.

She looked around the familiar living room with its harmonious blend of classic French design elements and a restrained colour palette that created an inviting and elegant ambience and the grand, marble fireplace with the ornate mantel adorned with an antique clock that quietly pinged the hour. Was she about to lose all this? They'd lived here some twenty years; this was home and the thought of losing it pained her. But if Eric left her, then what were the chances of holding onto it? It happened to Olivia, forced out of the house that had been their home for so long to end up living in a positive shack on the edge of town. But she did well out of the subsequent divorce and now lived OK, spending her money on clothes and looking fabulous.

Ten past seven, Tammy heard the key in the front door, Eric's familiar footsteps. He called out a hearty hello as he came in. He knelt down and kissed her on the cheek. Tammy breathed in, trying to see if she could smell *her* on him but no, he simply smelt his usual, old self.

'How was your meeting?'

'Oh, usual bullshit.' He proceeded to tell her about his meeting, about how clients start off by asking for *ABC* then, having drawn up all the plans, they decide they want *XYZ* instead. 'Infuriating,' he said in conclusion. More like she stood you up, thought Tammy.

She watched him as Eric took off his tie and removed his

jacket, placing them on the back of a chair.

'Any dinner on the go?' he asked.

'You said you'd grab something at work.'

'Oh, yes, I did, didn't I? Never got the chance.'

'I could do you an omelette if you like.'

'Perfect. Thank you, love.'

Tammy rose from her armchair. She opened her mouth, determined to ask him now but she couldn't do it, could not do it. Instead, she made her way to the kitchen to cook Eric's blessed omelette. She should poison it, she thought.

'They're showing *The Cruel Sea* tonight,' Eric shouted through from the living room. 'Jack Hawkins again. Shall we watch it?'

'Lovely.' Tammy had no desire to watch yet another dreary war film but didn't have the strength to argue.

After the film finished, Eric yawned and stretched.

'Are you having an affair, Eric?' She'd said it, just came out with it, hadn't planned it. Oh God.

He stared at her incredulously. 'Are you serious? Of course not.'

Olivia was right – it did take a nanosecond; Eric was not having an affair. 'I'm sorry,' she said. 'I don't know why...' She burst into tears.

'Hey, hey, hey.' He wrapped his arms around her. 'What sort of question is that?'

'I'm sorry. Ignore me.'

'Of course, I'm not having an affair. I love you, Tammy, and only you, silly.'

'I know. I'm sorry. Forgive me.'

'No, I'm sorry if I've given the impression... oh, hang on, it's all the late meetings, isn't it? That's why... Oh, love, oh dear. I'm sorry.'

Tammy had never known such a sense of relief. Why had she doubted him? She truly felt foolish now, but it didn't matter, not now, nothing mattered; Eric wasn't having an affair and that was all that mattered.

That night, Eric and Tammy made love. It was a half-hearted affair, as it invariably was nowadays but Tammy didn't care, she was thankful for the closeness. There were a couple of moments where she had to bite on her lip in order not to burst into tears again with relief.

As soon as they were finished, Eric rolled off her. 'I'm sorry,' he said. 'I guess I'm more tired than I thought.'

'It's fine, love. You work too hard.'

'Yes, I know. I ought to slow up a little.' He yawned and was asleep within moments. Tammy lay on her back, her eyes open, smiling to herself, watching the shadows of the branches from the elm tree in their garden dancing on her ceiling. The window was open but it still felt stuffy. They needed air conditioning; it was too hot and sticky to sleep.

The next morning, Eric sprung out of bed, keen to get to work as always. Eric loved his work; he enjoyed that combination of creativity and business. The morning sun streamed through the window. Eric had his usual shower, singing *Rhinestone Cowboy* loudly, the ensuite door open. Tammy sat up in bed and rejoiced that the dark cloud that had followed her around these last few weeks had finally evaporated and disappeared.

'Have you seen my linen jacket?' he asked, rifling through his side of the wardrobe. 'It's too hot for polyester. Ah, here it is.'

'Working late again tonight, love?'

'No, not tonight. Thank God. I'll be back nice and early. Hey, how about we eat out tonight?'

'Really?'

'Yeah, why not? We've not eaten out in ages. It'd be nice, don't you think?'

'Sure, why not? Good idea.'

'Great. I'll give you a ring later. Maybe you could make a reservation somewhere nice.'

Twenty minutes later, Eric left for work; he never had breakfast, preferring to eat at work, probably something unhealthy, knowing her husband. Tammy padded downstairs in her pyjamas, a spring in her step, fit to burst, relishing the sense of finally being free of the torment. She loved Eric; Eric loved her and she felt great!

She ate a bowl of cereal while reading the news on her phone but nothing held her attention. About to return upstairs for a shower, Tammy noticed Eric's jacket and tie where he'd left them on the back of the chair the previous evening. She scooped them up in order to hang the jacket up in the wardrobe.

She dropped the jacket on the bed and lay down. She loved the idea of eating out tonight, a chance to enjoy herself, to talk to her husband, to listen to him without that horrible niggling feeling that had eaten her up from the inside.

She needed that shower but maybe a few more minutes lying on the bed. She ought to phone Olivia and tell her the good news and thank her for giving her the courage to ask *the* question.

It was at that moment she heard an unfamiliar ringtone, an electronic version of Beethoven's *Für Elise*. What was that, she wondered. Where was it coming from? Eric's jacket, hell, it was coming from Eric's jacket. Quickly, she leaned across the bed and grappled with the jacket, checking its pockets until she found a small Android mobile. Unknown number.

Standing up, her heart thumping, she pressed the green button but didn't say anything as she put the phone to her ear.

'Eric. It's me. Is everything OK, darling?'

Tammy threw the phone on the bed as if it had just burned her hand. She could still hear the distant voice. 'Eric? Are you there? Eric, talk to me, darling.'

She stood shaking, the tears forming. She knew that voice all too well, the voice calling her husband 'darling'. That was Olivia's voice.

Chapter 9: Frida
Today

The Red Lion was almost empty but there again, it usually was. Frida McCleave had only been here a couple of times before and she didn't like it – she considered it an 'old man's pub' – heavy wooden furniture, dark, stained carpets, black and white photos of men with big moustaches, wallpaper that looked as if it hadn't changed since the seventies. They rarely played music and when they did it was usually a collection of dreadful songs from the sixties. But there was one framed print that made her smile, a colourful, vibrant self-portrait of a woman. She'd have approached it and had a better look but it was positioned above a table now occupied by two grumpy-looking men silently nursing their pints of bitter.

Diane had wanted to meet in town, somewhere off Oxford Circus or suchlike and as much as Frida would have preferred that, she couldn't risk it; she needed to remain close to home so she'd get back easily and on time. Diane walked in and didn't hide her disdain, saying, 'This place is a shithole.'

'I know but…' How could Frida explain? 'What would you like?' she asked quickly, wanting to change the subject.

They both had white wine spritzers. Frida had promised herself one drink at least but no more than that – she needed to stay alert, safer.

Having caught up with what they'd recently discovered on their Instagram feeds, Diane said, 'Have you got any jobs going at your charity shop?'

'No, I don't think so. I can ask. Only volunteers.'

'Yeah, that's alright.'

'OK, but sorting out old clothes and toys all day is fairly boring but I'll ask the boss if you like.'

'Please yes. I'll sort out old clothes all day. Anything. I just need something to do cos I get bored. I mean, I don't actually need the money.' She laughed. 'I got an inheritance last year. My grandma died and because she hates my dad, she left it all to me.'

'Kerching!'

'Yeah, absolutely.'

'What about your mum?'

'Oh, she died years ago. It's just Dad but he's a total waste of space. Haven't seen him in ages and I don't want to.'

'So, you don't really need a job?'

'Yeah, I do. Cos, like I said, I get bored. So, you'll ask?'

'Yeah, sure.' There was no way Frida was going to ask her boss. They finished their drinks.

'My shout,' said Diane. 'Same again?'

She'd love another wine but no, she daren't, she needed to keep her wits about her. 'A coke's fine for me, thanks.'

'What's the matter with you? I thought we were going to get smashed, find a couple of likely lads and get ourselves laid.' They both looked around the pub with all the dull, grey-coloured men and laughed.

'You can have first pick,' said Frida.

'I'd rather stab a cocktail stick in my eye. So, you're saying you only want a Coke?'

'Yes. Sorry.'

'Doesn't bother me. Cheap date. I'll be back in a mo.'

Frida was never quite sure why she was friends with Diane. They first met six months back. Diane had popped into the charity shop and bought a dog-eared copy of a Danielle Steel novel which Frida herself had donated. They got talking and somehow became friends. Diane wasn't the sort of person Frida would normally gravitate to but she didn't have any friends. Ade didn't like her having friends, wouldn't allow it. He didn't know about Diane. She only came out tonight because Ade was at the football. She liked it when he went to the football because it meant he was still fairly sober when he came home – as long as Arsenal won. He was unbearable if they lost. Thankfully, Arsenal were on a good run these days, rarely losing a game. Long may it continue. It was the 'pool' nights she dreaded, when Ade went to the pub with his mates to play game after game of pool. He always came back drunk and demanding sex, rough sex. Pretending to be asleep or even ill had no effect.

Diane returned from the bar bearing a spritzer, a Coke and a bag of crisps to share. 'Who's that picture of?' She pointed at the framed print Frida had spotted earlier. 'Do you know?'

Frida was delighted she asked. 'That's my namesake, Frida Kahlo.'

'Who? Never heard of her.'

'Mexican artist. She's really famous. That's who I'm named after. I spell my name the same as her.'

'Really? Weird. Thank God you haven't got her eyebrows.'

'No but she's beautiful, isn't she?'

'Well, if you like that sort of thing.'

They got talking about the yet unnamed BBC presenter accused of paying a young man for explicit photos. Time passed quickly, too quickly, and Frida, realising the time, almost jumped out of her seat. 'Shit, I've got to go.'

'Nah, go on, stay for another.'

'No, I can't. I have to go. I can't be late.'

'Can't be late for what?'

'It doesn't matter.'

'Gee, Frida, what's up?'

'It's... it's nothing but I have to go. I'm sorry. Thanks... you know, for a lovely evening.'

'It's OK. I guess.'

Frida rushed home, a good fifteen-minute walk, puffing on her strawberry-flavoured vape and swearing to herself. Normally, she was so careful. How could she have been so lax, so stupid? She'd only had the one glass of wine. She had to get home before Ade otherwise life wouldn't be worth living. It'd begun drizzling and she had no umbrella. It didn't matter, she'd be home soon. She checked her phone, not that she expected to see any messages. Ade never contacted her when he was out with his friends. Was it one of those football games that goes on forever with extra time and penalties, etc? Or was it just a normal game? She hoped to God, it was the former because that would delay his return by a good forty minutes or more, and she'd be OK.

She inserted her door key into the flat door and held her breath, beseeching God that he hadn't returned home before her. There was no light under the door so hopefully that meant she was OK.

She stepped inside. All the lights were off. Was he waiting for her in the dark? Please, God, no.

'Ade?' she called out quietly. No answer. 'Ade?'

She dared to hope. She switched on the lights, fearing the worst. But no, he wasn't here, the flat was empty. Oh, the relief, the relief.

Quickly, she removed her coat and hung it up in the tiny space next to the toilet, removed her shoes and put the TV on, settling on Love Island. Ade had no interest in it so he wouldn't question her about it, trying to catch her out. She sat down and tried to quell her breathing. She needed to look normal and relaxed.

Five minutes later, Frida heard the key in the door. Five minutes – too close for comfort. She'd learn from this. Ade came through and Frida knew immediately that Arsenal had won. 'Hi, babes. How did it go?'

'Three fucking nil. Bloody nailed it. Jesus scored twice. Top fella.'

'Well, yes, people speak highly of him but I didn't know he played football.' She knew he was referring to Arsenal's Brazilian forward, Gabriel Jesus, but she laughed at her own joke and then, with a heavy heart, realised how rarely she laughed within the walls of her own home. 'Do you want a bacon sandwich?'

'Nah, we got a burger on the way back.' Ade went to the loo, allowing Frida time to breathe a heavy sigh of relief. She'd got away with it.

Ade returned. 'Why's your hair all wet?'

Her heart tumbled within her chest. 'Is... it?'

'Yeah, it's wet. Why?'

'Oh, oh, I... I-I p-popped out to the shop.'

'At this time of your night? What did you buy?'

'One of those small vapes, you know.'

'Like fuck.' He gripped her hair, twisting it around his hand. 'Where were you really?'

'Please, Ade, don't hurt me. Don't hurt me…'

Chapter 10: Susan
Today

Her mother's death had clarified a few things in Susan's mind. Namely, that she was thirty-four years old and not getting any younger. She was pregnant with a married man's child and the two things she was certain of – she did not want to be a single mother and she did not want to lose this baby. Not this time. Her parents had been married thirty-eight years, almost a whole lifetime together. They adored each other, at least until dementia had stripped Mum of her dignity. Susan earned a good salary but she lived in rented accommodation and she needed to put down her roots. She'd grown up thinking she didn't need a man in her life to feel whole but now, pregnant, she realised how she envied what her parents had. She knew she couldn't put it off any longer; she needed to speak to Robbie. He needed to know. So, why was it so darn hard to phone him? She paced the length of her flat, her phone in her hand, urging herself to hit that button but unable to do so. She rang but only got his voicemail. She left a message, trying her best to keep her voice sounding light. Half an hour later, unable to bear it a second more, she tried again. But no luck. She had to ring him three times before he answered. He apologised but said it wasn't a good time but he did agree to meet her at Greenfield Park at twelve, during his lunch hour, although, he said, he couldn't stay too long.

On the way to the park and with time to spare, Susan decided to visit her father, see how he was getting on. They hadn't spoken since she told him she was pregnant and his reaction had shocked her. She shivered as she stepped out of the door. It may have been summer and parts of southern Europe were in the grip of a heatwave of Biblical proportions but here, in Highgate, it felt more like autumn than summer. She remembered a family holiday near St Ives in Cornwall during the relative heat wave of 1995. That was hot enough. Her mother complained about the heat the whole time they were there. Susan was eight years old at the time. They'd stayed in a small guesthouse, along with a German family, who included a boy a few years younger than her. Whenever she thought of that boy, she felt the embarrassment of having witnessed his humiliation. Susan, her sister and parents were heading out when they saw the German father next to his car, his face bright red with anger, as he shouted at the boy who stood with his hands behind his back, looking terribly small. In the blink of an eye, the dad fell to one knee, scooped up the boy, flung him over his knee, and spanked him before depositing him on the ground and storming off. Susan caught the boy's eye and felt his burning shame. Susan wondered whether her father remembered the incident. She knew how that little German boy felt now – the way her father talked to her when she said she was pregnant was like being slapped. *My daughter is carrying a bastard child and you expect me to be pleased?* And like the German father, her own father had left her feeling utterly humiliated.

She saw her father on his driveway, buttoning up his coat, striding with purpose. He jumped when she called his name. 'You're off somewhere, Dad?'

'Oh, Susan. I didn't see you there. Why aren't you at work?'

'Because my mother's just died perhaps?' If she expected a sympathetic response, she didn't get one.

'Anyway, if you've come to see me, as you can see, I'm off out.'

'Anywhere interesting?'

'No. J-just going out for a walk. I need to clear my head. I thought I might wander up to the cemetery. Not been there for years. Your mother used to love it there.'

Did she? Susan had never heard her mother mention the cemetery. 'I'll come with you if you like.' In truth, she didn't have time but for some reason, she wasn't sure why, she wanted to test her father.

'No. Very k-kind of you to offer but no. I-I need to be by myself. I'm sure you understand.'

Why was he lying to her?

'Anyway, Susan.' He started walking. Susan trotted to keep pace with him.

'Don't worry, Daddy, I'll head off at the crossroads. Leave you in peace.'

'So… how are you, you know, given your… your condition?'

'I'm pregnant, Dad, not ill.'

'You know what I mean.'

'Fine.'

'Look.' He stopped and looked at her. Reaching out, he

touched her arm. 'I'm sorry if I was a bit short with you when you told me. It's just…'

'I know. Bad timing.'

'Yeah. You could say that. But, Susan, what are you going to do? You can hardly bring up a child on your own. You'd have to give up work and I know how much it means to you.'

'I don't intend to bring the child up by myself.'

'Oh? I thought… You said–'

'He won't desert me,' she said, more to convince herself than her father. And the way he looked at her, she knew he wasn't convinced in the slightest. 'He's delighted at the prospect.' Now, it was her turn to lie to him.

'Good.' He flashed a smile. 'That's good to hear.'

'And even if I was by myself, I've got savings, I'd get maternity leave and, worst comes to worst, Mum said she'd remember me in her will.'

'She did?'

'Well, yes, Dad.'

'So, when can I meet the lucky chap?'

'Soon. Very soon.'

'Does he have a name?'

She didn't want to tell him, telling him somehow would mean committing herself and her baby to a man she wasn't even sure would stand by her. 'Robert. But everyone calls him Robbie.'

'Robbie? Right.'

'Have you heard from the police since?'

He cast his eyes down for a moment. Recovering himself, he said, 'No. Not a peep. We'll hear soon enough, I imagine.' He received a notification on his phone and checked it.

'Anything important?'

'Hmm? No. But I'd better go. Oh, by the way, Lizzie's arriving tomorrow.'

'Cool. I'll pop over and say hello.'

'Yeah. Sure.' He hesitated a moment before leaving. 'Look after yourself, Susan.'

'And you, Dad.'

He flashed her another quick smile before marching off. Susan did wonder if he was planning on strolling around the cemetery by himself, why he needed to rush off on receiving a notification on his mobile. He was meeting someone, she was sure of it. She had the inclination to follow him but lacked the time. She had a man to meet but first, she needed to do something.

Having let herself into her father's house, Susan went straight to her father's office, a small room at the back of the house that Eric had purloined as his office several years ago. She knew exactly what she was looking for.

The centrepiece of Eric's office was a sturdy oak desk positioned near the window to let in natural light and provide a pleasant view of the garden. On the desk, Dad's new laptop. He'd recently bought an ergonomic chair with lumbar support and adjustable height. On one wall, he had his bookshelves and above the desk an inspirational quote from Gandhi. But it was the filing cabinet that Susan concentrated on. It was locked but it took Susan a matter of seconds to find the key in the desk's slide-out drawer that contained pens, Post-It pads, paperclips and drawing pins.

The folders inside the filing cabinet contained Dad's paperwork going back years – no surprise there. And in the last folder in the bottom drawer, exactly as she remembered, Dad's diaries. But, flipping through them, she was disappointed to see that Dad had ceased keeping a diary from the moment they left France, so these all dated back years. She wasn't going to find out anything about his mysterious woman from here. Nonetheless, she flipped through the pages of a few old diaries, pausing occasionally to read an entry or two. Lots of anecdotes about Susan and her sister that made her smile, trips out to the theatre, a holiday in Sicily in 1996. Yes, she had vague memories of that – she was only seven. But then a name jumped out – Claudette. Who in the hell was Claudette? Her hand went to her mouth; this was a lover and here was Dad talking about it quite openly in his diary – spending the night with her while telling her mother he was at a conference. Another diary, 2003 this time, and yes, another name, another lover, and more. God, there seemed to be a different one every year. And here, in 2013, Olivia. There was a lot about Olivia, this one meant something to him. She skim-read the entries until she reached July of that year. 'Oh my God,' she said aloud.

Susan had read enough. She put the diaries back, locked the cabinet and returned the key to the drawer. She walked downstairs in a haze. She flopped onto an armchair in the living room. Her father had been a serial adulterer. Her poor, poor mother. She must've known, she must have had to live with this knowledge all her married life. How downright awful, how degrading. She shook her head in disbelief. 'You bastard,' she said. 'You utter, utter bastard.'

She remembered all too well the day in France ten years ago when she saw her mother visibly upset…

Chapter 11: Tammy
Annecy, France, ten years ago

Five minutes later and Tammy was still shaking, still too shocked for tears. She'd called him darling, not once but twice. Olivia. The very woman she'd confided in, the very friend who'd listened and offered advice. Stabbed in the back by her friend. The betrayal ran deep. How dare she? Why, she'd even suggested that when or if Tammy ever found out who the 'other woman' was that she 'kill the bitch'. Well, yes, thought Tammy, she'd bloody kill Olivia, her confidant, her so-called friend. How could she? God, of all people, Olivia knew how it felt to have your husband run off on you, never to be seen again. She knew the pain it caused, the devastation. And yet... and yet?

And what now? Would Eric leave her, run off into the sunset with Olivia? The thought of her husband, her gorgeous Eric, in the arms of another woman, left her gagging. The thought of Eric leaving was incomprehensible. Her future beckoned like a dark abyss. Didn't he love her? His words, uttered just last night, came back to her: *Of course*

I'm not having an affair. I love you, Tammy, and only you, silly. And she believed him, why wouldn't she? She loved him, God, she loved him. Maybe he *did* love her, but he loved Olivia too.

She sat on the bed and picked up the mobile. So this was why she'd found no evidence of Eric's infidelity on his phone because it was all here instead. The wallpaper showed Planet Earth from afar. Tammy had the feeling this was the default image that came with the phone. The only notification was the 'unknown number', Olivia's call a whole twenty minutes ago. Twenty minutes in which her world, her orderly existence had been turned upside down. She entered the passcode that he used on his 'main' phone but of course it didn't work, she hadn't expected it to. She tried a few variations – his date of birth, their daughters' births, her own. None of them worked. She wondered how long Eric had had this phone, how long had the affair been going on.

Tammy wasn't sure what was worse – the suspicion that Eric was having an affair or knowing for sure that he was. At least with the suspicion, there was always a chance you could be wrong, while at least with knowing, you knew where you stood, no more wondering, the worse had already happened. To think for a few precious hours last night, she truly believed him. Olivia's nanosecond theory had proved wrong but that was because Olivia would have told him, he had time to prepare.

So, what now, what to do this minute, today?

Simple, she was going to cause hell.

*

Tammy showered and dressed, taking time to choose the right outfit. She needed to look good when confronting her husband and his mistress. She opted for a pale green jacket and black trousers and her high-heeled shoes, not too high but high enough to look like a woman who meant business.

She had to assume Olivia would know that it was she, not Eric, who answered her call. She hadn't said anything but Olivia would surely have heard her gasp.

She ordered an Uber to take her to Olivia's address, about a ten-minute drive away. A few minutes later, she received a notification to say the Uber was just a couple of minutes away.

Tammy was locking the front door behind her when the familiar yellow Renault Clio pulled up outside. Susan. What did she want? Tammy tried to assess whether she could hide but it was too late – Susan had seen her.

'Hiya, Mum,' said Susan, slamming the car door behind her. 'You off out?' Susan approached, a jaunt in her step. 'I wondered if...'

'What?'

Susan slowed down. 'What's up, Mum?'

'Nothing.' She averted her eyes.

'You've been crying.'

'No. I haven't, no.'

'Mum.' Susan reached for Tammy's hand. 'What's happened?'

Tammy was trying so hard not to cry but it was too difficult. 'Ignore me, please, Susan, it's nothing.'

'It doesn't look like nothing from here. My God, Mum, what's upset you? Has someone died?'

'No.' Tammy tried to laugh. 'Of course not.'

'Don't tell me, Dad's having...' She stopped, her eyes widening. 'Oh my God, it's Dad, isn't it? He's upset you.'

Tammy couldn't and wouldn't have this conversation with

her daughter standing out here on the porch.

'Tell me, Mum, what's he done?'

Thankfully, the Uber arrived. 'This is me,' she said.

'What? Wait, where are you going?'

Tammy rushed to the car.

'Mum? Mum, tell me what's going on.'

Tammy slammed the door. 'Can we hurry, please?' she said to the driver.

She glanced out the rear window as the car pulled away. She saw Susan throw her hands in the air.

Ten minutes later, they were at Olivia's house. Tammy instructed the driver to wait while she knocked on the door. If it opened, he should drive off. If not, she'd need a ride into town. She sat in the back taking deep breaths while trying to formulate a plan of attack. But her mind was in too much of a whirl to focus; she'd have to wing it. It was another intensely hot day and she felt overdressed.

Tammy swallowed. Please, she thought, let her be in, please make her be out. She walked up to the door feeling like a condemned woman walking to her execution. She knocked on Olivia's door. She could hear footsteps but it wasn't Olivia who answered but her daughter. She hadn't thought of this scenario, she didn't want to confront Olivia with Francine in the house. She heard the taxi behind her drawing away. 'Mum's popped out,' said Francine. 'She won't be long; she'll be back in a minute.'

'Can I wait?'

'If you want.'

Tammy followed Francine into the house. Francine, without another word, pointed to the living room before jogging up the stairs. Tammy stepped inside. She could hear the thump thump of music coming from upstairs. Tammy hadn't been here for a long time, not since Yves had left. It was still, she had to admit, a nice space with hardwood floors with a cherry finish, a large mirror with an ornate frame, and soft, neutral tones, a series of ten-inch totem poles on the dresser. It felt welcoming. Tammy inspected the photos, the usual fair, including photos of Yves. There was a sweet one of Yves and Francine embracing on a beach, Francine grinning at the camera, Yves leaning down, planting a kiss on his daughter's cheek. Happier times.

Tammy sat, jiggling her leg. The minutes passed. Eventually, she heard footsteps outside, approaching the house, the turn of a key in the door. Tammy stood, her head held high, and braced herself.

Olivia entered the living room and stopped short on seeing Tammy on her feet, her expression one of shock. If Tammy hadn't felt so angry, she might have laughed at the expression on the woman's face. 'Tammy?' Her eyes shot upwards on hearing Francine's music upstairs.

'How long's it been going on then, Olivia?'

'What d-do you mean?'

'Don't play with me,' she said, her voice rising. 'I know. And you know I know.'

Olivia didn't answer, simply checked her handbag and carefully placed it on a chair.

'Well?'

'I'm sorry you had to find out.'

Oh, the way she said it, so calmly, shocked her. 'You're not denying it. You're sleeping with *my* husband. How could you? I confided in you.'

'I didn't ask you to.'

'I thought you were my friend.'

'I am. I was. It's not my fault I fell in love with Eric.'

'Love? You bitch.'

'It wasn't meant to happen but it did. I'm sorry for you, Tammy, really I am but we found a connection and I know it was meant to be.'

How could she be so calm, so calculating? She stepped towards her. 'Well, it's finished now. Keep away from him.'

Olivia shook her head. 'I'm afraid it isn't. Eric loves me.'

Tammy felt the stab in her heart. Had she really said that? Could it be true? 'No, no, he doesn't. How can he love someone like…'

'Like me? Someone who showers him with affection, with love? I want you to leave now, Tamsin.'

The surge of hatred rose through Tammy like lava; she'd never experienced such visceral hate. Her fists clenched; nothing she wanted more than to wipe that self-satisfied expression off the bitch's face.

'I said, get out of my house.'

It happened all in the blink of an eye, the dash for the dresser, her fingers closing around the totem pole figure, raising it above Olivia's head, bringing it down with as much force as she could muster. But through her bleary vision, she missed her target. Olivia's piercing scream tore through the air. Kill the bitch, kill the bitch. Tammy raised her hand again, ready to try again but Olivia gripped her wrist. Olivia lunged forward, her fingers gripping Tammy's wrist with a vice-like grip. Panic and anger surged within Tammy as she struggled to free her arm, pushing Olivia away with frantic desperation. The two women found themselves locked in an undignified embrace. Olivia was stronger, gradually forcing Tammy's trembling hand down, inch by inch.

Some unseen force from behind sent Tammy sprawling across the settee, the totem pole slipping from her fingers.

She scrambled to her feet, her breath ragged, her heart pounding, only to be confronted by Francine, her face red with anger. 'Get out.' Olivia, gathering herself, joined her daughter. 'Get out,' Francine repeated, her words cutting through the air, sharper and more threatening. 'Or I'll seriously hurt you.'

The girl looked demented, alarmingly dangerous. Tammy knew she was beat here. She gathered her handbag and stormed out. She strode to the end of the street, cursing the intensity of heat, and only when she'd turned the corner, she slowed to a stop and clamped her hand over her mouth as her tears poured.

Chapter 12: Eric
Today

Eric had to go see Angela but first, he had a phone call to make. Years ago, when Patrick and he were colleagues in a now-defunct architectural firm, Patrick was suspected of offering backhanders that could have cost him his job and a lot more besides. Eric told a story that had, in effect, saved Patrick's skin and his job, let alone his reputation. Bluntly put, Patrick still owed him and he knew it.

Halfway to Angela's, he stopped his car, parking in a disabled bay just off Kilburn High Road, and made his call.

The call answered on the second ring. 'Patrick? It's me.'

'I know, Eric. Your name came up. What do I owe the pleasure?'

'I need a favour.'

'What sort of favour?'

'Look, I've had some bad news. Tammy died last night.'

'Oh shit, I'm sorry to hear that. Are you OK?'

'Been better, to be honest. But the thing is, the police think it may be suspicious.'

'Hey? In what way suspicious?'

'As in… As in–'

'Christ, they don't think someone bumped her off, do they?'

'Well, yes, exactly that.'

'Bloody hell, Eric. Who'd do such a thing? I mean, God, Tammy?'

'I know. It's mad, isn't it?' Eric could see a traffic warden further down the street, arguing with a motorist. He needed to speed this up before the woman caught up with him. 'But anyway, Pat, I've put myself in a bit of a pickle. Do you remember Angela?'

'Angela?'

'Angela Wheeler.'

'Oh, yeah. Nice woman. Attractive. Hang on, no, no, surely not.'

'Well, yes actually.'

'Bloody hell, Eric, you dark horse, you. Up to your old tricks, eh?'

'Yeah, but it's not exactly a good look right now, what with someone killing Tammy.'

Patrick laughed. 'No, I suppose not.'

'Fact is, I was with Angela last night and I can't have Susan knowing. She'll kill me. So, mate, I wondered…'

'Oh, I see. The penny's dropped. You want me to say you were with me. Is that it?'

'It would help.'

'So, basically, if the police ask me, you want me to lie for you?'

'Yes, but the chances are, the police won't bother you. Look, I know it's a big ask but you know…' He left the sentence hanging.

He heard Patrick sighing, mulling it over. He too was remembering 'the' favour.

'You know I'm shit at lying, Eric.'

He could see the traffic warden heading up the street towards him. 'I'm relying on you, Pat.'

'Bloody hell, Eric. OK, I'll do it but don't blame me if it goes tits up.'

*

Eric hadn't seen Angela since Tammy's death. But it'd only been thirty-six hours. He needed to speak to Angela and say that it might be for the best if they cooled their relationship now. Frankly, Eric had been looking for the excuse for some time. Although he enjoyed seeing Angela and enjoyed the physical aspect of their relationship, he found her and her demands on him exhausting. Tammy's death was the perfect time to tell Angela he needed space, that he did not want to go to the latest art exhibitions or the bloody opera.

She opened her front door and he knew straightaway from her expression that she'd heard the news. 'Eric, my poor love.' She kissed his cheek. 'Come in, come in.'

She fussed around, plumping up the cushions and tidying up her magazines on the coffee table. Eric could tell she was nervous. 'How are you feeling?' she asked.

'Been better. It's all a bit of a blur, to be honest.'

'I bet. Have you told Lizzie?'

'Yes. She's on her way.'

'That'll be nice for you.'

'Yes.' He wasn't sure though. Eric had never had a particularly good relationship with either of his daughters, Elizabeth, especially. He hadn't seen her for a good year or more. He realised he wasn't relishing her return and he knew

Susan would feel the same. As sisters, they'd never been close.

Now that he was here, he wasn't sure why. She offered him tea and he said yes, simply so she had something to do and delay them sitting in silence, wondering what to say.

'I got those Madam Butterfly tickets,' said Angela, handing him his tea. 'But if you don't want to go now, I perfectly understand. I can always go with a friend.'

'I'm not sure.'

'Do you want to talk about it?'

'Tammy? I don't know.'

'How did she... I mean, what was the cause of...'

'Someone suffocated her.'

'Oh my, no. I didn't know... Oh my word, Eric. That's awful. Suffocated?'

Eric stood. 'Shall we go for a walk? I fancy some air.'

'Yes, of course. Yes. Shall we go to the cemetery?'

'Exactly what I had in mind.'

Angela had a membership card that allowed her and a guest free entry to Highgate Cemetery. The day was overcast, threatening to rain, so Angela brought an umbrella, just in case. 'I love coming here,' said Angela. Eric breathed in the fresh, damp air as they strolled along the paths flanked by the enormous tombs and sarcophagus, covered in lichen. 'It always puts things into perspective,' said Angela. 'I love all the Gothic tombs and graves. Spooky, don't you think? George Michael is here somewhere. And Charles Cruft.'

'Who?'

'As in Crufts, the dog show. And the chap who wrote *The Forsyte Saga*.'

They stopped at a tomb and read the inscription to a boy who died, aged eight, in 1889. 'How sad,' said Angela. She took Eric's hand. He didn't want her hand but felt as if he couldn't reject her, that she'd take it badly.

A woman and child passed, the girl holding aloft a Mickey Mouse umbrella. They exchanged good mornings. Angela paused at a monument, a mournful-looking angel perched on top, covered with ivy, its long tendrils obliterating the inscription. So many tombs had, over time, been dislodged by vines and roots, as if the dead were powerless to prevent nature from reclaiming its rightful place.

Eric's mobile rang. Susan. He ignored it.

'Are you having to arrange Tammy's funeral?' asked Angela.

'Not yet, not while the police have her… body.'

'I can't believe someone suffocated her, Eric. It's too awful for words. Who would do such a thing? Do the police have any idea who might have done this?'

'I don't know but I fear I might be their number one suspect.'

She stopped. 'You? Why would you think that?'

'Because… I'm worried they'll think I killed her out of mercy or something.'

'But you were with me, weren't you? I'll be your alibi.'

'I know but it's not a good look, is it?'

'No, I suppose not. Your wife dies while you're shagging your mistress.'

'Yes, alright, Angela. Let's not be too crude about this.'

'So who was there? Susan. You don't think—'

'Don't be ridiculous. Susan wouldn't kill her own mother.'

'Stranger things have happened.'

Eric's eye was caught by a sculpture of a dog lying at the foot of a grave so covered with lichen, it was almost green. 'The other thing is…'

'Oh no, what is it now?'

'Tammy recently changed her will, leaving everything to me.'

'Everything? What about the girls?'

'Exactly. Fact is, they don't know yet. But I figured they could look after themselves for a few years yet. Lizzie has got her business in Bournemouth which, by all accounts, is flourishing.' This wasn't true; he knew full well that Lizzie's business was struggling – and that was putting it mildly. 'And Susan has got her six-figure salary while I've been…' Now that he'd started the sentence, he didn't want to finish it, didn't want to admit his financial vulnerability to her.

'You're struggling, darling? Is that what you're saying?'

'Yes. A little.'

'I could always help. I have a bit put aside.'

'No, no. Everything we had, well, frankly, it was all Tammy's. I married a rich woman.'

'And Tammy was OK changing her will in your favour?'

'Yes, of course. It made sense.' He looked away.

'Eric? Was this before or after her dementia took hold?'

'OK, OK, don't ever repeat this but… yes, I might have…'

'Taken advantage of her mental state?'

'Yes. No. Maybe a little.'

'Oh, Eric.'

'It won't make any difference in the long term, that's the thing, because… because they'll get the house and Tammy's money once I peg off but meanwhile I need to consider my own situation.'

Angela paused next to a sleeping lion atop the grave, its head resting on his enormous paws. She linked arms with Eric and they walked in silence. After a while, they came across the 'Egyptian Avenue', a sloping enclosed pathway featuring a row of vaults with iron doors on both sides. They paused to allow someone to take photos with their camera phone.

'Let's think of the future, Eric,' said Angela with a smile.

'Future?'

'Give it a few months and then we can go public.'

Eric felt his heartbeat quicken. 'Public?'

'Eric, you're beginning to sound like a parrot. Yes, public, you and me.'

'No. Hell, Angela, it looks bad enough for me already without the police bringing you into the mix.'

'That's why I'm saying we just have to wait a few months. We wait until they find the real culprit and a decent amount of time has passed and then we'll be free to do whatever we want, darling.'

'But–'

'It's what we've always wanted, isn't it?'

Chapter 13: Benedict
Today

Benedict and Jessica approached Patrick Dunt's house when they saw a man with a huge beard leaving. Indeed, he held the garden gate open for them, his eyes glancing between the two of them. Benedict thanked him. 'We're looking for Patrick Dunt. Do you know–'

'That's me,' he said in a Scottish accent.

'Oh, excellent.' Benedict and Jessica introduced themselves, showing Dunt their badges.

'I don't really have time for this.'

'We can always come back, Mr Dunt, but it really won't take long.'

The man looked worried, glancing down the street as if planning his escape. 'OK, you'd better come in.'

Dunt showed the detectives into his living room, a drab affair, a number of cardboard boxes piled in a corner. 'I'm moving out soon,' he said. 'I've had enough of London.'

'Where are you planning on going?' asked Jessica.

'Found myself a little place outside Manchester. I'm sixty-five next year. I want to live out my twilight years somewhere nice. Can't trust anyone around here these days. They'll rob you as soon as they look at you.'

Jessica came from Manchester but she didn't volunteer the information.

'I'd offer you a coffee but–'

'It's fine. Thank you. Mr Dunt, we're investigating the death of Tamsin Fournier on Tuesday night. According to Eric Fournier, the two of you spent Tuesday night together.'

'Yes, yes, that's right. Yes.'

'Did you go anywhere nice?' asked Jessica.

'Yes, I mean, no. No, we didn't. Eric came around here. We chewed the fat, you know.'

'Do you often get together like that?'

'Not often but Eric and I go back years. He's about my only friend, to be honest.'

'Won't you miss him by moving up north?'

He shrugged his shoulders. 'Of course.'

'So,' said Jessica. 'Let's pin down the timings…'

Dunt detailed what time Eric Fournier arrived and left.

'So, you're saying Eric left here at ten thirty?'

'Er, yes. Maybe I've got it wrong.'

'Maybe you have, Mr Dunt, because Eric told us half eleven.'

Dunt's cheeks flushed. 'Did he? Well, yes, maybe he's right. I lost track of time.'

He was lying. Benedict knew it and he knew Jessica knew it too. 'What was Eric wearing, Mr Dunt?'

'What was he wearing? I don't know.'

'No? Not even the colour of his shirt perhaps?'

'I…I really can't remember. I'm sorry.'

'Try, Mr Dunt. He sat here for the best part of three hours, and you can't remember if he was wearing a blue shirt, a green one or a jacket perhaps. Maybe he was wearing shorts. It was a hot day Tuesday, after all. Like you just said, you don't see him that often so surely…'

'I think, yes, he was wearing a blue shirt with buttons and a collar, you know, quite smart.'

'What did you have to drink?'

'Drink? Oh, nothing. Just a cup of coffee.'

'Does he take sugar in his coffee?'

'Eric? Oh, erm, just the one.'

'Did you eat anything? A takeaway perhaps.'

'No.'

'What did you talk about?'

'I can't remember. Would you?'

'Some of it, yes.'

'How did Eric seem, Mr Dunt?' asked Jessica.

'Fine. I mean, he's concerned, or was concerned, about Tammy, naturally. But he was fine, his usual self.'

'He didn't seem troubled by anything?'

Dunt shook his head.

'OK. Enough now,' said Benedict. 'You do appreciate, don't you, that lying to the police is a criminal offence? We are investigating a suspicious death, the victim being a helpless elderly woman, murdered in her own bed. So, I'm going to pretend that we haven't wasted the last few minutes of our time and ask you again. This time, however, I'd think very carefully about how you answer. Do you understand?'

Dunt didn't respond.

'*I said*, do you understand, Mr Dunt?'

This time he nodded.

'Did you and Mr Fournier spend much of Tuesday evening in each other's company?'

Dunt looked down at the floor. 'No. We did not.'

Jessica raised her eyebrows at Benedict. 'So, why did you lie to us, Mr Dunt?' she asked quietly.

'He asked me to.'

'He asked you to. So, for the record, you're now saying Eric Fournier and you did not meet up with each other or see each other at any point on Tuesday evening?'

'No. I'm sorry.'

'So, when was the last time you saw Eric?'

'Oh, now you're asking.'

'Yes, I am.'

'I… I've not seen Eric for quite some time. A year or more. I'm not sure. Please, don't arrest me.'

'Don't worry, Mr Dunt,' said Benedict. 'I gave you a second chance, didn't I? And we're grateful for your candour. We're going to leave you in peace now but, a word of caution, I expect out of some sort of loyalty, you'll be wanting to ring Eric and inform him of our conversation here. I can understand. However, you are not to contact him in any way, whether by phone or in person. If you do, we will know, Mr Dunt. By definition, you can only have one second chance.'

'I understand. Thank you, Inspector.'

'No, thank you, sir. We'll see ourselves out. Jessica, are you ready?'

*

Alina Zhivkov lived in a small flat with her twins, whom she'd just picked up from their primary school. Still, in their school uniforms, the girls quietly settled down to watch children's TV, each with a plate of ham sandwiches and chocolate cookies with strict instructions from their mother that they had to eat the sandwich first before relishing the cookies. Given the size of the flat and that there were three of them here, the place was remarkably organised and clutter-free. Alina was obviously a woman who knew how to make good use of the limited space available to her. Her husband, she said, was in Bulgaria. Alina was Bulgarian, not Polish, as Eric Fournier had said. Although she and the twins missed him, economically, it made sense to keep their respective jobs.

'So, how long have you been cleaning for Mr Fournier, Alina?' asked Jessica.

'Not long. Six months. I once met the lady before me. She was very young. I don't remember the name. I'm not in trouble, am I?'

'No, not at all. I'm sorry if we've given you that impression.'

'It's such a terrible thing that happened to Mrs Fournier. Terrible.'

'It is. And we hope to get to the bottom of it. Tell me, Alina, what was Mrs Fournier like when you first started? I mean, was she already poorly?'

'Yes, but not as bad. She gets worse. But it's dementia. Everyone gets worse with time.'

'Was she bedbound six months ago?'

'No, but she was forgetful and always arguing with everyone, me, Mr Fournier, her daughter. It wasn't her fault, of course.'

'No. How did Mr Fournier treat her?'

One of the twins approached her mother and said something in Bulgarian.

'In English, please.'

The girl looked momentarily embarrassed but said, 'Mama, can we have another cookie?

'Hmm. What word have you missed?'

'*Please.*'

'You can have one more *between* you.'

'Yay.' The girl skipped off, happy with the answer.

'Mr Fournier was not always so nice to his wife.'

'What do you mean?'

'He could be rude to her.'

'Did he ever do anything that alarmed you?'

'No but sometimes he shout at her and sometimes Mrs Fournier will cry.' She suddenly looked worried. 'Please, please don't tell Mr Fournier I tell you this. I can't lose my job. I have to–'

Jessica put her hand up. 'Don't worry. Whatever you tell us is in confidence.'

'I love living here but it's not always so easy. I can't go home. My girls, you see, they have their friends here.' She looked over at her girls and smiled. 'They love the pop music here and the TV. It's much better than the TV we have at home.'

'Alina,' said Benedict. 'Did Mr Fournier ever do more than shout at his wife.'

'No, no. He never hit her if that's what you mean but he was horrible to her sometimes. I could hear, anyone in the house could hear, the neighbours too perhaps.'

'Did you look after Mrs Fournier yourself, Alina?' asked Jessica.

'No. I mean, I wash her sheets and things like that but I wasn't allowed to wash her or help her get dressed. I always wanted to apply a little make-up. I see the photos of Mrs Fournier when she was young so I know she liked her make-up but I didn't like to ask.'

'OK, Alina. I think that'll be all for now. Thank you for

your time.'

Alina smiled.

Back in the car, while Jessica fiddled with the ignition, Benedict watched a woman in a white coat speckled with colour, like splatters of paint, despite the heat of the day. She paused to light a cigarette, dropping the empty pack on the pavement.

Benedict turned to Jessica. 'We need to speak to Eric Fournier again and as soon as possible.'

Benedict received a phone call on his mobile. 'Ah, this is DC Kelly,' he said to Jessica. 'Hello, DC Kelly, how can I help?'

'Hi, boss. I've been doing a bit of background research and apparently in February this year, Eric Fournier reported a break-in.'

'Did he indeed?'

'Yeah, they lost a small TV, a laptop and half their knives and forks.'

'Knives and forks?'

'Well, they were silver.'

'Oh, I see. Silver service.'

'Thing is, boss, there was no sign of a break-in, no damage or anything. There was no follow-through. A couple of our guys had a look around, gave Mr F a crime reference number and that was about it.'

'OK, that's all good to know. Thanks very much, DC Kelly.'

Chapter 14: Eric
Annecy, France, ten years ago

Eric had just come out of yet another meeting when he checked his pockets for his 'other' phone. He couldn't find it. He searched each pocket, his jacket, his trousers, he checked his briefcase, the panic rising. 'Shit.' He checked again, frantically, before having to concede, he didn't have it on him. Damn. He tried to think – where in the hell could it be? Then, he remembered leaving it in the jacket he was wearing yesterday. He cursed his carelessness; there was always a chance Tammy would find it. He just had to hope for the best.

He made his way to his office, sat down at his desk and gazed at the silver-framed photo of Tammy and the girls. It'd always been there but he stopped noticing it. He picked it up and ran his finger over the glass. He had taken it at a funfair some three years ago, a rare family day out together, Tammy in the middle, a daughter on either side, all smiling, looking happy. Innocent days.

Jean, his secretary, knocked on his door and entered. 'A

couple of messages for you…' She reeled them off, looking, as always, as if she'd just sucked on a lemon. Jean was not Eric's biggest fan. Six months ago, she went for a job in a rival firm and returned from the interview in a positive mood, confident that she'd got the job. But she didn't. She blamed Eric, accusing him of writing a less-than-stellar reference. Eric denied it and even showed her what he'd written. It seemed fine to him but Jean was not impressed. 'There's no sparkle to it,' she'd said. 'It makes me sound dependable but utterly dull.'

'What do you mean?'

'Look at it,' she said, flinging the printout back across Eric's desk. 'I wouldn't employ me on the basis of this.' She got up from the chair, a scowl on her lips. 'Thanks, Monsieur Fournier, thanks for nothing.' Eric had the feeling that Jean still hadn't forgiven him.

Eric knew Tammy would quiz him about having an affair at some point but he hadn't expected it to be so soon. Luckily, Olivia had warned him. It had come as a shock but he should have anticipated it, Tammy always had an intuitive nature. He had tried to cover his tracks but somehow it was inevitable that she'd find out eventually.

So, what now? He knew exactly what to do – assuming Tammy would have him back, and that was to stick by her. He had no intention of leaving her and hoped she wouldn't leave him. Olivia was a lovely, intelligent woman and he liked her to no end but there was no way he'd want to spend his future with her. He sort of assumed that once they'd been found out, Olivia would be happy to call it a day but what she said at the restaurant was worrying him. *Yves left me. If you leave me too, I don't know what I'll do to myself.* What had she meant by that? Was there an element of emotional blackmail in there?

His desk phone rang. Who rang that nowadays? Still, he answered it. It was Olivia. 'Your wife has just tried to kill me.'

His heart shot up to his mouth. 'Oh, shit. What do you mean?'

'She was here, in the house, she just turned up.'

He put his head in his hand. 'Oh bloody hell.'

'She said I was to keep away from you. And then she attacked me.'

'What? You mean physically?'

'Yes, Eric, she did. If Francine hadn't been here and stepped in, I…'

Was she crying? 'Olivia?'

'I dread to think.'

Hell, he could do without this. 'Did you deny it?'

'No, I did not deny it. I told her the truth.' Eric slumped at his desk, groaning. 'She has to know, Eric. Even if I had denied it, she knew. I'd be very careful when you go home tonight. I think she's capable of anything. She could kill you.'

'Tammy? No, no way, don't be…'

'You should have seen the way she looked at me, Eric. It was like she was possessed by the devil; it was really frightening.'

'Oh, God.'

'You could stay with me, darling. Start as we mean to carry on.'

'No.'

'Please. I need to see you. We've got things to discuss, like what do we do from here. Can you come over now?'

'Now? No…' He thought about this. He had work to do, for sure, but he always did and he knew his concentration would be shot at for the rest of the day. Let's get this over and done with, he thought. 'OK, I'll be there within half an hour.'

He could hear Olivia's sigh of relief. 'I look forward to it, my darling.'

Eric put the phone back in its cradle. *You won't be looking forward to it when you hear what I have to say*, he thought.

As soon as he finished his call with Olivia, his mobile rang. Tammy. His finger hovered over the 'accept' button but he couldn't talk to her over the phone, this was too big. He'd speak to her when he got home. He let the call ring out then set his phone to the 'do not disturb' mode.

Having told Jean he was going out for an hour and to reschedule a meeting he had coming up, Eric caught an Uber to Olivia's house, a fifteen-minute ride away. He wasn't looking forward to this but he needed to stand firm, cruel to be kind. Someone had left a magazine on the back seat and he used this to fan himself. He always hated high summer in this part of France – far too hot. A part of him longed to return to England. He'd been in France long enough now, he loved it here, loved the life he'd built for himself and Tammy and the girls but his heart would forever be English. The idea of starting afresh in London appealed.

The taxi drew up outside Olivia's house. He paid the driver and, standing outside the house, puffed his cheeks. He'd not been here for a couple of years and he certainly hadn't laid eyes on Francine since God knows when.

Olivia answered straight away. She looked drawn, far from her usual stylish self. 'Thanks for coming over.'

'Is your daughter in?'

'No. Does it matter?'

He followed her into the living room where she stood

looking diminished. 'I can't believe Tammy was here.' He looked around as if searching for evidence of her presence. 'I thought I'd put her mind at rest.'

'It may have been my fault. I rang your phone and I think she answered it.'

'Didn't she say anything?'

'No.'

'Shall we sit?'

'No, I'm too agitated. How did this get so messy, Eric?'

Eric smoothed down his hair. 'I don't know.'

'You can sleep in my bed tonight.'

'Sleep in your bed? Why would I–'

'You can't go home now. You don't know what you'll be walking into.'

OK, thought Eric, he needed to be straight with her, however painful. 'Olivia, listen, you and me, we can't go on.'

She stared at him with uncomprehending eyes. 'What do you mean we can't go on?'

'Exactly that. This is the end of the road for us, you must see that.'

She stepped towards him. 'No, no, not at all.' She tried to reach for his hand but he whipped it behind his back. 'This is not the end, Eric. This is our beginning. Tell her tonight, now, phone her and tell her it's over between you.'

'No! You're not listening, it's over between *us*, not Tammy and me. Us, Olivia.'

'You don't mean that.'

'Do you really expect me to leave my wife for you?'

'Yes! Yes, I do.'

'I can't.'

'You can't just throw me to the wolves now. I need you, Eric.'

'I'm sorry.' He was itching to leave now. He'd said what he needed to say; no point hanging around making it worse.

'Do you want me to beg? Is that what I have to do? Do you want me to fall at your feet? Because I will if you want me to.'

'Don't be silly.'

'You don't love her.' There was a quiver in her voice now. 'You love me, my darling, *me*.'

'I'm fond of you, Olivia, very fond of you but…'

'But what? You don't love me?' The tears were coming now. 'Is that what you're saying?'

He nodded. 'I'm truly sorry it's come to this, really I am. You're a good woman and you deserve better than me.'

'Please, Eric, don't leave me.'

'I'm going to go now–'

'Back to *her*?'

'Yes, back to her, back to my wife.'

Chapter 15: Susan
Today

Susan made her way to Greenfield Park, concerned that she was already ten minutes late. She still felt numb from realising what sort of man her father had been. She'd been tempted to read more of her father's diaries but she couldn't face it. Just knowing her father kept his diaries left her feeling sullied. She could barely look at the man, knowing what she now knew, although, in truth, she'd always known, she'd just pushed it away. How her mother must have suffered all those years and even now, he was still at it. If only she'd known, she'd have been a better daughter for her mother. Did her father ever love Tammy? Her childhood, as she knew it, had been built on lies; a father who played at happy families, who presented himself as the loving husband, was, in truth, a despicable philanderer. It hurt. It hurt a lot. Every childhood memory was now tainted, every photo from that time spoiled. She felt adrift. Her mother was dead and the man she thought was her father was the sort of man she despised.

She and Robbie hadn't specified where to meet but they'd

met here a couple of times before and always at the same bench, the one near the public lavatories. The day was still grey but being the start of the summer holidays the park was busy. She found the bench empty and claimed it. No sign of Robbie. Maybe he'd been and gone. She'd give him two minutes before phoning. So, Lizzie was due tomorrow. What joy. That was not something to look forward to. How would she react to finding out she was pregnant? She'd be pleased, for sure, but also jealous. Lizzie had long wanted a baby and had been pregnant a couple of times with her previous partner but miscarried both times. She was thirty-seven, three years older than Susan. She knew time was against her.

So where was Robbie? Robbie worked as a mechanic. It was how they met. Six months ago, she'd taken her Volvo V40 in for a service and was charmed by his dark, good looks and easy Irish charm. And he didn't wear a ring. A week later, she heard a nasty, rattling noise coming from the engine and was delighted to have the excuse to return to the same garage but disappointed to be served by a different gentleman. But returning at the end of the day, the rattling noise having been dealt with, she saw him from a distance working on another car. He turned and caught sight of her and Susan found herself waving at him as a mother might wave to her child and felt immediately rather foolish by her girly behaviour. But, no matter, it worked. He approached and asked how she was. Within the week, they'd been out twice; within the fortnight, they'd slept together; within a month, he confessed that he was married. They'd been to the cinema. Afterwards, they went to the nearest pub and had a drink and there, Robbie told her that he was married to a woman called Margot. 'But you don't wear a ring,' said Susan.

'That's because it's no happy marriage, Susie. I haven't worn that ring since… God knows how long.'

'Why don't you move out then?'

He laughed. 'Because we can't afford to split up.'

'So, what about me, Robbie? Where do I fit in with your life?'

He took her hand. 'We'll work it out. I have to. I can't stay in a loveless marriage for the rest of my life.' He tapped his temple. 'It's doing my head in.'

'I'm not going to wait forever, you know.'

'I know, darling. I know.'

Was that really only six months ago? It seemed like half a lifetime. Yet, she was still waiting. Nothing had changed. Apart from the fact that she was pregnant again and terrified by how he might take it. Robbie and Margot were still together. Had he been lying all this time about the state of his marriage? She watched a small group of boys playing cricket, taking it most seriously. Their mums had settled on the grass and clapped in the right places, shouting encouragement while collapsing in giggles at regular intervals.

'Susan, hi.'

Despite expecting him, Robbie's sudden appearance made her jump. 'Oh, Robbie, hi.' He leaned down and kissed her on the lips before sitting next to her on the bench.

'You OK? Why this sudden need to see me?'

'Do I need an excuse?' She smiled, trying to soften the implied criticism.

'No, of course not. But listen, I can't stay long. I'm working on a big repair at the moment. The bloke's a right pain. How's it going at home?'

'It's all a bit weird, to be honest.'

'I bet. I still can't believe your ma died while we were

downstairs. Look, I've been meaning to say, I'm sorry I rushed off like that. I mean, hell, if I'd known...' He didn't finish the sentence.

She patted his hand as a way of accepting his apology.

'I can't believe someone killed her. It's incredible. I mean, it could've happened while we were there, Susie, actually in the house. It's been creeping me out. We didn't hear anything, did we? I certainly didn't. Are you OK? You look... Are you sickening?'

'No–'

'I'm sorry. It's because of your ma.' He took her hand and squeezed it. 'Tough days for you, eh? I get that. But listen, I'm here for you, baby.'

The boys playing cricket cheered. Robbie looked over. 'Never understood that game. Still, looks like they're having fun.'

'I'm pregnant, Robbie.'

He let go of her hand in an instant. 'Christ, what did you say?'

He looked shocked, she'd expected that but did he look happy shocked or appalled shock? Please, please, God, let it be happy. 'Yes, really.' She tried to smile.

He ran his hand over his hair. 'Jesus, oh, Jesus, Susan. I thought...' He stood.

'You thought what?'

'Are you sure?'

'Of course, I'm sure.'

He sat again. He'd turned pale. 'And, er, what... what do you plan on doing?'

'Me? Us, Robbie.' She reached for his hand but he quickly withdrew it. 'It's *our* baby, Robbie. You and me.'

'You can't keep it.'

His words tore through her. She tried to speak but the words wouldn't come.

Seeing her distress, Robbie relented a little and took her hand. 'I'm sorry, I didn't mean to be so blunt. But, Susie, please, you must see how... how impractical it'd be.'

'Impractical? Why?'

'Because... Hell, Susie, I'm married in case you forgot.'

'Yes but you said... you've always said you and Margot aren't happy.'

'Yeah but...'

'But what, Robbie, what?' She could feel the ache in the pit of her stomach.

'She needs me. She's not well.' He closed his eyes tightly as if in pain.

'But you will leave her, Robbie. You said.'

He shook his head and Susan had to bite her fist to stop herself from crying out.

'I can't. Not now.'

'What do you mean she's not well? You never said.'

He couldn't look at her. Speaking with his eyes cast down, he said, 'She gets depressed. I mean, really down. She's had a lot of shit to deal with and all that so I can't... I can't just up and leave.'

'She's had a lot of shit to deal with?' she cried. 'And I haven't? My mother's been murdered, I think my father's been seeing another woman and I'm pregnant. Pregnant with *your* child, Robbie. And I'm telling you this now, I am keeping this baby so don't ever again suggest otherwise.'

'I've got to go.'

She grabbed his arm. 'No, you can't. Don't go. *I* need you, Robbie and I'm the one that's pregnant.'

'Look.' He rubbed his eyes. 'Tell me what you want me to

do.'

'Do? I want you to leave Margot and commit yourself to me and your child.'

He looked at her with total incomprehension in his eyes. 'Oh, right. You make it sound so easy but we've only known each other for five minutes. Me and Margot, we've been married ten years.'

'So you've been lying to me all this time? All this stuff about it being a loveless marriage?'

'It is, it's exactly that but I told you, I can't just leave her – not in her state. Look...' He glanced at the time on his phone. 'I really must go. I'm sorry, Susie. I'm really sorry.' He stood. 'I'll give you a ring, OK?'

'Tonight. Give me a ring tonight.'

'Yeah. Yeah sure.' He didn't kiss her goodbye, simply walked off without looking back. Susan looked up at the grey sky and allowed the tears to fall.

The boys playing cricket and their mums had gone and Susan hadn't even noticed them leave.

Chapter 16: Frida
Today

Frida brought Ade his usual cup of coffee in bed, milk with two sugars. He sat up, bare-chested, as she passed him his coffee and he took it, neither looking at the other. She needed to get changed for work which meant changing in front of him. Luckily, he picked up his phone from under the bed and began scrolling. She slipped out of her pyjamas and into her clothes as quickly as possible, pulling a beige jumper over her head. Ade lit a cigarette. 'You're not wearing that old thing again, are you?'

'It's only for work.'

Recently, Ade had stopped having breakfast in an attempt to reduce his beer gut so at least Frida didn't have to worry about cooking breakfast any more.

Reading his phone, Ade said 'Yes' to himself, as if what he'd just read was a cause of celebration. 'Northern Star's odds have lengthened.'

'Is that good?' asked Frida.

'Bloody right it is.'

'No, Ade, I can't. I don't have any money left.'

He put his palm up. 'Calm it, will you? I'm sorted.'

She managed to stop herself from saying something sarcastic. The last two times Ade bet on the horses, he'd borrowed from her. The last time he lost and she never saw a whiff of her money again. The time before that he won on an each-way bet but he conveniently forgot that she'd paid for it. She never reminded him.

'Right, OK,' she said. She hadn't done her make-up yet but that was fine; she'd do it on the bus. 'I'll be off.'

But he wasn't listening, too engrossed in his phone.

Frida worked in a charity shop. Being the caretaker manager, she was the only paid member of the shop, the rest of the staff made up of volunteers. She enjoyed the work; she had a degree of responsibility but not too much to be stressful. The pay, whilst not great, was decent, at least it would be if she didn't have to support Ade. Ade got himself some occasional work as a labourer but nothing permanent. He was, by his own admission, work-shy.

As soon as she got to work, Frida knew she had a staffing problem for the day. One of her two volunteers called in sick, leaving only Stan for the first couple of hours and then from mid-morning 'grumpy' Mary. June, who was due to work the afternoon shift, couldn't come in earlier. So, Frida spent the next thirty minutes phoning the other volunteers. None were available, many on holiday – it was that time of year, after all. She rang head office and got no joy from there either. 'Looks like it's just you and me then, Stan.'

'Let's hope it's not busy then,' said Stan with a wink. 'But if it is, we'll cope, won't we?'

Frida smiled for the first time in the day. 'We sure will, Stan.'

Stan was quite the most endearing man she'd ever met, a kindly Jamaican gentleman in his late sixties, a widower of many years, a lonely guy who loved his volunteering. His eyes, a shade of soft, faded blue, hinted at a melancholy from the years spent alone. His neat hair and trimmed beard, mostly silver, framed his face with a distinguished air that added to his charm.

Unfortunately, it was super busy. As soon as Frida opened the door at ten o'clock, people started coming in, too many people. A whole lot of new donations had come in but Frida and Stan were too busy to sort through it. During a lull, Frida popped into the small staffroom at the back of the shop. Her phone rang. It was Ade. She'd take it; Ade was never one to talk on the phone, his calls never lasted more than a few seconds. 'I've got a job down Elephant and Castle today.'

'Oh, that's good. Labouring?'

'Yeah, just this site needs a whole lot of stuff shifted. Anyway, I need you to do me a favour. Northern Star is running at the twelve-fifteen at Newton Abbot. Can you put two ton on for me?'

'Two ton? Two hundred quid?'

'I'll pay you back. You know I will. She's five to one. That'll be a grand in the pocket.'

'I can't. I'm—'

'I'd do it myself but I've got to get down to Elephant and Castle. Remember, Northern Star, twelve-fifteen. Better go.'

'No, Ade, hang on…'

He'd rung off. 'Shit.' This was the last thing she needed today. The nearest bookmaker was a good seven-minute walk. She could do it on her phone but she'd never done so before, didn't even have an app and wouldn't know where to start. Stan popped her head around the door. 'I'm sorry to bother you, Frida, but we're getting busier.'

'Sorry, sorry, Stan. Give me a mo. Something's come up. I'll be there in a minute.'

'Take your time, love.' With a smile, he returned to the fray. That was Stan for you. Then Frida remembered Diane saying she had the day off today. She phoned her, willing her to pick up. She did. 'Oh, Diane, listen, I need a favour…'

Frida could tell Diane wasn't keen but, bless her, she said she'd do it, said there was a William Hill close to where she lived. Frida thanked her. Time to rejoin Stan in the shop.

The shop remained busy; the morning passed quickly. Soon, Mary turned up for her late-morning shift, replacing Stan. Frida didn't warm to Mary, whom she found condescending and quick to criticise.

Stan seemed to know this. Stepping up to Frida as he was about to leave, he whispered, 'Don't worry, Frida, her bark's worse than her bite.'

'Thanks, Stan,' she mouthed.

Two hours later, Mary declared she was going to lunch. 'Is it that time already?' said Frida. She looked at the time on her phone and realised with a jolt, that yes, it was exactly twelve – Ade's horse race was starting in fifteen minutes.

'Are you going out for lunch?' asked Frida.

'No, of course not as there's only the two of us.'

'Of course. Sorry, yes.'

Mary was right – Oxfam rule: never leave a member of staff alone in the shop, even if the other was out the back on break. There *had* to be two members of staff on the premises at all times.

Frida needed to ring Diane and make sure she got to the bookies OK but there was a woman in front of her trying to decide which of three skirts to buy. They were only a fiver each, for God's sake. Frida felt like saying *buy the whole bloody lot*. The seconds ticked by. Finally, the woman made her decision, paid her five pounds and left. Frida took the opportunity to ring Diane. No answer. Damn. She left a message – *Did you get to the bookies?* She wanted to ring her again but another customer, a man buying three paperback novels, prevented her from doing so. He started talking to her about one of the books, a novel by Cormac McCarthy, who'd just died. She felt her phone buzz in her jeans pocket. 'Have you read *No Country For Old Men*?'

'What?'

'*No Country For Old Men* by McCarthy. It's good. A bit gory in places and bleak as hell but, you know, it's a good read.'

'No, no, I've not read it.' She needed to check her phone.

'How long have you been working here?' he asked with a smile.

Was he flirting with her? He was old enough to be her father. 'Too long. Look, if you–'

'Actually, yes, I've seen you before. Do you like it here?'

'Listen, I don't mean to be rude but–'

'Oh, I'm sorry. I always talk too much. I'll see you again. I like to pop in every now–'

'Yes, yes, see you again.' She stepped away from him and finally taking the hint, he ambled off, giving her a silly little wave. She looked at her phone screen and swore. 'Shit!' People looked at her but she didn't notice, her heart was hammering too loudly. Diane had forgotten. *Sorry hun. Totally forgot. xx. Hope it doesn't win LOL!!!*

'Oh, Christ.' What to do? What to do? She went to the app store and tried searching for William Hill but her hands were shaking too much. She would have to download the app, set up an account with a password, verify the new account via email, and insert her payment details. The usual palaver. Then, she'd have to find the race and learn how to place a bet and all in… she checked the time again… eleven minutes. Oh God, oh hell. It'd be quicker to run to the William Hill on the high street. Bloody Diane. How could she have forgotten?

An old woman approached the counter bearing an oval-shaped metallic tray. 'Sorry, till's broke,' snapped Frida.

'You what, love?'

'You'll have to come back later.'

'Oh dear. Can you put it aside for me? I can—'

'Oh, just go away, will you?'

Her mouth dropped open. Frida barged past her, rushing for the door. Could she do this? Could she get to the cashpoint, draw out £200, get to the bookies, place the bet and be back in time *and* all that before Mary noticed? Nine minutes. She had no choice. Frida ran.

Chapter 17: Eric
Annecy, France, ten years ago

Eric had planned on returning to work having seen Olivia but this was too big; he needed to see Tammy straight away – his marriage and his future could well depend on it. Olivia had turned hysterical, sobbing, and wailing. Telling her to 'get a grip' only made matters worse.

When he tried to leave, she barred his way. 'Please, Olivia, don't do this.'

'I thought we had a future together, Eric,' she said, her eyes glazed with tears.

'I never at any point said I'd leave Tammy for you. Not once.' He didn't intend to say it so severely but his patience was fast running out. In a softer voice, he said, 'How can I do to Tammy what Yves did to you?'

'Don't mention that bastard's name in front of me.'

'You, of all people, know what it's like.'

'This is worse.'

'Worse? How can it be worse? You were married to… to him for *years*. You and I, we've only been going a couple of months.'

'If you leave me, Eric, I'll make your life miserable. I'll promise you that. You'll wish you'd never met me.'

'You're threatening me now?' He could feel his patience stretched to breaking point. 'I've had enough of this.' Brusquely, he pushed her to one side.

She called after him. 'Eric, no, please, Eric. I didn't mean it. Please... please...'

He could still hear her as he closed the front door on her and charged down the garden path. Reaching the gate, he paused to make sure he hadn't left his phone behind. He looked back at the house and, from the corner of his eye, saw movement from an upstairs window, a shadowy figure. Was that Francine up there? Olivia said she was out but he definitely saw someone. Had she heard everything? It'd have been hard not to. He could only imagine what it must have sounded like from her point of view, having to hear your poor mother's desperate crying, the hard-headed man rejecting her. Despite the heat of the day, a cold shiver ran down his back, someone stepping over his grave.

*

Eric caught an Uber south, back home, ringing Jean and informing her he wouldn't be in for the rest of the day. Jean huffed, evidently not impressed. He didn't care what she thought, the sour old bat. He sat in the back of the car chomping at a fingernail. He'd been a fool, a massive fool. Why had he done it? Yes, Olivia was an attractive woman but he didn't love her, never had. It was Tammy he loved, only ever Tammy, and if she booted him out now, as she had every right to do, he'd be destroyed. The thought of life without Tammy was unbearable. He needed her. Also, he couldn't face his daughters once they found out. He'd be such a disappointment to them and they'd hate him forever more. He cursed. He really had fucked up. The car drew up outside home. If he thought confronting Olivia was hard, this was going to be a hundred times harder. He felt in control of the narrative with Olivia but not here. If Tammy pointed at the door, he'd have no choice but to leave. The prospect filled him with dread. This, he realised, was a watershed moment…

Still only mid-afternoon, the day seemed to be getting hotter by the minute. He stopped at the front door and took a deep breath. He held onto that breath as he unlocked the door and stepped indoors. The house felt eerily quiet. 'Hello,' he called out quietly. He poked his head around the living room door. Tammy wasn't there. Nor in the kitchen or the dining room. OK, not to panic. He crept upstairs. He wondered whether he needed to knock on his own bedroom door. He didn't but eased it open gently. She was sitting cross-legged on the bed, her eyes red, her hand balling numerous tissues, the tissue box in front of her.

'Forgive me, Tammy. I'm so sorry.'

'Are you?' Her voice was hoarse.

He approached her as one might approach a foal. 'Can we talk?'

She nodded. She wore a baggy tee shirt and a pair of shorts. She looked terribly vulnerable sitting there on the bed.

'I'm not going to lie to you again, Tammy. I did something stupid and I regret it. I regret it so much.' He wanted to take her hand but thought it best not to, that it was too early. One step at a time. 'I could try and offer you a hundred and one excuses but it won't change what's happened. It did happen and I can't change that but it won't happen again, that I can promise you.'

'It's over?'

'Yes. It's over. I shall never see her or speak to her again.'

Tammy nodded but didn't seem capable of saying anything else. She looked exhausted.

'I…' He was about to say he'd heard about her confrontation with Olivia but decided against it. 'I've been such an idiot, a damn fool, and I'm sorry for hurting you, Tammy. I can't tell you how sorry I am.'

'So you're not planning on leaving me for her then?' Her voice was still so quiet, he had to turn his head to hear her.

'God, no, not in a hundred years, not ever. Unless you want me to go?'

She shook her head. 'No. I'd like you to stay.'

'Good. Thank you.' He wiped the sweat from his forehead. 'It's more than I deserve.'

'I'd like a little time to myself. Do you mind?'

'God, no, not at all. I'll be downstairs. I'm not going back to work. Call me if you need me.' He stopped himself from calling her 'love' and from leaning over and kissing her cheek. He'd achieved more than he'd dared to hope. With a quick smile, he left Tammy to herself. He returned downstairs and it was only as he fell on the settee, he realised just how close he'd come to everything blowing up in his face. Never again, he said. Never again.

His mobile rang, his 'normal' mobile. Olivia's number. He stared at the screen. Why was she phoning him? He ignored it, he had no desire to speak to her ever again. He turned the volume off.

An hour passed. Tammy came downstairs. Eric shot up from his chair. 'Hi. Tammy–'

'I want you to listen to me.'

'OK.'

'If you want this marriage to work, you are not to see that woman ever again. You–'

'I don't intend to.'

'Let me finish. You're not to see her or speak to her. Ever. After this conversation, we never mention her name again. It'll be like she never existed.'

'Fine by me.'

'I'm giving you a second chance, Eric. I will not give you a third.'

'I understand. Thank you, Tammy.'

'I've been thinking. I think perhaps we need a change.'

'Like what?'

'How about we start again in England?'

'I was thinking the same.'

'Could you start a new practice in England?'

'Me? Of course I could. Where would you like to go?'

'I don't know. East Anglia looks nice. But perhaps London to begin with.'

'I'd love to go back to London.'

'A new start for both of us.'

'Yes, yes. I couldn't agree more.' Was this the moment to hug her, he wondered. He didn't want to overstep the occasion. But he did, he stepped over and placed his arms around her, embracing her. She didn't respond at first but after a few seconds, he felt her hands on his back. He smiled. He'd done it, he'd survived this.

Chapter 18: Susan
Today

'You can't keep it.' That's what Robbie had said when she told him yesterday in the park that she was pregnant. 'You can't keep it.' How could he have been so cruel? It'd be impractical, he said. Impractical? What sort of word was that? This was a baby they were talking about, not a bloody dog.

Susan could not concentrate on anything. Lizzie was due at any moment. Her father had asked Susan to come around, presumably, she thought, so that he didn't have to face greeting her by himself. Any other time, she'd have told her father to 'man up' but given the circumstances, still only two days since Mum's death, she agreed. And frankly, given how wretched she was feeling after her confrontation the day before, she was pleased for the distraction.

She sat in her father's living room, scrolling through the news app on her phone. Robbie hadn't phoned her last night like he promised he would. She phoned him only to be put through to his voicemail. Tempted though she was to leave a rude message, telling him exactly what she thought of him, she resisted it. She hoped he would have got in contact now. He must know how she'd been feeling. Was he not just a little concerned for her?

Her father popped in looking like a man in search of something. 'Have you seen my address book, Susie? Listen, I've been speaking to the funeral directors. I'm thinking of having your mother cremated. Just a small affair, family and close friends, that sort of thing. Ah, here it is,' he said, holding up his address book. 'Are you OK? You look a bit…'

'I'm fine.' She looked hard at him and experienced a rush of anger; how she wanted to hurt him for all the things he'd done, for hurting her mother, for hurting *her*.

He nodded. 'OK, if you're sure. Lizzie should be here any moment. I'll see you in a bit.'

She thought Robbie would be delighted. How could she have got it so wrong? How many times had he said that he and his wife were married in name only? It was a 'loveless' marriage; they hadn't been intimate for months. Had he been lying to her all this time? She had no idea what to think. He said Margot was ill, gets depressed. Like hell she did. And even if she did, so what? Susan was pregnant and there was no way she was going to let Robbie shirk his responsibilities. It was as much *his* baby as hers.

She heard a car draw up outside. Lizzie had arrived.

Susan remained in the living room and could hear her father greeting Lizzie, asking after her drive from Bournemouth, saying how well she looked and asking whether she wanted a cup of tea or something stronger. Lizzie came into the living room, talking about a hold-up on the M3, her father behind her, and stopped short on seeing Susan. 'Susie!' she screeched as if her sister was the last person she expected to see. 'Is it true?'

Susan stood. 'Is what true?'

'That you're preggers, silly.'

'Oh, yes, it is true all right.' She tried to sound upbeat but feared she'd failed.

'Isn't that wonderful? Come here.' The sisters hugged. 'You look blooming. Look at your hair!'

'You look well too.' Why, Susan wondered, did she feel guilty? Guilty that she was pregnant and Lizzie, desperate to have a baby, was not. Wanting to change the subject and take the focus away from herself, she asked, 'How goes life in Bournemouth?'

Lizzie puffed out her cheeks. 'Oh, it's a long story. Anyway, we can get to that. Shocking business, isn't it? Poor old Mum. How beastly it all is. Have the police found the bastard yet, Daddy?'

'No, I've not heard a peep since they were here asking all their questions, looking at me suspiciously.'

Lizzie fell onto the settee. 'I'm exhausted. Three-hour drive that. And why would they treat you suspiciously, Daddy? Surely, they don't think you had anything to do with it. You loved Mum.'

'They always suspect the husband, don't they?' His mobile rang. 'Oh, I'd better get this, it's the funeral directors. Excuse me, ladies.'

'Ladies!' said Lizzie, laughing. 'Huh! So, who's your man then, Susie?'

Although she'd been expecting the question, it still took Susan by surprise. 'Oh, no one you know.'

'When do we get to meet him?'

'Soon. Soon.'

'Have you been together long? Any plans for marriage?'

'A while. And no, not yet.'

Lizzie pulled a face; it was obvious she didn't approve. 'What would Mummy say? Did she know?'

'There's a lot Mummy didn't know.'

'What do you mean?'

Could she tell her? Tell her sister what a bastard their father was; that he'd always been a bastard. No, she couldn't, she'd spare her, let her sister exist with her childhood memories intact. Why should their father infect all the women in his life?

'I did tell Mummy about the baby, yes,' she lied. 'But you know, she didn't take it in.'

'No. I suppose not.'

'So, how's life in Bournemouth?' asked Susan again, not that she cared much but she needed to change the subject.

Lizzie spoke about the summer influx of tourists in Bournemouth, pouring scorn on all the second homeowners and the knock-on effects on house prices there.

'How's your business going?'

Lizzie screwed her eyes shut. 'Not great, to be honest.'

'Oh?' Why did Susan experience a brief rush of glee?

'I thought I'd ridden out the post-Brexit slump but apparently not. One of my biggest importers, this firm in Luxembourg, has bailed out on me. It's shattering my profit margins.'

'Still, you'll have a cash injection from Mum's will.'

'I know. It sounds terribly mercenary but I shall need it. Hey, Susie, you couldn't help me out a little? I'm sorry to ask but I know–'

'No. Sorry, Lizzie but no.'

'OK.' She threw her hands up. 'I just thought…'

'You just thought what?'

'Well, you got your super salary and—'

'I'm about to have a baby, Lizzie. It's not cheap, you know.'

'I know, I know. Forget I asked, I'm sorry.'

'You could ask Daddy.'

Their father returned to the living room. 'Ask me what?'

'Nothing,' said Lizzie quickly.

'No, go on. What is it you want to ask me?'

Susan cleared her throat. 'We know it's a bit early to ask about such things but, you know, practicalities of life and all that...' She could barely speak to the man. It was like talking to a stranger.

'Spit it out, Susan.'

'No, it's fine,' said Lizzie. 'Susan, it's fine, really.'

'What's going on?' asked Eric.

'We want to know about Mum's will.'

'Oh.' He rubbed his chin. 'I see.'

It *was* too early to ask, thought Susan, he looked offended by the question. But guess what? She didn't care.

'It really doesn't matter,' said Lizzie.

Eric wiped his nose with the back of his hand. 'Your mother left her entire estate to me.'

Lizzie and Susan stared at him, the silence between them heavy with unspoken expressions of horror. Lizzie broke the silence: 'I thought...'

'I know. She changed her will. I begged her not to but...'

'But?'

'She had her reasons. Sound reasons, as it happens.'

'Such as?'

'Lizzie,' said Susan. 'You can't ask that. It's none of our business.'

Lizzie shot up from the settee. 'I'd say it was very much our business actually. So? Go on, Daddy, what reasons were they?'

Eric wandered over to the window. With his back to his daughters, he said, 'When your mother fell ill, I was here to look after her. But what if I get dementia too?' He turned around. 'Or got too infirmed to be of any use? Or dropped dead from a heart attack. It could happen. What then? Would either of you give up your career? No, I wouldn't expect you to but your mother could have ended up in a home or I could and that costs a lot of money. You know that.'

'Did you exert your influence, Dad?'

'What sort of question is that?'

'Lizzie, no,' said Susan. 'That's unfair.'

'It wouldn't be the first.'

'Well, I did not. Now, if you excuse me, I have a call to make.'

He stormed out of the living room. Lizzie shook her head. 'Nice one,' said Susan. 'You can't stop yourself, can you?'

'What do you mean?'

'You're back for two minutes and you throw a bomb into the fire. Daddy's lost his wife, for fuck's sake, and you accuse him of exploiting Mum. Christ, Lizzie. So typical of you. Welcome home.' Why, she wondered, was she sticking up for him? Because this was the nature of their relationship and now wasn't the time to break from that tradition.

'Yeah,' said Lizzie. 'And it's so typical of you to think the sun shines out of his arse. You can't bring yourself to admit what he's really like. Maybe you don't know, you buggered off to uni as soon as you could. But I was still here, wasn't I? And I saw how he treated Mummy. He bullied her, Susie. So, don't get all rose-tinted specs on me.'

'He wouldn't have done that.'

'What? Manipulated Mummy, you mean? Yeah, sure, Susie,

if that's what you want to believe, you go ahead, you keep your head in the sand.'

If only, thought Susan, if only.

Chapter 19: Frida
Today

Mercifully, there was no queue at the cashpoint. She had to pause a moment to catch her breath. Did she have enough funds? Yes, she was sure of it. Two hundred pounds – so much to draw out in one hit. To her relief, the money appeared. Now, the bookies. Four minutes. She ran along the high street but she'd forgotten exactly where it was. She asked a passer-by who didn't know. A second person however did. Pushing herself on, she finally found it. The time was twelve seventeen. Oh God. Was she too late? Maybe they had delayed starting the race, maybe you could still place a bet while the race was on. She approached the counter, a young, bored-looking woman behind it, her hefty bosom spilling on her desk behind the perspex front.

'Can I put a bet on the twelve-fifteen at Newton Abbot, please?'

'Twelve-fifteen? Oh no, sorry, love, you're too late for that. It's already started and we don't do in-play betting here.'

Frida felt her bowels loosen. 'Too late?'

'Yep. Sorry, love.'

'Please, I must. I have to.'

'What? You begging now? If you're too late, you're too late. What do you expect me to do? Stop the horses?' She motioned at one of the large TV screens behind Frida. 'That's the one.'

Frida stepped over to the TV, her eyes transfixed on the race. Her ears tuned into the commentator. Northern Star was out in front. 'Oh God, no.' She caught the attention of a couple of men who sniggered. One had an unlit cigarette behind his ear.

'What's the matter, darling? Don't you want Northern Star to win?'

'No. Anyone but him.'

'Our money's on Laptop Larry.' The men returned their attention to the screen. 'And yeah, he's catching up.' The men rubbed their hands. 'Come on, Larry. Come on, you old bugger!'

It was true, Laptop Larry was closing in on Northern Star.

Frida could tell from the increasing noise from the crowd and the rising excitement in the commentator's voice that the race was coming to an end. Northern Star couldn't win. Only Laptop Larry could catch him now. 'Please, Larry, please win,' she muttered. The men were shouting at the TV, urging Larry on. Frida too was screaming now, tears in her eyes. She'd never wanted something as much as this. Another half furlough according to the commentor. The two horses were neck and neck. Frida feared her heart was about to give way. Was Larry inching in front? Was he? Was he? The horses sped past the finishing line. Had he won? Had he? No! Northern Star had won it by a whisper. The two men swore. One tore his betting slip into two. His friend slapped him on the back. 'There's still the twelve-forty-five,' he said.

There was no twelve-forty-five for Frida. Northern Star had won. And she'd missed it. She felt sick. 'How much did he win?' she asked the man with the cigarette.

'I don't know, darling.'

'No, I mean, what were the… what do you call it? The odds?'

'Oh, the odds. What was it in the end, Bill?'

'Four to one.'

'So…' She didn't want to know the answer but she had to ask. 'If I put on two hundred pounds–'

'Yeah, eight hundred back. Is that how much you lost? Two hundred.'

No, she thought, she'd lost a lot more than that. But she nodded.

'Bad luck, love. Better luck next time, eh?'

She forced a smile.

She wandered back to work. She should have been rushing but she was so drained by the experience, her legs wouldn't let her. Ten minutes later, she approached the shop, praying that the shit hadn't hit the fan, that Mary was still out at the back quietly having her lunch, and that any customers still remaining hadn't rioted or looted the place. She was about to walk in when her phone rang. Her heart tumbled on seeing the name on the screen. Ade. She chose to ignore it. She couldn't face him yet, she needed time to think, time to work out a plan of action, namely, how in the hell was she going to find eight hundred quid in an afternoon?

She walked in to find the shop still busy with customers and Mary behind the counter, serving someone, red-faced and looking haggard. This, thought Frida, wasn't looking good. Mary finished with her customer and, turning to Frida, said, 'Oh, she's back. At last. Where the hell have you been, Frida?'

'I'm so sorry. I had an emergency.'

'Well, that's all very well but you could have told me. It's been so busy. I had to cut short my lunch, thanks to your disappearing act. You can't leave me by myself. You know the rules. What if something had gone wrong? Oh, and what's more, someone's complained about you.'

'Me?'

'Yes, you. You were rude to her, apparently.'

'Who?'

'A woman with that metallic tray. She said she's going to put in a formal complaint. Now, if you don't mind, I'd rather like to finish my lunch hour.'

'Yes, sorry, Mary. You go ahead. Like I said, it was an emergency. I–'

Mary put her hands up. 'Save it for management. I'm not interested.' Mary stormed off, throwing Frida a final look of disgust. Management? She was going to report this to management? And a formal complaint, too. But the gravity of the situation didn't register. She had bigger problems to worry about.

She served a young couple buying a baby's play station with lots of dangling mobiles and bells. They seemed delighted with their purchase. She needed an excuse, a damn good excuse. Bloody Diane, how could she have forgotten? Ade would go mad. Eight hundred quid. Her life wouldn't be worth living. But what could she say, what possible excuse was there? She had the two hundred in her pocket but where would she find the rest? She tapped the 'No Sale' button on the till, opening the drawer. There must've been about a further three hundred or more here. Could she? She glanced up at the CCTV camera pointing directly at the counter. No, too dangerous unless, that is, she could switch the CCTV off for a few minutes. She could claim they had an outage. This was desperate. What was she thinking about?

Her mobile rang. She couldn't ignore it again.

'Hey, Frida, Northern Star – what a star. We're in the money, babes.'

'Listen, Ade, the thing is–'

'What? You *did* put the bet on, didn't you? Please tell me you did.'

'No.'

'You what?'

'I couldn't get away, Ade. It was mad here and there was only the two of us and–'

'You are bloody joking me. You're having a laugh. Tell me you are.'

'No. See–'

'Come on, you're pissing me about.'

The tears came. 'I'm not, Ade. I'm so sorry. It wasn't my fault. I'm not allowed to leave the shop if–'

'I don't believe I'm hearing this.' He was yelling now. Frida could visualise him, pacing, his fist clenching, his face beetroot red. 'Eight hundred, for fuck's sake. You stupid, *stupid* bitch.'

'How much is this?' came a woman's voice. 'Miss, how much is this jumper? I can't find the price.'

'Have it,' said Frida. 'It's free. Just take it.'

'You sodding owe me eight hundred pounds, Frida.'

'I know, Ade. I'll pay you back, honest I will. I get paid in four days. I'll pay you then.'

'Free? I can't just take it.'

'Four days? Christ, Frida.'

'Are you sure it's free?'

'Yes! Just take the bloody thing.'

'Eight hundred quid, Frida. I'm not fucking about here. I want my money or you're dead, you got that?'

'Yes, yes. You'll have it, I promise.'

He rang off.

'You,' said the woman approaching Frida behind the counter. 'You, young lady, need to work on your customer relations. How dare you swear at me? What's your name?'

'Just go. Please, just leave me alone.'

Chapter 20: Eric
Annecy, France, ten years ago

The day after the reconciliation with Tammy, Eric went to work. He volunteered to stay at home but Tammy insisted she was OK. And so, somewhat reluctantly, he went. Having not looked at his phone since yesterday afternoon, he was shocked to see he had no less than twenty-two missed calls from Olivia, plus a couple from Jean.

He'd been at work only an hour when Jean knocked on his office door and popped her head around. 'Someone to see you, Mr Fournier.'

'Who?'

'She didn't want to give her name.'

'A woman?'

'Yes.'

'A client?'

'I don't think so. Shall I say you're free?'

'No, absolutely not. Tell whoever it is I'm out.'

'All day?'

'Yes, all day. And for the foreseeable future.'

Jean raised her eyebrows but said nothing. Eric dabbed his brow with his handkerchief. How much hotter was it going to get? It wasn't even ten in the morning yet.

A minute later, his office door swung open and there, in front of him, was Olivia.

He shot up from his chair. 'Olivia?'

'Out, are you? The way your secretary said it, I knew she was lying.'

Bloody Jean, why was she so disloyal? 'Olivia, you can't just come barging in.'

'What choice do you leave me with when you don't answer my calls?'

'I had my phone switched off.'

'Liar.'

'Tell me what it is you want then go.'

She sat. 'Is that how you treat me now? You used me, Eric. I see that now. You've had your way and now I'm to be discarded like a piece of trash.'

'I used *you*? You couldn't get enough of me–'

'Huh! Don't flatter yourself.'

'Actually, thinking about it, you used *me*. I paid for everything, I mean every single drink and meal.'

'Oh, if that concerns you, let me write you a cheque.'

'No, you just need to go. I'm sorry it's come to this, really I am, but I can't desert Tammy, and I certainly can't have you ringing me twenty-two bloody times in one night and morning.'

'You didn't answer.'

'There's nothing else left to say, Olivia. Look, I didn't mean to hurt you or Tammy–'

'Bit late for that now.'

'Yes, and I'm sorry about that.' He flung his arms out.

'What else can I say?'

She leaned forward in the chair. 'That you'll do the decent thing and leave her for me.'

'Why? Are you pregnant?'

She didn't answer straight away for a horrendous second, Eric feared she might say she was.

'No, of course not. I think I'd have mentioned it by now.'

'Good.' And he meant it. 'Listen, I've done the *decent thing* and I'm sticking by the woman I married. I'm sorry if Yves didn't measure up but I can't help that.'

'Oh, how noble you are.'

'So, look, if there's nothing else, I do have a lot of work to catch up on.'

She folded her arms across her chest. 'I'm not leaving.'

'What? Why? To what purpose?'

'I'm going to make you regret that you ever slept with me.'

Eric rose from his chair. 'I've had enough of this,' he muttered, circling around the desk. He grabbed her from under the arm and tried to pull her off the chair.

'Get off me. Get off.'

'Get out of here, Olivia, just leave, will you?'

She gripped the seat of the chair. However hard he tried, Eric couldn't dislodge her. 'Stop,' she yelled. 'Get your hands off me.'

'Leave then.' He tried again, yanking her up by the arms, but she was stronger than she looked and held on. He was covered in sweat now. Giving up, he stretched back, frustrated, annoyed and exhausted by the heat and the exertion. She grinned up at him and in his utter frustration, he slapped her.

Olivia's head spun back. She screamed.

'I'll call the police,' said a familiar voice. He looked up to see Jean disappearing down the corridor. How long had she been there? He ran after her. 'Jean, Jean, wait a minute.'

She stopped and turned around to face him. 'I saw you. I saw you assaulting a woman.'

'She's hassling me.'

'That's no excuse. You hit her. I'm calling the police.' She stormed off.

Eric ran after her, gripping her upper arm and pulling her back. 'Wait, will you?'

'Are you going to hit me too now, Monsieur Fournier?'

'Stop being so ridiculous.'

'Oh, so assaulting a woman is ridiculous now, is it? I saw it with my own eyes, you bully.' She marched off again and this time, Eric didn't chase her. He traipsed back to the office. Olivia was still there, her palm against the side of her face, tears coursing down her cheek.

'Forgive me, Olivia. I shouldn't have done that.'

'You bastard, Eric,' she cried. 'You utter, utter bastard.'

'Please tell my secretary you don't need the police.'

'I think I do. I've never been so humiliated.'

Eric fell onto his chair and had to stop himself from screaming.

Three minutes later, Jean returned. 'The police are on their way,' she said, barely disguising either her disgust or glee. Turning to Olivia, she said, 'Would you like to sit with me, madam?'

Olivia looked up at her.

'It might be safer.'

'Yes, yes, you're probably right. Thank you.'

Jean led the still weeping Olivia away but not before both women stole a look at Eric. Eric buried his face in his hands and groaned loudly.

It took twelve minutes for two uniformed policemen to turn up. They eyed Eric suspiciously as Jean showed them into the office. Eric stood. They introduced themselves but Eric didn't take the names in. The taller one said, 'We understand you've been hitting a woman, monsieur.'

'Well–'

'What is your name?'

Eric told them. 'Look, it's not how it looks–'

'No? Tell us how it does look then.'

'She was hassling me and she refused to leave. I asked her several times. And it was so hot and I got frustrated so I lashed out at her. I didn't mean to but…'

'So, you're readily admitting it.'

'No. Yes, but it's not as simple as that.'

Turning to Jean, the shorter one asked, 'Did you witness the assault, madam?'

'Stop calling it assault,' yelled Eric, the sweat pouring off him.

'You hit a person. There is no other word for it. Madam, you witnessed it?'

'Mademoiselle.'

He bowed. 'Mademoiselle. My apologies.'

'Yes, I did see Monsieur Fournier hit the woman you saw. You saw how red her cheek is.'

'Did he punch her or–'

'No, he slapped her.' Jean looked at Eric before adding, 'Hard.'

'This is madness,' said Eric.

'I saw what I saw.'

'Would you be prepared to make a statement, Mademoiselle?'

'Of course.'

Turning to Eric, the taller one said, 'Do you have a solicitor, Monsieur Fournier?'

'Yes. Why?'

'I suggest you call them now. I'm now going to caution you pending further questions. We'll need to take you to the station.'

'No, there's no need for that, surely. Look, I told you, I acted out of frustration and I've apologised.'

'No, Monsieur Fournier, that's nowhere near enough. We'll be taking statements from the witness and all those involved. Then, if the victim wishes to press charges, you will be arrested. Now, are you ready or would you like us to cuff you?'

Eric rubbed his eyes. 'I'm ready.'

Chapter 21: Benedict
Today

Benedict and Jessica were on their way to the Fournier home in Highgate, Jessica weaving her way through the traffic. They'd arranged the meeting beforehand. The post-mortem merely confirmed what they already knew – that Tasmin Fournier had been suffocated in her bed. Whoever killed her had used a pillow, there were minute particles of the pale-yellow pillowcase found in her nostrils and mouth. She had several drugs in her system but only the ones one would expect a woman in her condition to have, and none in any dosage that would raise questions. The forensics team had picked up numerous DNA samples but none that matched anything on the national database, in other words, they belonged to people who lived in the house. But it was still necessary to ask anyone who would have been in the bedroom to provide a DNA sample if merely to eliminate them.

Before leaving the station, Benedict had tasked one of his detective constables, Andrew Prowse, to check Tamsin

Fournier's will.

It was a warm summer's day, the sky clear. Jessica passed an ice cream van parked up and Benedict was tempted, being partial to the occasional ice cream but he was trying, rather unsuccessfully, to lose weight. The two detectives were discussing why anyone would kill an elderly person with dementia. 'It's got to be a mercy killing, boss,' said Jessica. 'Which means it has to be a member of the family.'

'You might well be right. There was no sign of a break-in, no damage.'

'And nothing stolen.'

'Anyway, let's see what they've got to say for themselves.'

Sitting in the lounge, the detectives spoke to Eric Fournier first. They started by asking Fournier about the break-in he suffered in February.

'Yes, it was annoying and a little worrying but ultimately, they didn't take much.'

'A TV, a laptop and your silver service.'

'Well, some of it, yes. We claimed it all on the insurance.'

'Do you, or did you, have any idea who might have been the perpetrator?'

'No.'

'But apparently, there was no sign of a break-in.'

'Yes but…' He sighed. 'I reckon it was probably Tammy pottering around and leaving the back door unlocked. I mean, I always check before going to bed but this happened in the middle of the day. I was out so, yes, there's every chance Tammy forgot to lock the door. She was already very forgetful by this stage.'

'I understand.' Next, Benedict asked Mr Fournier to relate his movements for the night Tammy died. 'You said you spent the evening with a friend.' Benedict consulted his notes. 'Patrick Dunt.'

Fournier blushed but didn't say anything.

'Mr Fournier? Is there something you want to say?'

'Yes, I was with Patrick, just like I said.'

'We've spoken to Mr Dunt.'

'Well, there you are then. And he told you we spent a jolly evening together.'

'He told us just the opposite, Mr Fournier.'

'What do you mean?'

'He said he hasn't seen you for quite some time. Isn't that right, DS Gardiner?'

'Indeed, boss. He said a year or more. He definitely didn't see you on Tuesday evening.'

'He said that?' said Fournier.

'He did, sir,' said Jessica. 'To be fair to Mr Dunt, he did try to lie for you but I'm afraid his acting skills leave a lot to be desired.'

'Do they? Right.'

'So, Mr Fournier?'

'Ah, well, yes. OK, hands up, I might not have been totally honest with you.' He glanced at the lounge door. Leaning forward from his armchair, he said, 'The fact is, I…' He hesitated.

'Go on, sir,' said Jessica.

'See, that night, I was with someone else, a…'

'Yes, Mr Fournier?' said Jessica.

'A lady friend.'

'OK.'

'H-her name is Angela. Angela Wheeler.'

'And where did you and Angela go that night?'

'Go? Oh, nowhere. We stayed at hers. I'm sorry, I couldn't say in front of Susan.'

'Does she know this Angela?'

'God no. She'd never forgive me if she knew.'

'We have to ask you this, Mr Fournier,' said Benedict. 'But can you tell us what sort of relationship you have with Ms Wheeler?'

'Is… is that necessary? I mean, what relevance is it?'

'Maybe none but we have to consider all angles, sir. So?'

Fournier ran his fingers through what was left of his hair. 'I think the expression is…' He glanced back at the door. 'Friends with benefits.' He shot a look at Jessica. 'Don't judge me. I know what you're thinking but…' He threw his hands in the air. 'Actually, it's as bad as it looks. There's no point in denying it. I'm sorry.'

'Is it a serious relationship, Mr Fournier?' asked Jessica. 'I mean, had you considered leaving your wife for Angela at any point?'

'God, no. You mustn't think that.'

'What about now, sir? Your wife's dead, there's no reason for–'

'No. I can't. I couldn't.'

'Is Angela married?'

'No. Divorced many years ago now.'

'So?'

'So what? No. Absolutely not.'

'Can we have Ms Wheeler's address and telephone number?' asked Jessica.

'Sure, sure.'

'So,' said Benedict, 'you returned from Ms Wheeler's at what time exactly?'

'Half past eleven, like I said before.'

'You returned home and found your daughter in this room asleep–'

'Yes.'

'You went upstairs and you found your wife dead.'

'Well, I wasn't a hundred per cent she was dead, not at first. But I called 999 straight away.'

'What proof can you give us, Mr Fournier, that you didn't kill your wife there and then whilst your daughter slept on the sofa here?'

Fournier shot up from his armchair. 'No, no.'

'No? There was no sign of a break-in, nothing. You're carrying on with another woman, and despite your protestations, I think Jessica's on the nail, you do wish to have a future with Angela Wheeler. And Tammy is ill, seriously ill. She'll never recover, she'll only get worse. You did her a favour in killing her, didn't you? Put her out of her misery.'

'Shut up, just shut up, will you? OK, I may not win any husband of the year contests, but we'd been together decades, Inspector. I loved her, I always have. There's no way I could have harmed her. No way. Time of death, what about that? That'll tell you.'

'We can't narrow down the time of death that specifically, Mr Fournier.'

'Mr Fournier,' said Jessica. 'Can you tell us what's in your wife's will?'

He sat down again and sighed. 'We had one of those wills, you know, we left everything to each other.'

'Nothing to your children?'

'I'm sixty-two, Sergeant. I want to enjoy my retirement.'

'So, everything to you?'

'Oh, for goodness' sake. You might as well arrest me now. I've got plenty of motives and apparently, I had the opportunity. You lot are beyond the pale.'

'Only doing our jobs, Mr Fournier,' said Benedict.

'In that case, I suggest you do your job properly and go out there and find the man who really killed my wife, and stop hassling me in my own home.'

'I'm sorry if our line of investigation comes across as harassment, Mr Fournier. So, now, can we speak to your daughter?'

Susan Fournier sat where her father had sat, her knees close together, her hands on her lap. They asked her to go through the events of that night in greater detail. They asked her what she did for a living and established that she earned a good salary and lived nearby in rented accommodation.

'Was the back door locked?' asked Jessica.

'Oh, I couldn't say for sure but it usually is. You don't think... oh dear.'

'The last time we spoke, you said you had a friend around to visit. Robbie, his name, yes?'

She looked down at her hands.

'Tell us about Robbie, Susan.'

'He's my boyfriend,' she said quietly.

Jessica and Benedict glanced at each other. 'You don't seem very happy about it,' said Jessica. 'If you don't mind me saying so.'

'No, no, it's fine. It's just that...'

'You can tell us.'

'Daddy wouldn't approve. Robbie is a mechanic, hardly what he would consider suitable. And, erm, I mean Daddy's not racist or anything but it doesn't help that Robbie is Irish. I suppose, as I'm in a confessional mood, I might as well tell you I'm pregnant too.'

'Oh, congratulations,' said Jessica.

'Thanks.'

She didn't seem at all pleased about it, thought Benedict.

'He's married.'

And that was the reason.

'Married?' said Jessica. 'As in married but separated?'

Susan picked at a thumbnail. 'Alas, no.'

'You know we need to speak to Robbie now.'

'Yes, I know. But…'

'Yes?'

'Please… can you speak to him without his wife there? Things are complicated enough as they are without making things worse.'

'We can't promise but we'll try our best.'

'I'd appreciate it.'

As Jessica drove back to the station, Benedict received a call from DC Prowse. He put Prowse on loudspeaker. 'DC Prowse, any news?'

'Yes, boss. I had a look at Mrs Fournier's will, like you asked me to. I spoke to the family solicitor and he told me that she's left the whole estate of about £110,000 to her husband. And the house is owned by both of them.'

'It's strange that the daughters aren't included.'

'Well, that's the thing, boss. They were. Years ago, Mrs Fournier had made up a will where she left fifty per cent to her husband and fifty per cent between the daughters but then she changed it.'

'Oh, I see. I wonder why. It seems rather drastic.'

'When did she change it, Andrew?' asked Jessica.

'Ah, that's the thing. Mrs Fournier only changed her will six weeks ago.'

Chapter 22: Susan
Today

Pacing the living room, Susan had to get out of the house. The two detectives had unsettled her with their damn questions. She needed a walk, to get some air. It may have been a large house but she still felt cooped up and being cooped up here with her overbearing father and her resentful sister was playing on her nerves. Her father had always been overbearing. He decided what school she should attend, what GCSEs she should sit, what universities to apply for. He always put curfews on what time she had to get home by when going out as a teenager. Mum was the laid-back one, perhaps something about her relaxed French nature. And Susan always did what she was told. Not so, Lizzie. Lizzie was able to stand up to their father. And he seemed to accept that while maintaining his say on how Susan ran her life.

It was eleven a.m. Susan decided to do what she'd been putting off – to ring Robbie. She'd hoped that since finding out that she was pregnant, he'd do the decent thing and ring her, see if she was OK. But no. Nothing. Not a peep. And that hurt. He knew, surely, that she was desperate to hear from him, even a short text, asking how she was. Steeling herself, she rang. No answer. She wasn't prepared and so didn't leave a message. She thought about what she wanted to say, even though she'd been through it numerous times in her head already, and then tried again. This time, she did leave a message: *Robbie, hi, it's me,* she said, trying her utmost to sound upbeat. *Listen, can you give me a ring? I really need to see you.* She paused for a moment, and then added, *Please, Robbie. Please.* Oh, god, she thought as she ended the call, did she sound as desperate as she feared?

Her mobile rang immediately. 'Yes!' She hadn't expected him to respond so quickly. Her heart beating, she rushed back to her phone and scooped it up. But it wasn't Robbie. It was someone from work. Susan's shoulders sagged with disappointment. Tempted not to answer, she did. Her colleague apologised for disturbing her while Susan was on compassionate leave, but could she answer an urgent query? Susan answered as best as she could while trying to hide her lack of enthusiasm.

She needed to go back to work and she wanted to return to her flat. Staying with her father and with Lizzie around was too much for her. Lizzie was still spitting teeth about the change in their mother's will. Maybe, under normal circumstances, Susan might have felt the same but she had far more pressing concerns.

'Are you OK, Susie?

Susan jumped; she hadn't heard her sister come in. 'Oh yes, sorry, just a work call.'

Lizzie threw herself on the settee, swinging her legs up. 'Will you take maternity leave when the time comes?'

'Yes, I suppose so. I hadn't really thought about it.'

'No? You? Ms Super-Organised? What are you hoping for? Boy or girl?'

'I don't mind either way.' It was true but even if she did have a preference, she wouldn't discuss it with her sister.

'Tell me,' said Lizzie, 'are you going to do the decent thing and get married beforehand?'

'I, er... probably not.'

'No? Oh dear. That'll upset Daddy, won't it?' She inspected her fingernails. 'He's a bit old-fashioned, you know what he's like.'

'Well, it's none of his business, is it?' It came out more harshly than she intended.

Lizzie noticed. 'Ouch!'

'Yeah, well.'

'For one about to have a baby, you seem very down at the mouth.'

'Maybe because we've lost our mother, Lizzie? Or had you forgotten that appalling fact?'

'She's in a better place, wouldn't you say? Look, are you sure you're OK?'

'Yes, I'm fine; stop asking me that.'

'OK, OK. So, look, an idea – Dad says he hasn't met the future father of his first grandchild, so why don't we have dinner and invite him around?'

'Robbie?'

'Why not? A sort of meet-the-family occasion. After all, he *is* family now.'

'I think he's away at the moment. Visiting his mother.'

'You *think*? What sort of relationship do you have with this man? It sounds very hands-off if you don't mind me saying so, Susie.'

Her father appeared in the living room wearing his usual

jacket and a pair of corduroy trousers she hadn't seen before. He faltered on seeing both his daughters.

'I was just saying, Daddy,' said Lizzie. 'We ought to invite Susie's man over for dinner, get to know him.'

'Yes, yes, good idea.' He fixed his gaze on Susan. 'Susan seems particularly cagey about him.'

'Not at all, it's just that…'

'What? What is it, Susie? Are you embarrassed by us? Or maybe you're embarrassed by him. So, yes, I think it's a grand idea. Invite him around.'

They all heard the front door opening. 'That'll be Alina,' said Eric.

Sure enough, Alina, wearing her usual dark blue tabard, popped her head around the living room door. Eric greeted her sullenly.

'Right, I'm popping out for a while,' he said, patting his pockets.

'Anywhere nice?' asked Lizzie.

'No, just meeting a friend for coffee then I'm off to see the florists to discuss flowers for your mother's funeral.'

'When will the police release her body?'

'They said this week sometime.'

'Who's your friend?' asked Susan.

'Hmm? Oh, no one you know. Right, I'll be off, ladies. See you later.'

'Actually,' said Susan. 'I was about to head out too. If you wait a moment, I'll come with you.'

'No, got to dash, running late already.' And with that, he made a hasty exit.

Is this the version of Eric that her mother had had to put up with for so many years? Did she know why her husband always behaved so secretively? Her mother's death had not slowed him up in the slightest. He was still his usual cheery self and this bothered Susan. He was still up to his old tricks. Saying goodbye to her sister, Susan decided to follow him.

The day was overcast but still warm. Susan could see her father striding ahead, walking fast for a man of advanced years. He waved at a woman on the other side of the street who shouted a pleasantry at him. Seven minutes from leaving the house, he took a left and walked up Highgate High Street, busy as always with shoppers, its cafés doing a brisk business. Her father dropped a coin into the upturned cap of a busker, sitting outside a mini-Tesco, playing *Waterloo Sunset* by The Kinks. Susan had to trot in order to keep up, zigzagging past people. She saw him turn right and ran to catch up. It was a wide residential street lined with trees in full leaf. He passed an ice cream van parked up waiting forlornly for its first customer. Soon after, he turned left down a street called Caversham Avenue. Finally, a good fifteen minutes after leaving home, Dad had reached his destination, a 1930s-styled, semi-detached, sandstone house halfway down the street. He knocked and waited. Susan crossed over to the other side of the street. The door was opened by an auburn-haired woman, perhaps in her early sixties, bright red lipstick, incongruous, thought Susan, at this time of day. She smiled on seeing Dad, her head tilted to the side. She welcomed him in.

This, thought Susan, was no ordinary friend, this was another of Dad's lovers.

Chapter 23: Francine
Annecy, France, ten years ago

The last few weeks at home had been hellish for Francine. Her mother hadn't stopped crying. Francine had been sympathetic and concerned to begin with. After all, no one wants to see their mother so distraught but after a while, the continual misery began to grate. She remained in her bedroom most of the time chatting online on various forums she was on and reading novels depicting teen angst. She'd also begun learning how to cook on account her mother had lost all interest in food. Olivia had always been slim but now, with the weight falling off her, she was looking positively skeletal. The large amounts of alcohol certainly weren't helping and she started smoking again, a habit she'd kicked when Francine was about ten. They rarely spoke and when they did it was always unpleasant; her mother's temper was awful. So Francine found it easier to avoid all verbal communication as far as possible, limiting it to the necessities of everyday life.

Francine knew why her mother was so upset; she'd heard it

all, the day that Eric, that awful man, came around and jettisoned her mother. She'd heard her mother's desperation: *You don't love me? I thought we had a future together. Please, Eric, don't leave me…* But he did. He left her and hadn't come back. She was upstairs in her bedroom and she heard it all. Standing at the window, she watched him leave. At one point, he stopped and looked back at the house. She pulled back from the window. Had he seen her? It didn't matter.

Of course, it wasn't the first time. She remembered when her father left some two years ago, Olivia collapsed then too. And that had been hard on her as well. She still desperately missed her father. She hadn't really thought about it when her parents were still together but after he left Francine realised how much more she loved her father than her mother. Her mother was always complicated and prone to these emotional outbursts. The older Francine got, the more she realised her mother was simply emotionally unstable, immature even. Papa, however, was a simple man, easy to love. Of course, as a teenager, she never demonstrated that love and that was a cause of regret now, but frankly, she wouldn't know how to express love; it simply wasn't in her nature. But now, she'd give anything for her father to return with that silly grin he always had.

Her father's leaving shattered Francine's life for a while. She was fifteen at the time, two years ago. She'd heard the arguing and witnessed the constant bickering so she knew things were bad. Olivia needed constant validation, a steady supply of compliments. *Well, you may not find me attractive any more, Yves, but there are plenty of men who would.* She heard that one several times. Her mother was always quick to criticise Papa, cataloguing his failures, his inadequacies.

And then one day, he left, just disappeared. Why, asked

Francine constantly with tears in her eyes. He changed his mobile number and didn't leave a forwarding address. It took a while before Mama told her that Papa had left her for another woman. Francine hated him for that but slowly, with time, she began to understand. Mama was difficult to live with, what with her fluctuating moods. For a few weeks before her latest setback, her mother had been high as a kite. Francine understood that was when this Eric man had come on the scene. She dressed up, wore make-up and went out a lot. Her subsequent fall was almost inevitable.

A month after Papa left, he rang Francine quite out of the blue. The fact that Mama was hard to live with was beginning to dawn on her. She burst into tears on hearing his voice. 'When are you coming back, Papa?'

'I'm sorry, sweet pie, I can't come back. I miss you though.'

'I miss you too, Papa.'

He was living in Paris, he said, almost 600 kilometres away. Francine assumed he'd left Mama for another woman and she knew that was still the narrative she held onto but Papa assured her that wasn't the case; he just left because he found living with Olivia so toxic.

They kept in touch but she never told Mama. She'd have a meltdown if she knew. About six months later, Yves invited his daughter to lunch. They met in a café in central Annecy. She cried on seeing him and felt so embarrassed. Papa told her not to be silly and he too had tears in her eyes. During dessert, a crème brûlée, Papa confessed that he had now met another woman, a woman called Isabella.

'Oh. Is she… nice?' She didn't know how else to ask the question.

'Yes, she is. Thing is though, Isabella is Spanish.'

'Is that a problem?'

He twiddled with the stem of his wine glass. 'I'm moving to Spain, Francine. Madrid.'

'No.'

'I'm sorry, I know it's not what you want to hear.'

'That's so far away.'

'I know. I'm sorry.'

'Does she have kids?' she asked, praying the answer was no.

'Yes,' said Papa. 'Two boys.'

Francine closed her eyes. 'How old are they?' she asked, hoping he'd say they were adults and had both left home.

'Twelve and ten.'

'What are they like?'

'They're great but… they're not *you*, sweet pie.'

She saw him one more time, the day before his move to Madrid. She felt as if her heart was breaking and she began to understand how her mother felt now. She hadn't seen him since.

Francine resigned herself to the fact that Papa was never coming back. But the thought of him being a proper father to another woman's sons caused an ache in her heart that she found hard to dislodge. Life was so damn unfair.

Now, six weeks on from the set-to with Eric, Mama seemed no better, if anything it was getting worse. One day, she summoned enough courage to ask about him. 'Did you love him?'

'I did,' said Mama. 'I still do.'

'What's his name?'

'Eric.'

'Eric who?'

'Eric Fournier. He's an architect in town.'

'What does–'

'I don't want to talk about him any more.'

That night, Francine rang her father.

'I want to live with you.'

'Why?'

'Because…' She started crying. 'I can't live with Mama. She's driving me mad, Papa.'

Papa laughed. 'Why do you think I left?'

'It's not funny. I want to leave too. Please, Papa, let me come live with you.'

She heard him sigh and she knew that wasn't a good sign. 'Oh, sweet pie, that'd be impossible. We live in a tiny house; there'd be no room for you. Secondly, the boys are a little, let's say, challenging. I don't think you'd enjoy it too much, and we're in Spain, sweet pie. You don't speak Spanish, it's not as if you could continue your studies here. Anyway, what about your friends? You'd miss them, surely?'

'I don't have any friends.'

'I'm sure that's not true.'

Yes, there were a couple of girls who might, on a good day, say hi but that was it – she really didn't have any friends; everyone at school found her weird, a little strange. Not surprising with a mother like Olivia.

Francine knew he was right but hearing him say no hurt nonetheless. It hurt like hell.

*

Another four weeks had passed; it was mid-December and winter had firmly set in. Francine hurried home from school, keen to get out of the cold. Soon, it'd be Christmas. The main thoroughfare through town was festooned with decorations and Christmas carols rang out from every shop. Francine was dreading it. The idea of having two weeks off school and spending Christmas Day cooped up with her mother was intolerable. At least Olivia had stopped crying now but she remained taciturn and frankly unpleasant to live with. This was going to be the most depressing Christmas ever. Half term was bad enough but at least that was only a week. She actually met up in town with a friend called Tasha and while not disastrous, it hadn't gone well. She didn't know how to talk to the girl and it was all rather awkward and embarrassing. Back at school, Tasha ghosted her. Francine hated school. She enjoyed English Language and was often complimented by her teacher on her ability but nothing else ignited any interest.

Francine arrived home and with a heavy sigh, put her key in the front door and stepped indoors. Whoa, it was cold. Had Mama forgotten to put the heating on? She called out for her mother but received no reply. Had she gone out? That'd be a rarity; her mother never went out now, not since Eric dumped her back in the summer. It seemed such a long time ago.

'Mama? You here? Hello? Mama?'

She went through to the kitchen, keeping her coat on. She noticed a folded piece of paper propped up against the kettle. Had her mother left her a note? That'd be a first. Dumping her school bag on the kitchen island, she read the note: *I'm sorry. Blame Eric.* That was it. Why was she… 'Oh, shit,' she said aloud. 'Mama? Oh fuck no, please, no…'

She rushed upstairs, her heart thumping, her footsteps heavy on the stairs. She flung open the door to Mama's bedroom. Empty, the bed made, the room unusually neat. She wouldn't be in Francine's bedroom, nonetheless, she checked. No.

'Oh God, where are you?'

The bathroom, there was nowhere else. Apart from the tiny

separate WC but the door to that was open.

She paused, swallowing down the bile that had formed in her throat. She knew. She already knew. Her mind empty, her hand shaking, Francine gently pushed the bathroom door open with the toe of her shoe. She heard the buzz of a fly or something against the window. She heard the slow drip, drip, drip of a tap. She stepped in. It took a moment to process what was in front of her... Olivia lying in the bath with her clothes on, her eyes open and glazed, staring straight ahead. Another step forward and Olivia saw the pinkness of the bath water.

Her hand over her mouth, she ran to the WC and flung herself on the floor in front of the toilet and threw up.

Chapter 24: Eric
Today

Eric walked briskly. Frankly, he was pleased to escape his daughters. Susan seemed to think he wanted her around, that he needed her. If anything, she made him feel worse. He'd be glad when she returned to her own place and left him in peace. And Lizzie had only been back a day, and she was already making him feel like she did whenever they spent more than five minutes in each other's company – self-conscious as if he was treading on eggshells. Eric wanted to be shot of them, to have the house back to himself. Sure, he'd missed Tammy but he felt as if he'd lost her a long time ago.

But what was really bothering him as he strode up Highgate High Street was the feeling that the police had him in their sights. Thanks to Patrick, they knew he'd lied about where he was on Tuesday night. So much for relying on Patrick. But on reflection, it had been a lot to ask. Yes, Patrick owed him but Eric had to acknowledge that it hadn't been a fair exchange of favours.

And now, he imagined, it wouldn't be long before the tall detective and his dyed-blonde assistant got to know about the change in Tammy's will. He so wished he hadn't done that now. What was he thinking of? Because now, that would put him under their direct glare. He'd done it because of Lizzie. He knew that Lizzie would have sunk the whole lot in one of her hair-brained business schemes, which effectively meant throwing it down the drain. Lizzie may have thought herself a smart businesswoman but the truth was everything she touched turned to dust. Even as a girl, she always overreached herself, coming up with clever-sounding plans but she never paused long enough to think them through. No, that wasn't Lizzie's way. Instead, she'd rush into things and end up in tears. Five years ago, Lizzie set up a digital marketing company. It lasted all of ten months before it all went tits up. He wasn't prepared to see Tammy's financial legacy lost in a ball of flames. And so, he couldn't cut Lizzie out of the will without cutting out Susan. He managed to persuade his solicitor that Tammy was still of sound mind to change her will. OK, no one believed it for a second but the man was an old friend and thus the deed was done.

He dropped a fifty-pence piece into a busker's cap, some scruffy urchin making an awful din. He vaguely recognised the tune, some hit from the sixties. He passed the café where he first bumped into Angela. They used to know each other years back, she and Tammy were friends for a while but Angela got married and moved away and the friendship fizzled out. But Angela, freshly divorced, had moved back into the area and Eric had bumped into her in this, one of many cafés along this street. She looked great, Eric remembered. She'd improved with age, was more confident in herself, she had a swagger about herself that was new. She even came around once, ostensibly to visit Tammy. But Tammy was ill by then and she had no clue who Angela was. He liked Angela, he enjoyed their casual relationship, he enjoyed the sex, but he had no desire to take it any further. Tammy had been his wife for thirty-eight years; he had no desire for anyone else.

And here he was, outside Angela's house on Caversham Avenue. This had to be his last visit. If the police were onto him, he had to show that he and Angela were no more.

Angela smiled on seeing him and led him through to her lounge. Her laptop was flipped open on her dining table, a picture of a quaint countryside cottage. Before he had a chance to remove his jacket, she embraced him and kissed him on the lips. 'Please, Ang.'

'What? Can't I greet my lover with a kiss?'

'Yes, well, maybe a cup of tea first.'

'Oh, listen to you. When did you get so staid, Eric?'

He unbuttoned his jacket. 'Perhaps since my wife died.'

'Ah, yes. I suppose. I'm sorry.'

He glanced back at the laptop. On closer inspection, it was one of those house-moving sites. The picture showed a whitewashed cottage with a thatched roof, prominent gables and a red front door. 'What's this?' he asked. 'Thinking of moving again.'

'It looks lovely, doesn't it? It's in a village called Chiddingfold in Surrey.'

'Yes, it looks great.'

'Take a seat and you can see all the photos of the inside and the garden. It's beautiful.'

'But why are you looking?'

'Because...' She looked awkward all of a sudden. Pulling on a strand of hair, she said, 'Look, I feel as if you've caught me out.'

'What do you mean?' Eric asked even though he knew exactly what this was.

'I know it may seem a little premature—'

'Premature? Telling me it is. God, Ang, Tammy isn't even her grave yet and you're planning a cosy little future for the two of us.'

'I know. I'm sorry. Don't be cross with me, I couldn't bear it.'

'Angela, I can't be seen with you. People will talk.'

'So what? Let them talk.'

'Tammy was murdered, for Pete's sake. I told you about the will and I told you I think I'm the number one suspect. They questioned me again yesterday and it was not a pleasant experience.'

'What did they say?'

'It doesn't matter. Look, Ang…'

She stepped closer to him. 'What is it, darling?'

He flinched at her use of the endearment. He took a deep breath. 'I can't see you any more.' There, he'd said it.

She paled and reached out for the back of a chair for support. 'Why not?'

'Tammy's death, it's…' He needed to ham this up a little, play the grief card. 'It's hit me harder than I'd anticipated.'

'I understand, darling. I do really but—'

'No, you're not listening. I need to… I don't know, to retreat into a shell, if you know what I mean. Somewhere quiet where I can grieve and remember. We had so many happy memories together. You know what she was like, she was such a… a happy, generous woman. And I miss her so much.'

Angela sat at her dining table, resting her head on her hand.

'I thought we had a future together, Eric, you and me. But obviously, I thought wrong. Terribly wrong. How silly of me.'

'No, not silly. I too thought that.' The image of Olivia flashed up in his mind. He pushed it away. 'But, hell, Ang, we were married thirty-eight years. I was always a one-woman man.' As soon as the words were out, he knew he was going to regret it.

'Apart from when you were fucking me, of course.'

'She was ill by then. The Tammy I knew and loved had gone.'

'So, that's it then?' She pulled a tissue from her trouser pocket. 'You and me... *poof.* Gone.'

'I don't mean to hurt you, Ang.'

She looked him hard in the eye. 'Oh but you have, Eric. You really have.'

Chapter 25: Frida
Today

Normally, Frida liked her boss, Sheila O'Malley, a woman in her forties who exuded a blend of professionalism, warmth and dedication. Her physical appearance was always polished and put-together, reflecting perhaps her commitment to maintaining a positive image for the charity shop. She typically wore smart business attire, favouring classic blouses and tailored skirts or slacks, which conveyed her sense of responsibility and leadership. They got on well and Frida knew that Sheila liked her in return and rated her. Not so now, however. Squeezed in together in the charity shop's office, the only private space in the entire shop, they sat uncomfortably close to one another, knees almost touching.

'You know this is going to have to go on your record, Frida. You appreciate that?'

'Yes, I know.' She looked down at her lap, unable to meet Sheila's eye.

'What were you thinking of? Telling one customer to, quote, *go away*, and telling another to, quote, *take the bloody thing*, is not what I expect from one of our shop managers. You can't speak to people like that.'

'I'm sorry. Honest. It won't happen again.' Frida tried her best to look contrite and any other time that's exactly how she would have felt but right now, as long as she kept her job, she didn't care. All she could think about was the eight hundred pounds she needed to find within a matter of hours. The sum hadn't stopped repeating itself in Frida's mind. The thought of the consequences left her reeling with weakness. That morning, she did the cash, as always, counting up the previous day's takings which added up to near enough five hundred pounds. Part of her was tempted. Take the money and run. She may have been desperate but she wasn't stupid; she knew she'd never get away with it. Still, she almost did it nonetheless. Better safe in a police cell than at the mercy of Ade's fists. The thought of it made her quake.

Sheila, however, hadn't finished. 'As for leaving Mary in the shop on her own, that is equally as unacceptable. She didn't even know you'd gone until someone knocked on the door. She's a volunteer, she's not paid to deal with angry customers, Frida. That's what *you* are paid for.'

'I had an emergency. I'm sorry.'

'And you couldn't wait until Mary was back from lunch?'

'No, it was… not life or death but almost.' She was close to tears now. She had to hold on, she couldn't cry, not now, not in front of her boss.

Sheila considered her for a while. Frida could tell she was softening. 'Frida, is there anything you want to tell me?'

Frida shook her head frantically, not trusting herself to speak.

'I am here to listen, you know.'

'Hm-mm.'

'Yes, I have a responsibility for the shop but I also have a responsibility to you, Frida. If there's an issue that's impacting your work and your personal life, I might be able to help, get you some time off to give you space to deal with whatever it is that's clearly upsetting you.'

'Thank you but I'm… I'm fine.'

Sheila nodded, utterly unconvinced. 'Fine. If you change your mind, you know I'm only a phone call away.'

'I know. Thank you.'

The rest of the day passed in a haze. But Frida got through it, smiling while inside she felt on the edge of a collapse. Fortunately, Mary wasn't in today, instead, it was Stan.

That afternoon, during a quiet period and with Stan holding the fort, Frida closed the office door and rang her mother who lived with her partner in Blackburn. She hadn't prepared. The idea of asking her mother for such a huge sum of money was so ridiculous that she couldn't bring herself to rehearse her words. Best, she decided, to wing it.

Her mother was a science teacher in some dreadful comprehensive school where her role as a teacher took second place to her skills as a social worker. Everyone knew teachers weren't that well paid but she was the head of department, so surely she had some money stashed away for a rainy day, like helping out a desperate daughter. She moved in with a man soon after Frida's father had died, indecently so. Frida, only sixteen at the time, protested violently but her mother was set, saying she needed a man in her life and ultimately, Frida had no choice but to put up and shut up. She hated the man and knew the feeling was mutual.

She hadn't spoken to her mother for some six months so there was a fair bit of catching up to do which was fine by Frida; it gave her time to ease the conversation in. 'So, how are tricks, Frida? Anything exciting happening in your life at the moment?'

OK, now, this was the moment… 'Mum, I've got a bit of a problem. Me and Ade are being evicted from the flat.'

'Oh no. What for? Have you done something wrong, love?'

'It's not that, the landlady wants to sell up. So, we're having to move. We've found somewhere already and… and we've got enough for the deposit and all that but, well, the thing is, Mum, we've not got enough for the first month's rent.'

She waited for her mother to say something, a word of encouragement, perhaps. But nothing was forthcoming.

'Can you lend me eight hundred pounds, Mum?' There, she'd said it. It wasn't so hard.

'I'm sorry, love. I… Look, maybe… I could spare you half that. Would that help?'

'Yes, God yes, that'd be brilliant.'

So, now Frida 'only' needed to find another four hundred. But with only half an hour to closing, she was rapidly running out of time.

She returned to the shop. Stan was talking to a woman about the pros and cons of a gas hob versus electric. Stan smiled on seeing Frida, but, there again, he always did. And the idea came to Frida. Stan. Could she do it? Stan liked her, that was obvious, and although she always presumed it was of a paternalistic nature, now that she thought of it, perhaps there was more to it. She busied herself tidying the rack of women's clothing, picking garments off the floor, brushing them off while planning her attack and whether it was a good idea. Stan had been a widower for some fifteen years or more – he'd mentioned it a couple of times. He lived alone. He was lonely, that much was obvious. When was the last time he'd been close to a woman? Frida would wager not since the day his wife died. Maybe she'd suggest a drink after work, get to know him a little better, get him a little tipsy. She'd hint that she found him attractive, maybe let a hand rest on his knee. Would she go the whole way? For four hundred pounds she would; to save herself from being battered she would, god, yes, she would. What choice did she have?

She caught Stan's eye across the shop. She smiled at him, different from her usual unconscious smile, this was a different smile, a smile that conveyed something. Sure enough, Stan's return smile quickly faded as he turned away and busied himself with something, a hint of puzzlement in his expression.

Half an hour later, Frida slammed the bolts securely, locking the shop. She'd taken the till reading and put today's takings into a cloth bag which she then put in the safe in the office at the back, ready to be counted before opening up tomorrow morning. She checked her banking app. Her bank account was four hundred pounds better off. 'Thanks, Mum.' She was halfway there.

Returning to the shop, Frida found Stan waiting for her, as she expected, buttoning up his usual duffle coat, somehow managing to look halfway between scruffy and dapper. Her heart was somersaulting. How does one ask a man like Stan out for a drink? It was a ridiculous idea but she was in danger, actual physical danger. She had to do it.

Chapter 26: Francine
Annecy, France, ten years ago

Today, a week before Christmas, was the day of Olivia Lenoir's funeral, taking place in a small, Catholic church a ten-minute walk from home. The day, although cold, was sunny. Francine had plenty of black clothes to choose from, although most were a little small for her now, a throwback to the days she flirted with trying to be a Goth. It wasn't a phase that lasted long. She knew her peers thought her weird enough so why make it easier for them?

Following her aunt and uncle, Francine entered the church. Her Uncle Jacques and Aunt Violette genuflected before the altar. Francine couldn't remember the last time she'd been inside a church, certainly, her parents had never been churchgoers. She was disappointed to see the place almost empty save for a small huddle of people she didn't recognise. She looked around for her father hoping he might appear from the shadows with his booming voice, But no, no sign of him. A couple of women smiled at her as she took her place beside her aunt and uncle in a pew at the front. The place was dimly lit, with sunlight filtering through the coloured panes of the stained-glass windows, casting vibrant hues upon the weathered wooden pews. The scent of aged wood, candles, and incense added to the atmosphere. A small, weathered crucifix hung above the altar. In the corner, a large Christmas tree and in front of it a table with a display depicting the nativity scene.

Ten days had passed since her mother's death. The time had passed in a haze. Having been sick in the upstairs toilet, Francine had staggered downstairs and stood shaking, freaked out that her dead mother was lying in the bath above her. She wondered whether the water was still warm.

Pulling herself together, she rang the emergency services. An ambulance arrived within ten minutes, followed soon after by a doctor who confirmed that Olivia Lenoir was dead. Soon after that, a couple of policemen and a young policewoman who hugged Francine as she cried into the woman's chest. Further police officers arrived dressed in ghost-like white suits and a woman with a huge camera.

The policewoman allocated to look after Francine asked lots of questions, like how old she was, and others which Francine tried her best to answer. She showed her Olivia's note. *I'm sorry. Blame Eric.* 'Who's Eric,' the woman asked. She asked whether Francine had any living relatives whom she could stay with. 'My father lives in Madrid.' 'Hmm, anyone closer?' 'I suppose there's my aunt.' Olivia and her elder sister, Violette, had never been close despite living only thirty kilometres apart. Indeed, Francine could count on the fingers of one hand the number of times she'd met Aunt Violette and her husband, Jacques. She didn't much like them. The policewoman asked for Violette's number which Francine found in her mother's address book. 'We'll give her a ring and ask her to come pick you up.'

'Why?' asked Francine. 'I don't want to go there. I can stay here by myself.'

'No, I'm afraid we can't allow that. You're still only seventeen. You need a ward until you turn eighteen.'

'But that's only six months away.'

'I don't make up the rules.'

The men and women in their white suits were still busy at work and had asked Francine to wait outside when, an hour later, Aunt Violette drove up in her battered Citroën van.

'Oh, Francine, you poor, poor girl,' her aunt screeched, having parked up, rushing towards Francine with her arms open. Francine allowed herself to be hugged. Aunt Violette hadn't changed much, thought Francine, still plump with a large crucifix on her massive bosom, still that untidy and tousled hair and her pinched expression giving her the look of someone who disapproved of everything. 'What happened?'

'Mum's topped herself.'

'Oh.' Francine knew Violette wouldn't like her turn of phrase and found it disrespectful. She didn't care. 'Oh my, how awful. Did you find her?'

Francine nodded.

'You poor girl.' Aunt Violette hugged her again. 'Have you phoned your father?'

'Not yet.'

'I'll do it if you want.'

'No, I want to do it. I'll do it after the men in the white coats have gone.'

Still barred from returning indoors, Francine and Aunt Violette waited in Violette's car facing the house, watching the various comings and goings. They had to wait for almost an hour during which time Violette spoke of her childhood growing up with Olivia. She seemed to speak highly of her sister, more than Olivia ever did. The only silver lining on this particular cloud was that Violette and Jacques had no children of their own and that, as far as Francine was concerned, was a mighty relief. They lived in the countryside. Francine remembered the house from, she thought, her only visit one Christmas when she was about ten. She remembered the house backed onto a woodland and that they kept chickens. 'We still have the chickens,' said Aunt Violette.

Stepping out of the car, it took Francine three attempts before her father picked up. She told him the news. He swore and said how sorry he was. When Francine said she was now obliged to live with Violette and Jacques, she heard Yves' sharp intake of breath.

'What?'

'Jacques. The man's a neanderthal.'

'What do you mean?'

'He's a fascist and he's a dick and his wife, your aunt, is a religious nut.'

Francine looked over at Violette, still in the car, who gave her a double thumbs up. 'Great.'

'Don't worry, give it a few months and you can return home.'

'Or I could move to Madrid and live with you.'

'No, Francine. You know that's not an option.'

'Oh, Papa, please…'

'It's not possible. I'm sorry, Francine.'

'Will you come to Mama's funeral? Please, Papa. Please.'

'I'll see.'

'I've not seen you for two years, Papa. Please come. *Please.*'

'I'll try, OK. Work is a bit full on at the moment but I promise I'll try my best. Can't say fairer than that.'

'No.' She heard someone calling his name from a distance.

'Anyway, sweet pie, I'm sorry for your loss.' And with that, he rang off.

Once the forensics team had finally finished, the police officers allowed Francine back inside. And so, Francine packed up two suitcases, four cardboard boxes and a large canvas bag full of her belongings and with Violette's help, piled them into the Citroën. She had to sit with one of the cardboard boxes on her lap as Violette drove the thirty kilometres back to her countryside home out in the sticks, as she called it. 'That's the way we like it, no nosey neighbours, but the village is only a kilometre away.'

Uncle Jacques was at home to welcome Francine. 'Here she is!' he said. 'My, you've grown,' he said, his eyes taking in his niece. 'Sorry to hear about your mum. Tragic that. You're welcome to stay with us for as long as you want, my dear.'

'Thank you,' said Francine, thinking he seemed OK.

'How are your cooking skills?'

'Terrible.'

He laughed at that. Stepping into the house Francine felt as if she was being transported into a bygone era, with weathered wooden beams overhead and uneven, worn stone floors. The whole house felt rugged, with tatty, old furniture, a stone fireplace in the main room, a huge wooden crucifix above it, and far too many pictures of Jesus and religious scenes. Everything felt dank and depressingly drab. It even smelt dusty and ancient. She took an immediate dislike to the place.

But by the end of that first evening, Francine decided she quite liked Uncle Jacques. Yes, he had a tendency to invade her personal space and he said things that caught her off guard but on the whole, she didn't consider him a fascist or a dick.

Four days after Mama's death, the police rang Aunt Violette to say they had completed the post-mortem and could now release the body for her funeral. Olivia Lenoir had died by her own hand by slashing her wrists. She'd bled to death. There were no grounds for suspecting third-party involvement.

The funeral started. How strange it was to see the coffin, so large for such a slight woman. She couldn't equate the fact that her mother was encased inside that solid wooden box. She hoped she might feel *something*, a regret that she hadn't been a better, more loving daughter, a sense of her own grief, a sense of longing. But nothing, nothing emerged from within her, just a feeling of emptiness. Glancing to her right, she caught Violette bowed in prayer and, to her left, Jacques inspecting his fingernails.

The service was coming to an end when Francine heard the heavy church doors opening. Her father, it had to be her father! He'd come after all. She whipped around to see. There was someone, a man, a silhouette caught in a beam of sunlight. Her heart skipped. The man closed the church doors. Francine's eyes adjusted. Her heart sagged as she realised it wasn't her father at all. But whoever it was, she recognised him. It took a few moments before she realised just who it was. It was Eric Fournier.

Chapter 27: Susan
Today

Susan had paced up and down and hung around outside the woman's house for a good fifteen minutes. Quite why, she didn't know. Did she intend to confront her father when he reappeared? Part of her was tempted to walk up to the door and ring the bell, but she knew she'd never have the guts. She felt as if the woman's neighbours were noticing her now, this strange person pacing the pavement, looking like she was up to no good. She decided to call it a day. She walked back up to the high street and without realising at first, found herself peering into a small, independent clothing shop that specialised in children's clothes. Don't go in, she told herself. Don't go in. She went in.

The shop was deserted. A pretty young shop assistant, who could have been no more than seventeen, greeted her cheerfully. She found herself drawn to the baby section. Her heart lurched on seeing the array of pink and sky-blue outfits: sleepsuits, a knitted romper, frilly dungarees, a tiny pink sweatshirt with bunny rabbits on it and, oh so adorable, a pair of blue booties with ears. She could feel her eyes pricking. 'Anything I can help you with?' asked the shop assistant in a high-pitched voice.

'Oh, no, thank you. Just... just browsing. Thank you.'

'No worries. Take your time.'

These items weren't cheap but they were all handcrafted and beautifully put together. Whoever knitted these items, did so with love and care.

Her heart ached with wanting. Her first baby had been a boy, a stillbirth at twenty-four weeks. Five and a half years ago. An issue with the placenta, she was told, insufficient blood flow. Still, to this day, she blamed herself. She'd been suffering from vaginal bleeding but she'd been up against a deadline at work and tried to ignore it. By the time the deadline had passed, the bleeding had stopped. So, when it occurred again, she assumed it wasn't anything to worry about. How wrong she was. Des, her partner at the time, was with her all the way through the grief. He helped ease the pain. She assumed he'd be there forever, and that they'd try again. Again, how wrong she was. He left her two years back. There wasn't another woman involved. How much easier that would have been. No, he simply said he'd fallen out of love with her, that the stillbirth had changed her too much. It was true; she couldn't deny it. She'd always been a worker but after the stillbirth, she threw herself into work like a thing possessed. Des never got a look in. The truth was, she'd fallen out of love with him as well. Without realising it, they'd stayed together out of some sort of misplaced loyalty, a loyalty born from their shared grief. And perhaps that was one of the things that had contributed to the breakdown of their relationship – Susan was so wrapped up in her own grief, she never gave Des a chance to express his own feelings. Poor old Des; he deserved better. She hadn't heard from him since. She hoped he was doing OK.

She picked up an all-in-one naval suit complete with fake braces. She shook her head; it was to die for. This time, she was determined to do everything right – she'd cut out caffeine, ate healthy meals, not a drop of alcohol, she slept on her side, not her back. This boy was going to live, even if he didn't have a father.

She thanked the cheery assistant and left, her heart still fluttering.

Standing at a deserted bus stop, Susan tried Robbie's number again. Still no answer. This time, she didn't leave a message. Curse him. How dare he blow her out? Didn't she deserve more than this?

She caught a 31 bus and from the stop on Kentish Town Road, made her way to the garage. She recognised the young, plump lad behind the reception desk, a lad they called Tucker who, according to Robbie, had sawdust between his ears. 'Hi,' she said with a smile. 'Is Robbie about?'

'Oh, I dunno. I'll go check.'

She waited in the empty waiting room, its wall dotted with old-fashioned posters featuring classic cars and grinning auto enthusiasts. Even here, the place smelt of engine oil. She picked up a tatty, year-old copy of *Hello!* and flipped through its pages wondering why she'd never heard of any of these celebrities and minor royals, although she did know Hugh Jackman.

'Sorry,' said Tucker, returning from the garage. 'He's taken the afternoon off. Something about his missus.'

'Oh. Right. OK.' She knew she was looking dumbfounded. Recovering her composure, she thanked him and left. Something about his missus, indeed.

OK, she thought, she'd had enough of this. Damn him. What was it that her mother used to say? If the mountain won't go to Mohammed, then Mohammed must come to the Mountain...

It was either a couple of buses or a particularly long walk to Robbie's and frankly, Susan was too tired for either, so she called an Uber via her phone but ended up ordering a Bolt, simply because it came more quickly.

Robbie and his wife lived in a very ordinary red brick, two up two down, in a very ordinary street, the sort of street where Susan held that much tighter to her handbag and did not risk checking her mobile phone. She was being paranoid, she was sure, but better paranoid, she thought, than regretful. She slowed up as she approached the house. This wasn't the first time today she found herself outside someone's home wondering what was happening inside. If she thought it was stressful enough with her father, this was a thousandfold worse. This was the future here and the thought of what she might find left her feeling hollowed out.

She decided to give Robbie one more chance and ring him. Again, he didn't answer. How many times had she tried? She was fuming now, livid with him. She'd had enough. Striding up to the front door she pressed her finger to the doorbell only to realise it wasn't working. She knocked instead, a solid rap on the plastic door. She could hear unfamiliar footsteps coming from the inside – those were not Robbie's steps; they had to be hers. This was it. She braced herself. A woman, barely five feet four tall, answered the door. She had slightly ruddy skin, a freckled face, not unattractive, and her hair, a shade of strawberry blonde, looked rather dishevelled. She carried an aura of weariness.

But what shocked Susan was the fact the woman was clearly pregnant.

Chapter 28: Eric
Today

Eric made his way home, drained but relieved. It was true what he'd said – he hadn't wanted to hurt Angela; she was a good woman with a kind heart. He hated leaving her, crumpled. He expected it to be difficult but not *so* difficult. Seeing her so upset, he almost weakened – almost said it was merely a matter of time and he'd be back to his old self. Thank God, he didn't. Too often in his life, he'd made promises he had no intention or means of keeping. And it would have been unfair on her. Yes, he enjoyed her company but… not *that* much. It was alright while Tammy was alive, he and Angela adhered to an unspoken but obvious boundary, Angela knew and understood where she stood. But with Tammy gone, Angela's indecently timed play for him was too much. And there was no way he wanted to move to some tiny village in the backend of nowhere. He liked it here in Highgate, he liked having all of London at his fingertips, even if he did prefer to stay at home. He liked seeing Angela occasionally but the thought of the two of them living cheek-by-jowl in some small cottage in a village where they knew no one, was not an attractive proposition by any stretch.

He arrived home to find Lizzie conjuring up some lunch in the kitchen, Radio Four on in the background. 'Omelette,' she said. 'Is that OK with you?'

'Lovely. Thank you. Alina gone?'

'Yep, you just missed her.'

He made his escape, planning on going upstairs for a rest, deciding he needed a short nap to recharge his batteries after his emotionally bruising encounter with Angela but no soon as he'd left Lizzie, he bumped straight into Susan and he knew immediately that she was not happy.

'Can I have a word?' she said as if addressing one of her underlings at work.

'What about?'

'Shall we go through?' She marched to the living room and Eric felt he had no choice but to follow.

He closed the door behind him. 'Anything wrong?' he asked nervously.

'Who is she then, Dad?'

'She?'

'Don't play the idiot with me, Dad. I followed you. I saw her.'

'You *followed* me?'

'Was she the same woman you saw the night someone murdered my mother, the night you said you were meeting your so-called friend, Patrick?'

'It's none of your business, Susan.'

'No? I think it is. So, what's this woman to you? Is she, what, a lady friend, is she–'

'She was a friend to Tammy, all right? I went to see her to

tell her the bad news, that is all, Susan. I don't see why I should justify myself to you but there you have it. She was, still is, a friend to both of us.'

Susan glared at him. 'I don't believe you.' She stormed out, slamming the door behind her.

Eric swore. The quicker she went home and left him in peace the better. He went upstairs, desperate for the sanctuary of his bedroom.

For the last year, he'd been sleeping in the spare bedroom but now with Tammy gone, he thought about returning to the main bedroom with its wooden floor and tall sash windows that overlooked a picturesque view of the quaint London street below. It smelt of almonds, that wood polish Alina always used to mop the floor. He sat at the end of the queen-sized bed staring at his reflection in the large, framed mirror on the dresser, adorned with delicate porcelain figurines and antique trinkets, a reminder of Tammy's personality. The walls were painted in a soft, muted shade of pale blue, creating a soothing atmosphere. The crown moulding and intricate cornices added a touch of Victorian charm to the room. A plush, neutral-toned rug partly covered the polished wooden floor, providing warmth and softness underfoot. They'd been happy here, he and Tammy. She kept her jewellery in a silver-plated box in the dresser, plus more in smaller, felt boxes. She liked her Art Deco, did Tammy. Before she became ill, Tammy loved her necklaces and brooches and she had a ring on virtually every finger. But as she became more ill and thinner, the rings slipped off and they ended up in the dresser. He especially remembered the silver ring with a large amber stone, a recent anniversary present. Was it their silver anniversary or their thirtieth? He couldn't remember. Tammy loved it. He'd bought it in a small jewellery store on Bond Street and presented it to Tammy on their anniversary trip to Tuscany.

He waddled over to the dresser, wanting to see the ring, to rest it in the palm of his hand and remember the occasion. Retrieving the tiny key from the small drawer beneath the mirror, he pulled open the bottom right dresser drawer and… to his surprise found it empty apart from a small notebook Tammy used to keep. But no jewellery box. She must've moved it. He tried the drawer above and found a brochure from some financial management company but still no jewellery. Eric slammed the drawer shut and flung open the top one, his panic rising within him, quickly followed by the three drawers to the left of the dresser. Lots of small items and knick-knacks but no jewellery, nothing at all. It *had* to be here. He checked again, six drawers. How could that be? He'd definitely seen her silver jewellery box here not so long ago. Tammy would never have thought to move it, surely.

Perhaps, he thought, the box was in one of the wardrobe drawers, or a box stacked above the wardrobe, maybe, under the bed, anywhere. It had to be here somewhere. He heard Lizzie calling up from downstairs, saying lunch was ready. Ignoring her, he frantically searched through everything a second time, a third time. A knock on the door. Lizzie popped her head around. 'Dad, didn't you–'

'It's gone,' he wailed. 'It's all gone.'

'What's gone?'

'All your mother's jewellery. It was here, in the dresser, where it's always been but it's not there now.'

'Are you sure?'

'Of course I'm bloody sure.'

Lizzie checked as well, checking each drawer as if she might conjure it up from nowhere.

'See,' said Eric when Lizzie had come to the same inevitable conclusion.

'Maybe it's downstairs, maybe she put it in the bank, I don't know.'

'No.' He rubbed his eyes. 'Someone's stolen it. My God, yes, some blighter's taken.'

'Whoever killed her.'

'I thought I'd checked.' He tried to think; he did check occasionally, but had he checked since Tuesday night? He couldn't remember. The last couple of days were a blur. The police didn't find anything missing but had he mentioned it to them? 'Unless…' He sat on the bed. 'It's Alina. I remember I overheard them talking about the jewellery once, Tammy and her. Alina was admiring it all and Tammy was telling her where she'd got various pieces.'

'That'd be it then, Dad.'

'I've never liked her, never trusted her. I always wanted to replace her but Tammy wouldn't let me.'

'You can't just accuse her, Dad. Not without any proof.'

'Maybe not but I'm going to fire her anyway. I don't need her any more. It's a waste of money.'

He sensed Lizzie bristle on hearing the word, 'money'.

'You need to tell the police, Dad.'

'I know.'

'But after lunch, hey?'

'Yeah, I'll be down in a minute. I've got a phone call to make first.'

Lizzie left him alone.

He took his mobile and looked up the number.

'Alina? Hello, yes, it's Eric Fournier here…'

Chapter 29: Francine
Annecy, France, nine years ago

Francine's Aunt Violette and Uncle Jacques lived a primitive life out in the sticks. They didn't believe in computers, refused to use the internet and didn't have access to any wi-fi. They only believed in living a simple life as God willed it. Francine couldn't bear it. Their house was perpetually cold, icicles hanging from the eaves. The glass in all the windows was cloudy with age, making it difficult to see outside. Thin, tattered curtains hung limply, barely providing any warmth. Built of weathered, grey stones, the house made Francine think of Cathy's bleak home in Wuthering Heights. Outside was even more depressing, especially the yard behind the house. The yard was a barren expanse of uneven ground, devoid of any greenery or signs of life, the puddles frozen over. A gnarled and leafless tree stood sentinel in one corner. Near the house, a dilapidated wooden shed leaned precariously to one side, its door hung askew, half-open, revealing a jumble of rusty gardening tools and broken pots inside. The shed's roof was tattered and patched with mismatched pieces of metal, struggling to keep out the relentless rain and snow. To the far side of the shed, a well, just a circle of bricks about three feet high. Francine peered in but saw nothing but the darkness. She shouted down and listened as her voice echoed back to her. A rusty, forgotten bicycle leaned against the side of the house, its tyres flat. The yard was enclosed by a low, crumbling stone wall. A rusty, creaking gate hung loosely on one hinge. The chickens ran amok, littering the mud-packed yard with their droppings.

Francine hated every aspect of the place, and the more she got to know her aunt and uncle, the more she despised them. She hated how Aunt Violette never wasted an opportunity to take a swipe at her father. The man, she said, was a waste of space, a shirker, a lazy good-for-nothing, an idiot and not fit to lick Olivia's shoes. Uncle Jacques, Francine realised, liked his drink. He always had three bottles of beer each night which left him maudlin and sometimes argumentative. He'd make embarrassing comments on Francine's clothing: 'You look like you're going to a bloody funeral' or, one day when she was wearing a top that was slightly too clingy, he remarked, 'You ought to be careful, love, you'll have my eye out with those.' Aunt Violette laughed loudly.

Francine was obliged to change school and as much as she dreaded it, school was OK. In fact, away from her new home, it was a place of refuge. Her English skills continued to improve.

She thought a lot about Eric Fournier turning up at her mother's funeral. He remained at the back and slipped away the moment the service was finished. He didn't speak to anyone. She Googled 'Eric Fournier architect' and found the address of his business, she found him on LinkedIn and Twitter and Facebook. She spent an unhealthy amount of time looking at his photos on Facebook, pictures of him with his wife and daughters, looking happy, a man without a care, satisfied with his life. How dare he look so happy when he'd destroyed her mother? She became impossible to live with and that was his fault. One day, however long it took, she'd have her revenge; she'd single-handedly destroy *him* and his family.

Christmas Day was a miserable affair. Aunt Violette bought Francine a book on French medieval history. Francine was so appalled that she could barely muster the effort to thank her. She did, however, receive a generous voucher from her father to spend in a popular high street store. She tried to ring him a couple of times but didn't get through. Christmas dinner was nice enough – that was about Aunt Violette's only saving grace in Francine's books: her aunt knew how to cook, far better than her mother ever did. Her uncle started drinking earlier than normal and held forth on his favourite subject – criticising the government. He hated the French president, François Hollande, with a passion, hated everything he did and everything he stood for. As soon as dinner was over, Francine excused herself, saying she wanted to make a start on her new book.

She ran to her bedroom and flung herself on her bed. She scrolled through her phone, viewing hundreds of Instagram posts from friends and people she knew enjoying their Christmases. How she envied their 'normal' families and their happy lives.

She heard a gentle tap on her bedroom door. Her uncle came in, a smile on his face, one hand hidden behind his back. 'What are you doing?' he asked.

'Nothing really.'

He sat on the edge of her bed. 'Are you missing your

mother?' It was the first time anyone had spoken of her all day and she was grateful for it.

'I am.'

'Yeah. Lovely woman. Lovely. Lovely.' He slapped her thigh. 'So tragic. She used to be the life and soul, you know?' He didn't remove his hand, just left it there resting on Francine's thigh, the warmth of his palm burning through her dress. She wriggled to one side but the hand remained. 'You take after your mother. Did you know that?'

She shook her head.

'She was dead attractive too. Sorry, I shouldn't have said dead.' He laughed. 'You might not know this but your mother had a thing for me.' He giggled. 'Don't tell your aunt.' He edged closer to her, far too close, one hand still behind his back. Leaning towards her with his foul, beery breath, he whispered, 'She once told me she wished I'd married her. I bloody should have instead of being lumbered with the ugly sister. Now, you and me, we're not related by blood so, er… you know, if you ever… you know.'

'I want to be left alone now, please.'

He put a hand up. 'OK, fair enough, fair enough. But before I go, I want a Christmas kiss.' He winked as he held up a sprig of mistletoe. So that was what he'd been hiding.

'No, please, Uncle Jacques.'

'Hey, come on, don't be shy, it's traditional. Christmas mistletoe and all that.' He tapped his cheek. 'Come on, just a peck here.'

'I don't want to.'

'One kiss and I'll leave you alone.' He crossed his heart. 'Scout's honour.'

Francine leaned up and, holding her breath, pecked his cheek.

He laughed. 'Is that it?'

It happened so quickly that it took the breath out of her. He pinned her down on the bed, his wet lips reaching for hers. She couldn't breathe; he felt so heavy on her. With horror, she felt his hand needling her breast. She retched as she twisted her head left and right as his lips searched out hers. 'Get off me. Get off.'

'Jacques?' Aunt Violette's voice came rattling up from downstairs. 'Where are you?'

'Shit,' he said, lifting himself off her. 'Coming, my love,' he shouted. He wiped his mouth with the back of his hand. 'Cor, you're as bad as your mother. Our secret, OK?' He tapped the side of his nose.

'Jacques, I need help with the washing up.'

'Yeah, yeah, alright.' He stood and pulled his shirt down. 'Next time, eh?' He winked at her again. 'Next time.'

Chapter 30: Benedict
Today

Angela Wheeler had a kind face, thought Benedict, her eyes bracketed by laughter lines and perhaps a few challenges along the way. She had curly, red hair which seemed to convey a sense of energy. She invited Benedict and Jessica through to her sitting room, a large, tidy space, with a high ceiling and ample natural light streaming in through large windows. The walls were adorned with an eclectic collection of art, showcasing a wide range of styles and mediums. Framed paintings, sculptures, and photographs created a gallery-like atmosphere, adding a vibrant and dynamic touch to the space.

Benedict began. 'Ms Wheeler–'

'Call me Angela, please.'

Benedict smiled. 'Angela. I'm sure you've worked out why we're here.'

'Tammy's tragic death. Poor Eric

'Yes, indeed. Now, regarding Eric. We believe he spent much of Tuesday evening here with you. Is that correct?'

'Ahuh, he did.' Leaning forward, she flashed him a smile.

'Can you confirm the times.'

'Oh, let me think... He must have got here around, say, half past eight. Maybe a bit earlier. And he left at ten.'

'Ten?' Benedict didn't mean to show his surprise and was embarrassed by his reaction which he should have kept hidden but Eric Fournier had definitely said he hadn't left Angela's until nearly half past eleven. 'Are you sure of this? It is rather important that we get this right.'

She rubbed her chin in what Benedict thought was a conscious effort to appear that she was carefully trying to remember. 'Yes, ten o'clock. I remember because just after Eric left, I put the radio on and the ten o'clock news bulletin was on.'

'What was on the news?'

'Oh, Inspector, I don't know. I wasn't listening. I just had it on in the background. I always have the radio on. I like the company. I do live by myself, as I'm sure you're aware.'

Jessica cleared her throat. 'How was Mr Fournier on Tuesday evening, Angela?'

'How do you mean?'

'I mean, did he appear his normal self to you or was he agitated at all? Anxious perhaps?'

'Well, yes, actually. He was on edge. I asked him several times if he was OK but he said he was fine, just brushed it off. But I thought at the time he was evading it, that something was troubling him.'

'But you don't know what?'

'No. I mean, I knew he was finding it difficult looking after Tammy. They never really got on, despite what others might say. But you won't find many who'll admit it. No one likes to speak ill of the dead or the terminally ill, do they? It's like a taboo. But I feel it's important you know.'

'They were married for some thirty-five years.'

'Thirty-eight. Wouldn't you be sick of someone after that long? I got sick of my first husband after six months. I managed to put up with number two for a lot longer but still.' She laughed to herself. 'I'm sorry, would you like a coffee or something?'

'No, no,' said Benedict. 'Most kind of you but we won't take up too much of your time. When you say Mr Fournier was finding it difficult looking after Tammy…'

'Oh, he was most circumspect with what he said but it wasn't difficult to read between the lines, Inspector. He found it a strain. Tammy was never an easy woman, even when she was healthy, and she became intolerable to him as she became increasingly ill.'

'Intolerable?' said Jessica.

'I'd say so. I mean, Eric wouldn't admit it in a month of Sundays but he and me go back many years. I could tell,' she said with a wink.

'Did you like Tammy?' asked Jessica.

'Hmm.' Her eyes slid sideways as she thought about the question. 'In a word – no.'

'Can I ask why not?'

'She was…' She rubbed the back of her neck. 'Tammy was a manipulative woman and she could be very selfish at times. Very demanding. It's what drove poor Eric into my arms.'

Benedict tried to hide his surprise at the casual way she brought that into the conversation. 'Can you expand on that?'

'Must I? It's rather personal.'

Not so personal that you mentioned it without prompting, thought Benedict. 'It might be helpful.'

She crossed and uncrossed her legs. 'Can I speak in confidence?'

'Yes,' said Benedict. 'Absolutely.'

'Eric and I are in love. There, I've said it. We want to be together. I'm sorry that Tammy met her end in such a gruesome way but…'

'Go on,' said Benedict.

'Well, obviously, it clears the path for us. We know we can't act too hastily; it wouldn't look right. But once the dust's settled, there's no reason why we can't make it official, he and I. Eric was about to ask Tammy for a divorce when Tammy fell ill. So then, of course, he couldn't bring himself to do it. What would people say? What would his daughters say? We plan to put his house on the market. We want to live together, be a proper couple, maybe get married. I'm not so bothered but Eric is… well, he's old-fashioned like that. In fact, he's promised that as soon as we've had Tammy's funeral, we'll go to Hatton Street and buy ourselves our rings.' She smiled at the thought. 'Husband number three. My poor mother; she'll be turning in her grave. Still, we all deserve to be happy.'

'Indeed.'

'Eric often used to say…'

'Yes? What was it he said?'

'Oh dear, I guess I shouldn't say this,' she said with a little laugh. 'But he used to joke about how much easier his life would be without Tammy. I mean, don't get me wrong, he'd never have hurt her or anything but… put it this way, I don't think Eric will be in mourning for too long.'

Benedict thanked her for her time.

Sitting in the car, Benedict puffed out his cheeks. 'What do you make of all that?'

Jessica scratched the back of her head. 'Bloody weird, actually.'

'Wasn't it? I mean, there's telling the truth and telling the truth but…'

'Yeah, that's what I thought. So, through that, we've now totally established Eric Fournier's motivation and we now know, according to Ms Wheeler, that he left hers at ten, not half eleven, as he told us.'

'Can we believe her though? She must've realised that everything she said simply put her lover more in the frame than ever.'

'Exactly. But we do know Tammy Fournier only changed her will six weeks ago.'

'I think we need to speak to Mr Fournier under more formal circumstances. I'll give him a ring and invite him in for an interview.'

'He'll need his solicitor.'

'Exactly. All the evidence we have against him is, at this stage, fairly circumstantial but, you know, I don't think it'll take much to make him crack. And when he does, case closed.'

Jessica started the car. She smiled. 'If only every case we had was as simple as this.'

Chapter 31: Frida
Today

Frida rang Diane. She didn't need to get home on time tonight as Ade was out again watching yet another football match in the pub with his mates, and she needed a friend to talk to. Diane answered. Was she free for a drink, asked Frida. Yes, Diane was. They agreed to meet in half an hour in the Red Lion again, even if Diane did consider it an 'old gits' pub'. Frida simply needed a friend to talk to. Diane wasn't exactly a friend but she had no one else.

Ade hadn't forgotten about the money; indeed, he hadn't stopped reminding her. But he hadn't raised his fists for a couple of days and as far as Frida was concerned, that was a win.

Frida was still reeling from her encounter with Stan. 'Fancy a quick drink, Stan?'

He stepped back, unable to disguise his surprise. 'A drink?' Frida knew immediately that she'd overstepped some invisible line.

'Yes, if – if you have time. I mean, it d-doesn't matter.' She could feel her cheeks burning. 'I just thought…'

'What did you think?' he asked, his eyes narrowing.

'Well, I thought we…' This was pointless and utterly embarrassing. Stan was a harmless, lovely old guy and in her desperation, she was totally ruining everything. 'You know what, forget it.' She didn't mean for it to come out so harshly but too late now.

'OK. I'm sorry, Frida, I don't understand.'

'No, you're right. I'm sorry. Look, I'd better go. Sorry, Stan. I shouldn't have asked.'

'Is everything all right, Frida? If you don't mind me saying, you seem upset about something. If you want to have a chat over a drink, I have time. I always have time.'

He looked so trusting, so kind. She could ask him now, just four hundred quid. But he was retired, alone. What sort of person was she becoming? She forced a laugh. 'No, I'm fine, really, all's good.' She couldn't wait to leave now. 'I'd better go. Sorry, Stan. I'll-I'll see you next time you're in, yeah?'

'Yes, of course. I'll be here. You know me, never sick, never late.'

'I know, and I appreciate it. Good night, Stan,'

'Yes, good night, Frida.'

She scampered off, head down, knowing that he was watching her. She disappeared into the high street crowd and once she was sure she was out of sight, she paused and caught her breath. 'Idiot, idiot,' she muttered to herself. What had she been thinking about?

Thirty minutes later, the flush of shame was still burning her up from the inside but now, at least, she could have a drink with Diane and try to shelve this humiliating and misguided experience. She dreaded now seeing Stan again but that was a worry for another day.

The Red Lion was still fairly quiet at this early stage of the evening, a young couple leaning towards each other, whispering, three middle-aged women at another table, their mobiles on the table before them. Frida silently acknowledged the portrait of Frida Kahlo. She spotted Diane sitting by herself in the corner reading *Metro*, the free newspaper given out in tube stations, a pint of beer in her hand.

'God, are you all right?' asked Diane looking up and seeing Frida approaching. 'You look like shit.'

'Long day,' she said, sitting down. 'I need a drink.'

There was no queue at the bar and she returned with a gin and tonic.

They talked about a B-list celebrity who'd been caught kissing someone whom he shouldn't have been kissing and shared anecdotes they'd read about on Instagram and TikTok.

Diane got herself a second beer, offering to buy Frida a second G&T but Frida said no. Returning to the table, Diane said, 'So, did you ask about me working in your shop?'

'Yes,' she lied. 'But no luck. I'm sorry.'

'Oh well, doesn't matter.'

Frida remembered Diane talking about the inheritance she got from her grandmother. Surely then she could spare her a few hundred quid but asking was so difficult, like standing on a cliff face and not being able to throw oneself off. She thought of Ade, out with his mates, getting wasted, one drink after another. He'd be back late, drunk as a skunk, demanding sex and violently reminding her again about the money. Her deadline was fast looming but she knew there was at least something she could do as a last resort to buy herself perhaps a whole week's grace, something she hated doing, something she'd dearly hoped she wouldn't have to do but with her options running out, the prospect was real. Diane was now her only hope.

'Where do you live?' Frida asked.

'Me? I live in a top-floor flat in Camden Town. It's quite decent. Not cheap though but where is unless you're living in some shithole somewhere like… Edmonton.'

'Do you live alone?'

'No, I share. Why?'

'Oh, just wondering,' She took a sip of her drink. 'Actually, I am looking for somewhere, a house share or something.'

'I thought you lived with your boyfriend.'

'Yeah but…' She placed her glass carefully on the table. 'Fact is, Di, I need to move out. We don't get on so well and he's…'

'He's what?'

'Violent.' There, at last, she'd said it.

'Oh, shit, is he?'

'Yeah, and it doesn't help that I owe him a wad of money at the moment.'

'That's not good.'

Frida waited, desperately hoping Diane would pick up on that and offer her a handout. Instead, Diane declared she needed the loo and promptly disappeared. Frida waited, hoping that Diane was thinking about it right this moment. She was tempted by another drink but couldn't risk feeling tipsy, not with Ade coming back drunk.

Diane returned. 'I should get going.'

'You couldn't help me out, could you, Di?'

'Help you out with what?'

'With a…' God, this was hard. 'An IOU.'

'Me?' She laughed. 'Fuck off.'

Her words felt like a punch. 'I'd paid you back.'

'If you don't have any money now, you're not likely to be better off anytime soon and I'd never see it again, would I? Nah, sorry, no way, Jose.' She stood and scooped up her coat.

'Please, Diane.'

'Shit, are you begging me now? God, have some respect, girl.' She checked her phone and smiled. 'See ya.'

And with that, she was gone leaving Frida with tears in her eyes. So, that was her last hope.

*

Frida returned to the flat she shared with Ade. It'd be several hours before Ade returned. She spent the evening in front of the television, her mind going over, as it frequently did, on how she could escape him. As much as she hated her mother's new partner, she had asked a few months back whether she could move in. It would have meant giving up her job but anything was better than living with Ade. Her mother's boyfriend said, according to her mum, that hell would freeze over first before he gave her headroom. She checked the online rental agents but there was nothing, literally nothing, she could afford. Coming up in a deposit and the first three months of rent was just a pipe dream.

She was stuck, truly stuck, and there was absolutely nothing she could do about it.

She'd suffered two humiliations today and now, in order to buy a few days' grace, she'd have to endure one more.

Chapter 32: Francine
Annecy, France, nine years ago

If Francine thought her life with her aunt and uncle was miserable before, now, following the incident with her uncle on Christmas Day, it was infinitely worse. She was terrified of him, constantly on her guard. She prayed it was a one-off occasion, that he was drunk on Christmas cheer, and it'd never happen again. But their relationship changed for the worse, not that it was exactly rosy to begin with. She couldn't bear to be in his presence while Uncle Jacques took every opportunity to seek her out. If Aunt Violette left the lounge to, say, go to the kitchen, Francine would follow, asking her aunt if there was anything she could help with. She started wearing baggier clothes and less make-up, anything to appear more drab.

One day, Francine bought a basic sliding lock for her bedroom door. Taking a screwdriver from the shed, she fixed it on. It'd gone within a couple of days, removed by Jacques who told Violette who, in turn, berated Francine for making unnecessary holes in the door and frame.

On New Year's Eve, Francine's father rang. She burst into tears on hearing his voice. Naturally concerned, he asked what on earth was the matter. She couldn't tell him, too ashamed to speak the words. Instead, she just said she missed him. 'Please, let me come live with you, Papa.' She could tell he hated her asking him because it made him feel bad but it'd be impossible, he said, repeating the same barriers as before. She cursed that she'd chosen English at school. Spanish had been an option but she never even considered it. English was the language of commerce, she was told, the international language, it made more sense. Her father asked how she was enjoying living with his ex-wife's sister and her husband. What could she say?

'Hey, something I learnt recently. Your mother was assaulted by some bloke she was seeing.'

'Assaulted?'

'Yeah, he hit her. Would you believe it? Your mother pressed charges but he got away with a suspended.'

'A suspended what?'

'It just means he got his knuckles rapped and told not to do it again. Some chap by the name of Fournier. What a bastard.'

Francine stiffened on hearing the name.

Francine didn't go out on New Year's Eve, no one invited her anywhere. Uncle Jacques was steadily getting drunk and this worried Francine no end. She had nowhere to hide. She suggested to Violette that Jacques had had enough to drink but her aunt just laughed and said he had every right to 'let his hair down'. Francine went to bed at ten knowing she'd never get to sleep. Come midnight, she heard Jacques climb the stairs. She braced herself, her arms wrapped around her knees and willed him to walk past her door and onto his own bedroom further down the landing. He did. She dared to hope that Christmas Day had indeed been a one-off.

The new term at school couldn't come around fast enough. Francine had never been so happy to return to school. What a miserable holiday that had been – she hadn't spoken to a single friend of her own age.

Early February came and Francine finally began to relax a little. Uncle Jacques had kept a respectable distance and didn't do or say anything else to make her feel uncomfortable. Indeed, life was getting a little better – she'd made a few friends at school and one Thursday, one of them, a girl called Ines, said she and a couple of her friends were going out on a bike ride the coming Saturday and would Francine like to join them. Francine didn't have a bicycle but there was an old 'bone shaker' in the yard. That evening, she rushed home and changed into her home clothes before heading outside. The bike had seven gears. Yes, the tyres were flat, the chain rusty and the back brake missing a pad although the front brake was fine. Using her phone, she googled instructions on how to fix up a bike. She concluded it was too much work but there was, according to Google, a bike repair shop in town. She didn't relish the thought of pushing her bike a kilometre into town. She was going to have to swallow her pride and ask Uncle Jacques to throw the bike on the back of his truck and take her.

So engrossed on her phone, Francine didn't hear a thing. At the last moment, she was aware of a shadow, someone behind her but before she had time to react, two hands were on her breasts. She screamed, dropping her phone. Uncle Jacques stepped back, laughing. 'That made you jump.'

'You pig.'

That stopped him laughing. 'What did you call me?'

'You heard me.' Scooping up her phone, she barged past him, her eyes smarting with tears, and ran indoors. By the time she slammed the front door behind her, she was crying.

Aunt Violette emerged from the kitchen, drying a saucepan. 'You all right, Francine?' she asked. 'What's the matter?'

'Uncle Jacques...' She couldn't get the words out.

'What about him?'

'He... he... he grabbed my...' She stopped. Would her aunt believe her?

Violette's eyes narrowed. 'Grabbed your what exactly?'

Francine wiped her tears. Looking skywards, she said, 'I can't say it.'

'How can you expect me to help you if you don't tell me?'

'He grabbed my boobs.'

Violette flung the saucepan on a table. 'You little devil, you!' she shouted.

Francine stepped back, surely her aunt had to believe her. 'He did.'

'Why, you... you little twollop, how dare you make up fibs.'

'I'm not fibbing, honest to God, he... he crept up–'

Aunt Violette moved so quickly, Francine had no time to react. Violette slapped her across the face. Francine fell back, shocked by the sting.

'You wash your bloody mouth out, miss. Who do you think you are, coming into my house and making up such filthy lies under the eyes of the Lord?'

Uncle Jacques appeared, closing the door behind him. 'What's all this shouting?'

'Nothing for you to worry about, love. Francine is going to her bedroom now to ask the Lord for His forgiveness.' Turning to Francine, she said, 'And you're not to come out until I say so. God does not like little girls who lie about their elders and betters, and the quicker you learn that, the better. Now, be off with you. The sight of you makes my stomach churn.'

Francine traipsed upstairs to her room. She sat on her bed and reached for her phone. Seconds later, Violette barged in and snatched the phone out of Francine's hands. 'You can't contemplate your sins while you've got this.'

'Please, Aunt Violette.'

'No, you don't need this. Do you see me and your uncle with these stupid things? They rot your brain. This,' she said, holding the phone up, 'is why you are such a devilish girl.' She dropped the phone on the wooden floor and stamped on it several times, destroying it.

Francine screamed.

'You'll thank me one day.' And with that, she stormed off leaving Francine a trembling wreck. She knew that without her phone she was utterly isolated. She also knew that while she lived in this house, she remained at risk from her uncle. She'd run away. But where? She had no money, no friends and nowhere to run. No, running away wasn't an option. That meant she had only one option, and that was to deal with her uncle so that he never bothered her again.

Chapter 33: Susan
Today

Margot was pregnant. Susan still couldn't grasp it. The moment she saw her, Susan's world collapsed.

All the words Susan had planned simply vanished; she stood in front of the woman gawking as Margot stood there with her hands cupped beneath her belly. 'Yes?' said Margot eventually. 'Can I help?'

'I, er…'

'Are you OK?' She spoke with an Irish accent, not dissimilar to Robbie's. She had a harsh face and grey, hard eyes. She wore an all-in-one velour tracksuit and white trainers.

'Who is it?' came Robbie's voice from within the house.

'Whatever it is,' said Margot to Susan, closing the door, 'we're not interested.'

Susan stood stock still, her mouth open, not believing what she'd just seen.

A moment later, the door opened again, and there was Robbie. If the situation hadn't been so horrendous, Susan might have laughed at his shocked expression. Glancing back indoors, he quietly closed the front door. 'What the fuck are you doing here, Susan?' He took her by the elbow and gently led her away from the house, back onto the pavement. 'Susan, answer me, what are you doing here?'

'You didn't answer my calls. I didn't have a choice.'

'Yeah, well. Look…'

'You're going to be a dad.'

He couldn't look her in the eye. 'Yeah.'

'Twice over.'

'Yeah, look, about that…'

'Yes?'

'I always meant to tell you but the time never seemed right. It wasn't meant to happen like this.'

'But it has.'

'Please, don't tell Margot. I'm begging you, Susie.'

'You lied to me. All this time, I believed you. I'm having this baby, Robbie. I thought, you and me, I thought…' Damn it, she began crying.

Robbie glanced up and down the street, desperate to be shot of her. 'Look, I'm sorry. You go home and I'll try and pop around later. We can talk then.'

'You will?' She hated the pleading tone in her voice.

'Yeah, absolutely. I promise.'

Margot reappeared on her doorstep. 'What are you doing, Robbie? Who the fuck is that?'

'No one. Give me a minute.'

Margot returned inside.

'So, I'm *no one* now? Funny that, I thought I was the mother to your future child, one of them, at least.'

'Sorry about that, really. I'd better go. I'll see you later.'

'Don't let me down, Robbie. I'll come back tomorrow if

you don't. Trust me, I'll tell her, I'll bloody tell her everything.'

'I'll come around about eight, yeah?'

'You'd better, Robbie, you fucking better.'

And now, approaching eight o'clock, Susan, curled up on the sofa in the living room, waited, a knot in her stomach. Her father kept popping in and out, saying he was about to head out while Lizzie had just returned from meeting a friend. Susan wondered where her father was going, whether it was his woman friend. She'd asked but right now, with her life falling apart at the seams, she didn't care. Both women had told Eric that they were heading back to their respective homes tomorrow. 'That's fine,' he said. It was obvious Eric didn't need them any more if indeed he needed them in the first place.

'Are you OK, Susie?' asked Lizzie.

'I'm fine,' she snapped. She hadn't mentioned Robbie's impending visit partly because it was a case of believing it when she saw it. But ten minutes later, the front doorbell rang. Susan rushed to the door.

'Susie.'

'You'd better come in.'

He followed her through to the living room. He stopped short on seeing Lizzie sprawled on the settee. Lizzie almost dropped her phone on seeing the handsome Robbie suddenly appearing in front of her. Eric, on hearing voices, came through. Susan made the introductions, introducing Robbie simply by his name, not the fact he was supposed to be her boyfriend. But it was obvious. Robbie glanced around at the three of them, looking like a man who'd inadvertently walked into a trap. Susan hadn't planned it but now that it had happened, she wasn't sorry.

Eric, squinting, said, 'Are you…'

Lizzie, standing, finished the question. 'You must be Susie's intended. Lovely to meet you at last.'

Robbie pulled on his ear lobe. 'Yeah, well…'

Susan helped out. 'Robbie's wife is expecting a baby.'

Lizzie covered her mouth with her hand. 'Oh, I'm sorry, me and my mouth. I thought…'

'He is,' said Susan. 'I'm also expecting Robbie's child.'

Lizzie and Eric exchanged shocked expressions. 'I don't understand,' said Eric. 'What do you mean?'

'You tell them, Robbie.'

He looked down at his feet.

'Go on,' shouted Susan. 'Tell my father and my sister how you've managed to impregnate two women and what a shit you are.'

Lizzie shrieked.

'Is this true?' said Eric, his face red. 'Well?'

'It wasn't meant to happen.'

'What wasn't meant to happen? So, are you saying you're actually married?'

Robbie nodded.

'And your wife, she's… pregnant?'

'Yes.'

'And… my daughter, you're the…'

'Yes. I'm sorry.'

'Oh my God,' said Lizzie, unable to hide her glee at her sister's misfortune.

Eric looked as if he might burst a blood vessel. 'And what do you intend to do? I hope you plan on standing by my daughter.'

'Yes but…'

'But what?'

'I can't leave my wife but I will…' He waved his hands about. 'I'll make sure Susie's looked after.'

'Well, isn't that a relief? We can all sleep easy now. What is it you do?'

'I'm a mechanic.'

'Do you own your business?'

'No.'

Eric threw his hands in the air. 'Great. Bloody brilliant. So, on your mechanic's wage, you plan to look after all your harem and their offspring. Incredible. Susan, what the bloody hell were you thinking of? Got seduced by that easy Irish charm, did we?'

'I didn't know, did I, Robbie? The marriage was over, you slept in different beds, hadn't been intimate for months and barely talked. That's what you said, wasn't it? God, how stupid I've been, how bloody stupid.'

Lizzie put her arm around her, an uncharacteristic show of affection from her sister. Susan was about to brush her off but her heart just collapsed within her and she fell into her sister's embrace and allowed the tears to come. What a fool she'd been, an utter, utter fool.

'Well,' said Eric. 'I'd been looking forward to meeting and shaking you by the hand and welcoming you into the family. But right now, the only thing I want to shake is your neck. So, my first grandchild is to be born a bastard, an Irish bastard at that. I hope that job of yours pays well because you…' He jabbed Robbie in the chest. 'Will not be shirking your responsibility.'

'I won't, sir.' Robbie too looked close to tears. 'I won't.'

Lizzie guided Susan to the settee, sitting down with her.

Eric looked at his watch. 'I've got to go. Well,' he said, looking at Robbie. 'I would say it was a pleasure to meet you, young man, but frankly, it isn't and this has come as a terrible shock. And you, Susan…'

'What?'

'We'll have words tomorrow.'

Why was he talking to her like this? Was this her fault? But she had nothing left in her, no fight, no energy. She watched her father storm out. So was he going to see that bitch of a woman, his lover? The word felt like poison on her tongue.

After Eric had left, Robbie remained on his feet, unsure what to do or say next. Lizzie was looking at Susan with such pity, it almost reduced Susan to tears again.

Lizzie, breaking the ice, said cheerfully, 'So, what are you hoping for, Robbie? Boys or girls, one from each maybe? What about you, Susie, do you have a preference?'

But Susan wasn't listening; she was thinking about her father, about how he'd mistreated her mother for all those years, about how he carried on even as she lay in her bed ravaged by that cruel disease; how he was *still* at it before her mother had been even been put in her grave; how he'd manipulated her into changing her will. What started off as a simmering anger was rapidly coursing through veins, threatening to explode. She shot up from the settee. 'I'm going out,' she snapped.

'Where are you going?' asked Robbie.

But Susan didn't answer him. She'd deal with Robbie later; right now, she needed to confront her father for once and for all.

Chapter 34: Eric
Today

Eric stormed down the street, his head whirling, still reeling from the emotional onslaught of finding out the truth about Susan's boyfriend. Nine o'clock, it was still light and the night warm but the streets around here were largely deserted. He was going to drive but after that bombshell, he felt in need of a walk and the chance to clear his head.

How had he got his life in such a mess? In a matter of days, he'd lost his wife, finished with his lover and now realised that his youngest daughter's life was as much of a mess as his. But his mess would recede with time while Susan's problems were only just beginning. How could Susan have been so irresponsible? It beggared belief. How would Tammy have reacted? Tammy had always been the laid-back one, the perpetual hippy. But even Tammy would have been shocked by this turn of events. She would have hugged Susie and said something like, *Don't worry, darling, we'll get through this together.* Poor Tammy. But despite her outward liberal attitude, Tammy could be a closet snob. At least Eric was honest about his snobbery. Tammy would have been quietly appalled… no, not appalled but certainly *disappointed* that Susan's choice of suitor was a mechanic. Hardly the sort of occupation with a future.

Eric checked his watch again as he turned onto Highgate High Street. He passed a pub, its customers sitting outside enjoying the balmy evening, their voices happy and loud. He passed a young Asian woman wearing a sweatshirt that bore the painting of Monet's famous painting of the lily pond and the Japanese bridge. He smiled at her but she didn't notice. Angela loved Monet; indeed, she'd recently been to Monet's home and garden in Giverny in Normandy.

Would Angela mind him turning up this late and out of the blue? No, probably not. Indeed, she'd be delighted. He hoped he wasn't going to regret this but the fact was, he was going back to her, cap in hand, ready to bow at her feet and beg her forgiveness. He'd been too hasty, too much in shock, when he spoke to her last, saying their relationship was over. In the couple of days since, he had the chance to reflect and he knew he was an idiot. A good woman like Angela was a rarity and the thought of never seeing her again was too unbearable for words. He was going to ring her but he decided to man up and speak to her in person. He wished now he'd thought of it earlier and had a chance to buy a generous bouquet of flowers but it was too late for that now and so he was going to have to face her empty-handed but with a full-hearted apology.

Perhaps he could stay the night? She always used to hate it when, after their lovemaking, Eric left to go home, back to Tammy. It made her feel cheap. But he didn't have a choice, did he? Not then. But now? Yes, if Angela wanted him to stay the night, he'd be more than glad to oblige.

They'd have to keep their relationship quiet for now; it wouldn't look good so soon after Tammy's death. But give it a year, perhaps even six months, and they could come out, so to speak, make it public. She could sell up and move in with him, make a real go of it. Lizzie would be fine with the situation. She wouldn't care too much; Susan perhaps less so but given her circumstances now, she'd have greater things to worry about.

Leaving the high street, Eric took the turning onto Caversham Avenue, Angela's street. The excitement of seeing her again was building. He quickened his pace, keen to see her, keen to feel her arms around him; keenly anticipating her reaction when he reappeared on her doorstep, contrite and begging her forgiveness for his stupidity.

No, for a man who'd just lost his wife, Eric Fournier's future seemed positively rosy. He smiled to himself.

He heard footsteps behind him, alarmingly close. He turned. 'Hello? Oh my God, what are you doing creeping up on me like that?' He chortled nervously. 'Really, you gave me a fright there.'

'It's time.'

'Time? Time for what?'

An abrupt dull pain in his stomach. What was that? Ah, OK, it was getting worse, an inexplicable stomach pain. The figure simply about-turned and walked briskly away. 'Wait,' he called. What was happening to him? He clutched his stomach. Something sticky. What was that? His eyes blinked, a sudden feeling of light-headedness. He felt sick. His legs were giving away now. That stickiness, what was that? Shit, oh no, that was blood, his blood. God, he'd been stabbed. This wasn't happening; it couldn't be happening. There was no one about, people in their houses, no one on the street. He needed help, he needed it now. His phone. He'd ring 999. But he couldn't coordinate his movements, couldn't get his brain into gear. The pain was intensifying. Oh shit, no, this was bad now. He had to hold on. He staggered up a pathway towards someone's door, every step taking it out of him. He rang the bell, clutching his stomach, trying not to cry out with the pain, the tears streaming down his face. He would have slammed his fists against the door but totally lacked the strength. He couldn't bear his weight any more. He sank to his knees, squealing in pain. He was scared now, he couldn't die, not now, not like this. The door opened, a shaft of light. Thank the Lord for that. He reached his hand up. The woman looked down at him, her expression blank with confusion. And then she screamed.

He was dying, he knew that now. Angela would never know; she'd go to the grave thinking he'd spurned her. She'd hate him forever. Of all the regrets he had, of all the things he'd done right or wrong in his life, this was all that worried him now at the very end, that Angela would think bad of him. The woman of the house was still screaming. A man was beside her now. Was he phoning for help? It wouldn't get here on time, not now. It was too late. Too late.

Why? God, why? He didn't deserve to die like this. Why?

But even in his very last moments, Eric Fournier knew why. He knew exactly why.

Chapter 35: Francine
Annecy, France, nine years ago

Another week passed, and Francine had barely spoken at home, only speaking when spoken to. Aunt Violette did not attempt to hide her disdain for her, almost throwing her dinner plate on the table in front of her, looking at her as Uncle Jacques offered his usual mealtime prayer of gratitude. She never got the bicycle repaired and hence missed the day out with Ines and her friends. When she returned to school the following Monday, no one mentioned it. Francine did think of approaching one of the friendlier female teachers and telling them about Uncle Jacques but she knew, ultimately, it'd be her word against his. And they were never going to believe her, a sullen schoolgirl, disturbed by her mother's suicide, against the word of a God-fearing man. She desperately missed her phone but there was no way she'd ever be able to afford a replacement.

The following Saturday Uncle Jacques declared he was going to chop up some wood as they were fast running out. Aunt Violette was off to town to do her weekly shop. Francine begged to go with her. 'I think not,' came the curt reply.

'I can carry your bags for you.'

'I can manage quite well by myself, thank you. And anyway,' she added, lowering her voice. 'For one thing, I wouldn't want to be seen with a liar, and secondly, you…' She jabbed Francine in the chest, 'are still grounded. Remember?'

As soon as she left, Uncle Jacques put his coat on. 'You can help me,' he said.

'No, you're alright.'

'It wasn't a request, young lady. It's about time you started earning your keep around here. Come on.'

'But it's going to rain any moment.'

He made a *pft* sound. 'A bit of rain's not going to harm you. Go on, get your coat. Put some gloves on too. You'll need them against splinters.'

She followed him out, disturbing the chickens. The clouds darkened. 'Right,' said Uncle Jacques. 'You bring me a log at a time and as I chop them up, carry them over there,' he said, pointing to the side of the shed. 'Then, we'll take a supply inside and cover the rest. Go on then, let's make a start before it pours down.'

After a few minutes of silent working, Jacques said, 'You missing your mother?'

'Yeah.' She wasn't going to say anything further. Yes, she did miss her mother. She may have become impossible to live with and she could be complicated but she was still her mother and yes, she did miss her very much. Life with Mama could be hard but it was infinitely better than this.

'Ah, you're better off here,' he said, swinging his axe.

'I don't think so.'

Straightening up, he glared at her. 'You know, you're an ungrateful little madam. That's your problem. We didn't have to take you on. We could have left you to rot in some home with all the other delinquents but no, you don't think of that, do you? You don't know how lucky you are, young lady.'

Lifting his axe, he chopped a small log clean into two. It began raining and even the chickens ran for shelter but Jacques didn't seem to notice. Soon, they were both wet through. But undeterred, Jacques kept chopping. They worked in silence for another fifteen minutes until Jacques asked, 'So, how's it going at school?'

'It's all right.'

'Got yourself a boyfriend yet?'

'No.'

'No? Pretty girl like you. Not surprising is it, though? The way you mop around with all hair all lank and looking miserable as sin. What do you expect?'

'I don't want a boyfriend.' As soon as she said it, she regretted it.

'No? Like an older man, eh? Someone with a bit of experience. Is that it?'

'No.'

He laughed. 'It's tipping down,' he said, looking up and stating the obvious. 'I think we'll stop. Look at you, girl, you're wet through. Look, why don't you have a bath? I'll come rub your back.'

'No, thanks.'

'Go and have a bath, girl. Like I said earlier, it's not a request.' Leaning the axe against the pile of unchopped logs, he stamped his boots. 'Go on, you go run the bath. I'll finish off here. I'll only be a minute.'

Jacques disappeared into the shed. Francine stood in the rain, watching the puddles form in the mud. Her mind devoid of thought, as if she was watching herself from a distance, she picked up the axe and felt its weight. She stood to the side of the shed door, the rain lashing down on her face, washing away her tears. She could hear her uncle inside, rummaging around.

A minute later, he emerged from the shed, looking up at the rain. He paused for a moment, shaking his head. He screeched as the axe sliced into his left shoulder. He dropped to his knees, screaming, his right hand on his shoulder, trying without success to stem the shocking torrent of blood. Francine lifted the axe over the head ready to strike again but his screams were so shatteringly loud, so shocking and pitiful, she couldn't do it. Instead, she calmly placed the axe back where she found it and walked around her uncle to face him. His eyes were screwed shut, his hand drenched in blood. The wound was nearer to the neck than she'd thought.

'Call for help,' he gulped through gritted teeth.

'I can't, can I? Aunt Violette broke my phone, didn't she? Here, let me help you to your feet.'

She struggled to get him to his feet. 'Call for help.'

'Let's get you to the well. You can sit there while I run to the phone box in the village.' She half pulled him, half pushed him to the well, his feet dragging on the mud, propping him up, bearing his weight. She finally got him there. He sat on the low stone wall, gasping for breath, crying, groaning, still clutching onto his neck while Francine caught her breath. A new wave of pain wracked his body. He screeched, stretching back, throwing his head up. With her uncle leaning back, it was simply a matter of a gentle push and Uncle Jacques fell backwards. He screamed as he hurtled down the well. Francine was surprised by the loudness of the thud, she expected to hear a splash, not a thud.

She leaned over, squinting but couldn't see a thing. She

could hear him groaning and crying. After a while, his voice echoed up to her: 'Help me, Francine. For the love of God, help me…'

Chapter 36: Benedict
Today

Having spoken to his boss, DCI Lincoln, Benedict had permission to bring Eric Fournier in for a formal interview. But he wasn't answering his phone. If Angela Wheeler was to be believed, and he wasn't entirely sure she could be, then Fournier had some further questions to answer. It was always a tricky situation, suspecting the next of kin as the potential killer. A detective's first priority was, obviously, to unmask the killer so tough questions needed to be asked. But if the next of kin was indeed innocent, then it seemed rough to subject them to such an ordeal. But, ultimately, needs must.

So, together with DC Kelly, Benedict drove up to Fournier's house. Susan answered the door. She didn't look well, thought Benedict. Had she been crying? 'I'm sorry to turn up unexpectedly but is your father in?'

'No, he went out. He left about half an hour ago.'

'Do you know where he went?'

She shook her head. 'I'm sorry, I've no idea. Although I suppose you could try that fancy woman of his.'

'Thank you. We will.'

'You don't know who I'm referring to.'

'We do. Did he say when he'd been back?'

'No. Sorry.'

He thanked her.

'Oh, Inspector, before you go.'

'Yes?'

'I thought you ought to know something. Yesterday, Dad realised that all of Mum's jewellery had been stolen.'

'Has it indeed?'

'Yes, unfortunately. He said he was sure it was there when Mum died and he reckoned it was his cleaner.'

'Alina?'

'Oh, you know her? Yes, Alina. He phoned her and said unless she brought the jewellery back within twenty-four hours, he'd sack her and report her to the police.'

'I see. And has Alina brought the jewellery back?'

'Well, no, because, apparently, she said she never took it in the first place.'

'Did your father believe her?'

'Not for an instant.'

'And what do you think?'

'Me? No way. Alina didn't take it.'

'So, who did?'

Susan shrugged her shoulders. 'I wish I knew.'

'How much was it worth, would you know?'

'No clue but there was a lot of it and she'd had some of it for as long as I remember. As a kid, I used to play dress-up with some of it.'

DC Kelly drove the five minutes to Caversham Avenue. Turning into the street, they saw an ambulance parked up, its blue light still flashing silently. Kelly drew the car up to an abrupt stop. 'Come on, Kelly,' said Benedict. 'Let's see what's happening here.' They could see a scrum of people at the front door, a figure prostrate on the ground, a couple of paramedics kneeling over, a couple of people, presumably the householders hovering inside the doorway of the house.

'No coppers here yet by the looks of it,' said Kelly.

They approached the house, their ID badges at the ready. 'Kelly, mind where you step, keep to the edges.' He didn't want to disturb any possible evidence, blood trails or footprints or anything that might be of use.

The woman of the house, a woman of about forty, started talking over the top of the figures on the ground between them. 'He just appeared out of nowhere, blood all over him.' She was clearly shaken, her partner or companion just behind her, white as a sheet.

Benedict looked down and, with a start, saw Eric Fournier, the very man he was about to arrest for the murder of his wife, lying there, the bright porch light shining down on him. He was still alive, just about, his white shirt shocking red from blood, probably his dark blue jacket too. The paramedics were frantically attending to him. Leaning down, he whispered into the female medic's ear, 'Can you save him?'

The woman shot him a fierce look and shook her head.

'Can I speak to him?'

'No, you bloody can't.'

'Just for a second. Please.'

'Don't be so stupid.'

Benedict stepped back. Yes, it was stupid but he still didn't like being called out in front of his detective constable. DC Kelly looked suitably embarrassed.

Fournier looked dead, a spittle of blood spewing from the

corner of his mouth, his eyes rolled back, his chest still. Benedict wanted to speak to the couple but couldn't bring himself to step over Fournier and the medics blocking the way. The woman had turned and buried her head into the man's chest. Benedict and the man acknowledged each other.

Benedict and DC Kelly had no choice but to wait while the paramedics tried their best to save the man. Meanwhile, two squad cars appeared, their sirens shattering the peaceful night air. Four uniformed officers jumped out of their cars. DC Kelly, his palm up, stopped them at the garden gate and explained what was happening. Benedict heard Kelly advise the officers to block off the street and start an initial search of the immediate area.

Suddenly, Mr Fournier raised an arm a fraction, his mouth open. 'He's trying to say something,' said Benedict. 'Please, give me space,' he said to the paramedics.

'I'm not sure,' said the female medic but her colleague nodded to her and, reluctantly, she acquiesced.

Kneeling down next to the stricken man, Benedict said, 'Mr Fournier, Inspector Paige here.'

The man's mouth opened, releasing a further trickle of blood. The disconcerting sound of gurgling rose from inside his throat.

'I'm listening, Mr Fournier. I'm listening.'

'S-Su…' He swallowed, his eyes still closed. 'Susan…'

'Susan? What about her?'

But his mouth closed, the effort had been too much.

'Stand clear now,' said the female medic. The two of them resumed their desperate efforts to revive him as Benedict stepped back and stood next to DC Kelly.

Only a couple more minutes passed when first the man and

then the woman paramedic rose to their feet, both shaking their heads. 'We tried,' said the woman.

Her colleague slapped her on the shoulder. 'That was tough.'

The six of them stood silently looking down at the pathetic man dead on a random person's doorstep, his features contorted, his eyes, now open, glazed with outright shock and fear. It made for a pitiful sight. Benedict shook his head.

'We'd better move him,' whispered the female medic.

'I'll get the stretcher,' said the man.

'No,' said Benedict. 'We can't move him. We'd risk compromising the evidence.' Turning to the couple, he added, 'I'm sorry. But we're going to have to wait.'

Benedict asked the medics for a quiet word, away from the couple. 'What are your thoughts?' he asked.

'He was stabbed,' said the man. 'One fatal wound from what we can see. And from what we can tell, we were here within three and a half minutes of the lady of the house making the call. But we were still too late.'

Three minutes later, Benedict and DC Kelly stepped over Fournier's corpse, conscious that it might appear rather undignified, and stepped into the house. They listened to the couple as they related their tale. 'I shall never forget it,' said the woman, reaching for her partner's hand. 'The blood, it was everywhere.' She dabbed her eyes. 'That white shirt of his, it was like something out of a horror movie.'

'Did you see or hear anyone or anything else?' asked DC Kelly.

'No. We had the TV on though. We always have it loud cos Tony here is a bit hard of hearing, aren't you, love?'

Tony nodded, looking rather embarrassed by the fact.

'So the first we knew of it was when I opened the door.

And I just saw him there like some Dracula victim and I screamed.'

'I suppose you got to let people know now,' said Tony. 'Like his wife or whatever.'

'Yes,' said Benedict.

'Blimey. What a job. I don't envy you that.'

'No. It's not the easiest of things.' Slapping his knees, he stood and, turning to DC Kelly, said, 'And sadly, I think we should make a start.'

Chapter 37: Frida
Today

Frida lay on her bed, weeping. She knew she had to get up and get to work but she couldn't face the day. She was tempted to call in sick but she'd rather be at work than stuck in the flat dwelling on what Ade had made her do last night. She was still dreadfully sore. She loathed anal sex but it did provide a temporary lifeline – another week to find that wretched money. Thanks to her mother she had half of it, but she had absolutely no idea how to raise the rest apart from asking the bank for a loan. But the interest would cripple her.

Ade was out for the morning – a half day's labouring on a building site in Lambeth. It'd be one o'clock by the time he got back.

However she looked at it, her future seemed bleak. It hadn't always been this way. Ade was actually a decent enough person when she first met him four years back. She fell for his good looks, his green eyes and finely arched, almost feminine eyebrows and the decorative tattoos that ran the length of his arms and the centre of his chest. Her mother always used to warn her against the good-looking boys, invariably fine on the outside, rotten within. The sad thing was she had a lovely boyfriend at the time, Ray, slightly dull, his eyes too close together, his nose a tad too big but he adored her, nothing was ever too much trouble when it came to pleasing Frida. She ditched him for Ade. What a fool. She saw him recently down the refrigerated aisle in Tesco and was shocked by how it affected her. He seemed to be spending an awfully long time deciding which pack of frozen peas to buy. Her heart melted a touch. She would have loved to say hello, ask how he was but she didn't trust not to break down there and then in front of him. So, with a pebble in the pit of her stomach, she turned and walked away.

Ade simply changed. It happened so gradually that she never noticed until it was too late. He became more demanding, more critical and sarcastic. But she was fine, she could cope with all that – until the day he first hit her. That's when her life changed – for the worse.

Wincing, she pulled herself up from her bed and padded over to the bathroom to have a shower. She relished the hot water and the time to herself. She got dressed and, as always, set about clearing Ade's mess. The man was incapable of putting his clothes or indeed anything away. From his underwear to a pizza box to his razor, everything was always left out and it was always down to Frida to put it away. She usually checked his pockets in the hope of finding some incriminating evidence of him playing away. She'd be delighted; let another woman bear the brunt of his anger. Alas, she had yet to find a single thing.

There was a pair of black jogging bottoms under the bed. She yanked at it and heard the tiniest of little clunks, something she'd inadvertently dislodged. She looked at the digital clock on the bedside table. If she didn't leave now, she'd be late for work and she couldn't afford another telling-off from Sheila. But curiosity had got the better of her. She lay on the floor and reached under the low-slung bed, her hand patting the wooden floorboards until she hit something metallic. A box maybe? She retrieved it. She let out a gasp. Was this what she thought it was? Opening the latch and flipping open the lid, her eyes widened on seeing the array of treasure within – necklaces, brooches, pendants, rings, so many rings. And all so tasteful, much of it she recognised as the Art Deco design. How much was this worth? A thought occurred to her. Using the torch from her phone, she scanned the dark cavern beneath the bed and yes, there were more. She extricated them – three small boxes, felt boxes. More treasure. My god, what was all this? She knew for sure she wasn't meant to find it and if Ade knew, there'd be hell to pay. If she viewed her boyfriend in a kinder light, she might have thought Ade was planning a massive surprise for her – after all, her birthday wasn't too far away. But no way. She'd be lucky to get a Mars Bar and a birthday card recycled from two years ago. No, Ade was hiding it for a reason. He'd stolen it. Her heart thumped so loudly it drowned out her thoughts. She could use this. Not sell it, that'd be far too risky. But somehow, she had to take advantage of this.

The idea hit her straight away. Not wanting to lose a moment, she rang Sheila, said she'd be late to work today, she was awfully sorry. She could hear the intake of Sheila's breath, her obvious annoyance. But when Frida explained she had to go to the police station to report a crime, Sheila's demeanour changed immediately.

Using her phone, she Googled police stations in Camden and worked out the nearest was in West Hampstead, Fortune Green Road, a couple of bus rides away. She dressed quickly, applied only the faintest touches of make-up and placed all the jewellery boxes in a small rucksack and left the house. She kept the rucksack pressed against her bosom, excited by the adventure of it all, excited that perhaps, just perhaps, she might have found a way out.

Thirty minutes later she was there. She spoke to the woman at the front desk who took surprisingly little interest in Frida's haul, and rang through for an officer. A man in uniform appeared and invited her to an office at the back. His name, he said, was PC Chiles, a clean-cut man not much older than Frida with short dark hair, neatly groomed. He asked for Frida's name.

'So, where did you find this?' asked PC Chiles, once he'd looked at the jewellery. Frida noticed he only moved things with the end of a pencil. Of course, she hadn't been so careful.

'Under my bed.'

He laughed loudly at that. 'Seriously?'

'It's not that funny.'

'So, dare I ask how all this stuff got under your bed?'

'My boyfriend put it there.'

'Really? OK.' He was taking this more seriously now. 'Do you know why?'

'I suppose because he's hiding it. It's not his.'

'What are you saying here? Do you have reason to believe your boyfriend stole it?'

'Yes. Hopefully soon my *ex*-boyfriend.'

PC Chiles raised his eyebrows at that. 'OK, so you do think he stole it?'

'Yeah, he must have, otherwise, why would he be hiding it?'

'Yes. You appreciate what you're doing here?'

'Of course.'

'OK, let me take down some details.'

Having taken all of Ade's details and how Frida found the jewellery, PC Chiles said he'd run it through the database and see if anything came up. 'I imagine with this much, someone will have reported it. If so, we'll be able to reunite it with its rightful owner and your boyfriend, or ex, will have some serious explaining to do. Would you have anything on you right now that might have your boyfriend's fingerprints?'

'Erm, I don't think so. Oh, perhaps my debit card. He uses that quite a bit.'

'OK, it might be worth a go.'

'Can't you arrest him now?'

'Not straight away, no. We'll need a bit more to go on.'

'But you have to arrest him today and keep him on remand or whatever you do.'

'I'm afraid, miss, it doesn't quite work like that.'

'But when he realises what's happened, he'll kill me. I mean, literally, he'll batter me black and blue. It doesn't take much for him to hit me.'

'I'm sorry to hear that, Frida.'

She loved the way he used her first name; it made her feel safer already. She warmed to his man.

'I could refer you to a women's refuge nearby. They can usually take women at short notice and it will provide you with a safe, temporary accommodation.'

Frida felt her shoulders drop. The relief. 'Yes, that'd be great. Thank you. Thank you so much.'

He smiled. 'A pleasure, Frida.'

Chapter 38: Francine
Annecy, France, nine years ago

Francine stood in the yard, the rain lashing down on her, her whole body shaking. The rain almost drowned out Uncle Jacques's pleas. Aunt Violette would be back soon, she needed Jacques to quieten before she returned, not that anyone would hear him unless they were almost standing at the well but it worried her nonetheless. Grabbing a handful of grass, she wiped the axe clean of blood. Good thing, she thought, that her uncle had advised her to wear gloves to protect her hands against splinters. There were hints of blood in the puddles, not that anyone would notice unless they were looking for it. It'd soon wash away.

She leaned over the well and called down into the darkness. 'Don't worry, Uncle Jacques, help is on its way. We'll soon have you out of there.' Why had she done that, she wondered. There was no need to torment the man but it pleased her that his final moments would be spent in agony, hoping to be rescued in time. Indeed, she was amazed he'd survived the fall. She had no idea how deep the well was but it was a long drop. She rather assumed there'd be water down there but he must have broken a few bones. With any luck, he'd broken his neck. Serves the bastard right.

'Help me, Francine. Please…' His voice was weaker. It wouldn't be long now. She smiled.

She had that bath, just as Uncle Jacques had suggested. While submerged, she heard Aunt Violette's Citroën truck drawing up outside and a couple of minutes later, her footsteps coming into the house. 'Hello?' she called. 'Anyone at home?'

'Having a bath, Aunt Violette.'

'Oh, OK. Have you finished with the wood?'

'For today, yes. It's too wet.'

'Where's your uncle?'

'He said he was going for a walk.'

'In this weather?'

'I know.'

Twenty minutes later, feeling refreshed and clean, Francine joined her aunt in the kitchen. 'Do you need a hand with anything?'

'Why do you always ask that just as I finish? I'll be heating up yesterday's soup for lunch. Your uncle will like that. Did he say where he was going or how long he'd be?'

Francine shook her head.

'He must be mad, walking in this rain. He needs his head examined, the stupid pup.'

'He told me that my mother had a thing for him.'

Aunt Violette scoffed.

'Do you think that's true?'

'In his dreams.'

'He said Mama wished she'd married him and instead he got lumbered with you, the ugly sister.'

Aunt Violette glared at her. 'You really do have the devil inside you. How dare you lie about such things? Go on, get out of my sight.'

'That's what he said.'

'Out, out, out.'

Francine went to her room and lay on her bed, flipping through the pages of a book she'd found downstairs on dinosaurs. He'd be dead by now, she was sure of it.

Half an hour later, Aunt Violette barged in without knocking. 'It's lunchtime. Where is he?'

'I told you, he–'

'He wouldn't miss lunch. Are you sure he didn't tell you where he was going?'

'Nope. He just went off, saying he wanted a walk. He said I should have a bath and that he'd come rub my back.'

'Stop with the fucking lies, you devil girl.'

Francine tried to hide her shock on hearing her aunt swear. 'I'm sure he'll be back soon, Auntie.'

'If he's not back in an hour, you can call the police.'

'Shame we don't have a mobile in the house.'

'Don't get clever with me, girl.'

An hour passed. Francine wolfed down the onion soup with a large hunk of bread. Aunt Violette didn't eat a thing, simply sat at the table, her hands resting on her bosom, glancing continually between the clock on the wall and the front door which she could see from her place at the table. Finishing her soup, Francine offered to walk to the phone box in the village.

'Let's give it another hour.'

'Fine by me. I'll be upstairs when you want me to go. But I'm sure he'll be back soon. Don't worry, Auntie.' She patted Violette's hand. Violette flinched at her touch and whipped her hand away.

The second hour passed. This time, Aunt Violette tapped on Francine's door before entering. 'Can you go now?'

'He's not back?'

She shook her head.

'Maybe he went to visit someone, a friend perhaps.' Francine stood.

'Jacques? He doesn't have friends.'

'A prostitute maybe?'

Violette slapped her.

It stung. Francine rubbed her cheek. 'That's the second time you've done that.' She stepped up to her aunt. 'If you ever do it again, I'll fucking hit you back, you understand?'

She stepped back, shocked. 'You really are Satan's disciple.'

'Do you want me to ring the cops or what?'

'Yes, yes. Go now.' She paused and then added a 'please'.

'I need some change.'

'You don't need change to phone the emergency services.'

'I didn't know that. I've never used a phone box before. I always had a mobile until you stamped on it.'

'Just go, will you?'

The rain had eased off now, just a fine drizzle. It was a good kilometre to the village. The phone box stood in the centre, next to a stone wall, in front of the church. An old woman in a headscarf wished her a good day as she passed, pushing a shopping trolley on wheels. Francine made the call, making sure she sounded sufficiently concerned. 'How long's he been missing?' she was asked.

'A good three hours.'

'That's not long enough.'

'My aunt is very concerned.'

'Be that as it may, three hours is not long enough. If he was a child, it'd be different. Is he vulnerable in any way?'

'Vulnerable?'

'Does he... does he have any issues, mental issues or disabled, that sort of thing?'

'No.'

'OK, look, we don't have the resources to go around searching for adults who've gone AWOL for a couple of hours. If he's not back by, say, seven, give us another ring and we might send someone around. OK?'

'Aunt Violette won't be happy.'

'It's the best we can offer right now.'

'OK. Thanks.' She rang off.

She relayed the message to her aunt who threw her hands up in the air in despair.

The afternoon dragged by. Francine spent it in her bedroom, listening to her aunt pacing downstairs. Francine heard her go out at one point. She rushed to the window and watched Aunt Violette in the yard, disturbing the chickens, checking the pile of logs and checking the shed. She even glanced down the well at one point. Francine's heart stopped. But Violette turned away without expression.

At seven, Francine returned to the phone box. This time, she was told, they'd send a couple of officers around.

They turned up at eight, two men in uniform. Aunt Violette cried as she told them that her husband was missing. Had Violette tried his mobile, they asked. Francine stifled a laugh. They asked about potential friends he might be visiting. Francine volunteered that she was the last person who saw him. No, he didn't say where he was going or how long he'd be. They said there was little they could do now but if he hadn't turned up by the following morning, they'd ask around the village. Someone, they said, must have seen him.

That night, Francine lay in bed, a smile on her face, as she listened to her aunt sobbing in her bedroom.

Chapter 39: Benedict
Today

Benedict and Jessica had arrived at Eric Fournier's house forty minutes earlier. In that time, they interviewed a teary-eyed Lizzie. An officer had come the night before to break the news to Lizzie and her sister – their father had been murdered in the street, a mere fifty metres from Angela Wheeler's house. Lizzie had no idea who Angela Wheeler was and Jessica was obliged to explain which only added to Lizzie's anguish.

Now, the detectives remained in the living room and waited for Susan. They could hear Lizzie calling for her sister. Benedict smiled at Jessica. She raised her eyebrows in return. Benedict admired a framed painting hanging above the mantelpiece depicting a nineteenth-century man in a large red cloak upon a wild-eyed horse.

Finally, after a good four minutes, Susan appeared. Offering no apology, she perched on the edge of an armchair and twisted a handkerchief around her fingers. 'First my mother and now this,' she said, her voice hard. 'This is beyond cruel. Where's it going to end? I'm going home today. I've had enough of this place. Are Lizzie and I in danger too, do you think? We need protection, Inspector. You have to give us protection. We could be next. Have you any idea who's responsible?'

Ignoring everything she said, Benedict said, 'Susan, I don't know if you know, but I was with your father last night.'

'What do you mean?'

'I was on my way to talk to Angela Wheeler–'

'That bitch.'

'When I came across your father as he… Anyway, the ambulance had already arrived but unfortunately, they weren't able to save him. I'm very sorry.'

'Did he say anything?'

'Actually, yes, and I wanted to ask you about that.'

She leaned forward.

'He said just the one word – your name.'

Her mouth dropped open. 'My name?'

'Yes.'

'Oh my God. Why did he say my name?'

'We were rather hoping you might tell us.'

'He said nothing else?'

Benedict sighed. This wasn't an easy thing to tell a grieving daughter. 'No. I mean…'

'Yes?'

'He… he tried but…' He shook his head.

Susan stood and strolled to the window and looked out. It was an overcast, quiet day out there.

'What was he trying to tell us?' asked Jessica. 'Was he calling for your help or…?'

She spun around. 'Or what?'

'Was he accusing you?' Benedict was impressed by how

coolly Jessica had said it.

Susan's eyes narrowed. 'Fuck you.'

'According to your sister,' said Jessica, 'you left the house very soon after your father last night.'

'So?'

'Why don't you sit down?' said Benedict.

'I'm alright, thanks.'

'Did your father say where he was going?' asked Jessica.

'No.'

'Did you *know* where your father was going?'

'No, but I had an inkling.' She leaned against the windowsill.

'And that was?'

She hesitated. 'I think… I reckoned he was going to see *that* woman.'

'Angela Wheeler.'

'Yeah, her.'

'Why did you follow him?'

'How do you know I was following him?'

'Weren't you? If you weren't, where were you going?'

'Nowhere. I was feeling stressed by everything. I just needed a walk, get some air. Look, what are you getting at here? Are you seriously suggesting I followed my own dad and killed him in the bloody street? You're mad, both of you. You've no idea what's going on. Christ, talk about clutching at straws.'

'OK,' said Benedict, taking a deep breath. 'Finding out your father has been sleeping with another woman must have hurt.'

She didn't answer, simply stared at him with undisguised hatred.

Benedict continued, 'Is that what you wanted to speak to

Eric about? To have it out with him out of your sister's earshot.'

'No, nothing of the kind.'

Jessica asked. 'Have you met Ms Wheeler?'

'No, of course I haven't.'

'We understand you're pregnant,' said Benedict.

'What's that got to do with anything?'

'Congratulations.'

'Yeah.'

'But your father wasn't happy, was he? Not when he realised you're carrying the child of a man who is married and whose wife is also expecting.'

Susan rolled her eyes. 'Great. Thanks a bunch, Lizzie.'

'The fact the father to your child earns his living as a mechanic certainly didn't impress your father.'

'I'm not staying to listen to this bullshit–'

'Yes, you are, Miss Fournier, you most certainly are.'

'So, my dad could be a snob. So what?'

Jessica said, 'It was our understanding your father was concerned about how this man was going to support you and your child. I'm assuming this is the man you told us about, Robbie?'

'Was he right to be concerned?' asked Benedict. 'Has Robbie pledged to help you or will he be standing by his wife?'

Susan glared at him, her arms folded across her chest.

'Especially as your mother cut you out of the will,' added Benedict. 'I imagine that came as quite a shock.'

'You and Lizzie were a bit upset about that, weren't you?' said Jessica.

'Only because Dad manipulated her.'

'Not a problem now, I'd imagine,' said Jessica. 'Your father told us you and your sister are the only beneficiaries of his will. I mean, this house alone…'

'I did not kill my own father.'

'Will you sell the house? Rent it out maybe? You probably haven't had a chance to discuss yet, your sister and you.'

'You think I killed my father so I could lay my hands on this house? You're mad, completely stark-raving mad. Is there anything else?'

'No, I think that's enough for now,' said Benedict. 'Thank you for your time, Miss Fournier.'

Benedict and Jessica sat in the squad car and exchanged wearied looks. 'What do you think?' asked Benedict in a whisper.

'Defensive as hell but I don't think she's our woman.'

Benedict rubbed his chin. 'I'm not so sure.'

Chapter 40: Benedict
Today

'There's every likelihood that Tamsin Fournier's death was directly related to the theft of her jewellery,' said Benedict addressing Jessica in the squad car outside the home of Alina Zhivkov. 'I'm hoping we'll be wasting our time here. Alina doesn't seem the type to resort to stealing from an old woman with dementia.'

'Yes, it takes a special type of scumbag to do something like that.'

Alina looked terrified as she showed the detectives into her flat. Her twins, she said, were at school. She was expecting her husband at the weekend.

'That'll be nice,' said Jessica.

'Yes.' She didn't seem very sure. 'He won't be happy when I tell him I lost one of my jobs. We need every *stotinka*.'

'*Stotinka?*'

'It's Bulgarian. The same as your penny. Did Mr Fournier send you? He thinks I stole Mrs Fournier's jewellery. But I didn't.' She seemed close to tears. 'I would never do that. He thinks—'

Benedict put his hand up. 'OK, let's slow down a little.' He smiled in an attempt to put her a little more at ease. 'We're not saying we agree with Mr Fournier but we wouldn't be doing our job if we didn't ask you about it.'

'OK.' She nodded, looking slightly calmer.

'Did you notice the jewellery missing, Alina?'

She shook her head. 'I never opened Mrs Fournier's drawers. *Never.*'

'Of course, of course. Tell me, what day or days did you work for the Fourniers?'

'Every Wednesday morning.'

'I see. Did Mr Fournier explain why he thought you'd taken it?'

'No, he just thinks I did because I clean in Mrs Fournier's room but I promise you I never did. Here, search the apartment, please, look everywhere, I don't mind. You won't find anything.'

Jessica patted Alina's hand. 'We believe you, Alina. We believe you.'

'You do?'

Benedict smiled at her.

Alina put her hands on her heart. 'Thank you. Will you tell Mr Fournier?'

'Ah, we have some news about Eric Fournier, Alina…'

Alina had to stifle a cry when Benedict told her that Eric Fournier had been killed.

'That is so awful. First Mrs Fournier and now Mr Fournier. But why?'

'I'm afraid we don't know – yet.'

As Benedict and Jessica were about to leave, Alina said, 'Oh, I remember something. Do you remember I couldn't remember the name of the young girl who worked as Mr Fournier's cleaner before me?'

'Oh, yes?'

'I saw her near the house on Wednesday morning, my last day. Not that I knew it was to be my last day,' she added forlornly.

'Near the Fournier's house?' asked Jessica.

'Yes, yes. She look funny, I mean, *acting* funny. I say hello but she walked away without a word. I thought maybe she doesn't know me.'

'OK. So, what's her name?'

'Oh, I can't remember but I saw her – outside the house. Could it be important?'

'Maybe,' said Benedict. 'We'll ask one of the daughters. Susan, especially, will remember her name, I'm sure.'

Benedict and Jessica sat in the car. 'Where next, boss?'

'I think we need a review of where we are right now.' Benedict's phone rang. 'DC Prowse,' he said to Jessica.

'Boss, good news. We've found Mrs Fournier's jewellery.'

'Really? That is good news. Let me put you on loudspeaker. OK, tell me more.'

'Yes. So this morning this woman turns up at West Hampstead station with one large box and several smaller boxes of stuff, necklaces, rings, the lot. So, they ran a search on it and bingo! Every piece, every item is accounted for.'

'Good God. Susan and Lizzie will be pleased. Tell us about the mysterious woman. Where did she find it?'

'Under her bed.'

'What?'

'Yeah. Her name is Frida McCleave. She told them at Hampstead that she reckoned her boyfriend stole it. Apparently, she's going to be staying at a women's refuge for a while because she's frightened of the boyfriend. I'll send you her deets and the boyfriend's.'

'Yes, do. Excellent stuff. Thank you, DC Prowse. Well done.'

'I think,' said Jessica. 'I should go straight to Alina and tell her the news in person.'

'Yes, good idea. I'll wait for DC Prowse's text.'

By the time Jessica returned to the car, Benedict had received the text. 'Right, so we need to speak to one Adrian Burchill, boyfriend of Frida McCleave, aged twenty-nine. Here's the address.'

'Excellent. I know it. Shall we go?'

Benedict and Jessica drove the two miles from Alina's flat in Hampstead to Camden Town and to a side street where Ade Burchill lived in a top-floor flat with, until today, his girlfriend although he might not be aware that Frida had left him.

'I've gotta go out,' said Ade at the flat door. 'So, if you don't mind.'

He tried to shove past the detectives. They stood firm. 'It won't take long, Mr Burchill,' said Jessica. 'We'd like to come in, please.'

'Now,' added Benedict.

Burchill reluctantly backed down, showing the detectives through to the tiny interior of his flat. It may have been small but it was immaculate, thought Benedict.

'Do you want a beer?'

'No, thank you. Take a seat, Mr Burchill.'

He sighed as he sat. 'So, what's this about?'

Jessica showed Burchill a few photographs on her mobile, swiping through them slowly. He recognised the jewellery, thought Benedict. He couldn't hide his surprise, the redness creeping up his neck, his fidgeting fingers. 'Do you recognise any of this stuff, Mr Burchill?' she asked.

'No. Should I?'

'No? It was stolen from a house in Highgate recently and today it was found under *your* bed.'

He laughed. 'You'd better ask Frida. She's me girlfriend. She'll be at work right now. Works in an Oxfam. She'd be there now if you want to speak to her.'

Benedict knew that Jessica had to tread carefully here and not compromise Frida any further than she already was. 'Are you saying,' said Jessica, 'that your girlfriend might be responsible for this?'

'Yeah. You see, Frida's got... she's got an *issue*. I tell her it's stupid but she can't help herself, you know? She's one of those... what do you call it?'

'Kleptomaniac?'

'Yeah, one of those. Like I said, she can't help it. It's like an illness with her. She sees something, she has to have it, especially something shiny like those in the photos.'

'Like a magpie,' said Jessica.

'Yeah, exactly.'

'How is your relationship with... Frida, did you say?'

'Yeah, Frida. It's alright.'

'How long have you been going out.'

'A couple of years. What business is it of yours?'

'Mr Burchill,' said Benedict. 'Where were you on Tuesday night?'

'Tuesday? Erm, let me see... er, I guess I was with Frida. Yeah, I would've been. You ask her.'

'What were you doing?'

'I don't know. The usual. Watching TV and stuff. Why you asking?'

'No reason for now. And what about last night, at nine o'clock?'

'Ah, last night I was out with me mates. We had a bit of a pub crawl. You can ask them. They'll tell you.'

'Can we have the details?' asked Jessica.

Burchill listed all the names of the friends he was with and, as best as he could, the different pubs they passed through. Jessica thanked him.

'Now, Mr Burchill, we are going to have to ask you for your fingerprints.'

'Really?'

'You don't have to, but it would look odd. Do you mind?'

He did mind, he minded very much, but he did it.

'That's everything,' said Benedict. 'Thank you for your time, Mr Burchill.'

'Oh, is that it?' He looked mightily relieved.

'Yes,' said Benedict. He paused. 'For now.'

Back in the car, Jessica said, 'Did you see his reaction on seeing the photos?'

'Yes. He couldn't hide it. Guilty as hell.'

'Yeah, and how noble of him to try and pass the buck onto his girlfriend.'

'Indeed. Well, once we have the results from the fingerprinting, we'll be able to arrest him.'

'Fingers crossed.'

'I think we should pay this Frida a visit.'

Jessica rang Frida and agreed on a time to go see her. So, first, the detectives headed back to the station.

On sitting down at his desk, Benedict noticed a long telephone number written on an orange Post-It note stuck to the side of his computer monitor, a number beginning with +33. That was France.

DC Prowse shouted over. 'Oh yeah, boss, that note's from me. A copper in a place called Aniseed in France.'

'Aniseed?'

'Something like that. Anyway, he's called Pierre something and he wants you to ring him back on that number when you can.'

Benedict thanked him and dialled the number which was answered by a gruff-sounding man called Pierre Lescot, based in a police station in Annecy (not 'Aniseed'). Benedict fancied himself as rather good at French so he began as he meant to continue… *'Bonjour, Inspecteur Lescot, je m'appelle Inspecteur-Détective Benedict Paige. Je comprends que vous avez appelé.'*

'What did you say?' said the Frenchman in perfect English.

Benedict repeated himself. To his ears, he sounded fine.

'I'm sorry, I cannot understand your accent. Can you speak in English, please?'

So much for that! Feeling somewhat deflated, Benedict said, 'I'm so sorry. I'm Detective Inspector Benedict Paige from CID in Camden in London. I understand you called.'

'Ah yes. Thank you for ringing back so soon. We heard about the unfortunate death of one of our former residents, Eric Fournier. Very sad.'

'Yes, very sad. Unfortunately, Mrs–'

'Monsieur Fournier was once charged with assaulting a woman. Nothing came of it. No proof. This was ten years ago. Soon after, the woman killed herself, Olivia Lenoir, her name. She left a short suicide note which said, *Blame Eric.*'

'Oh?'

'Yes, indeed. Now, Olivia Lenoir had a daughter, a peculiar young lady called Francine. I had to interview her once. She was not of age when her mother passed so she lived with her uncle and aunt. Soon after Francine moved in, the uncle was killed, one Jacques Philipe. He was known to us as a man who… erm, let us say, liked his girls *young*. He was pushed down a well where he lived in this remote shack. He'd been missing for four months. I was based around there at the time and I was part of the investigating team. We couldn't prove it but I was convinced then and I am convinced still that Francine Lenoir killed this man. His wife, Violette, thought so too. Maybe he showed too much interest in Francine. We shall never know. Again, no proof. Too much time had passed, you understand?'

'I see.'

'A year ago, Violette died and that's when I learned that Francine had moved to England. So, this morning, when I learned of Monsieur Fournier's passing, I decided to check up on Francine so I rang her father who now lives in Paris. He told me Francine works as an au pair for a Monsieur and Madam Cleverly in Northwich.'

'Northwich?'

'No, not Northwich, *Norwich*.'

'Ah yes.'

'So, I just rang Madame Cleverly and she says no, Francine no longer works for them because she got a new job in London.'

'She has?'

'Yes, as a… cleaner.'

'And do you happen to know, Inspector, the name of Francine's new employer?'

'Yes. Francine went to work for Eric and Tamsin Fournier…'

Chapter 41: Benedict
Today

Pierre Lescot, the French detective, sent Benedict a photograph of Francine Lenoir. It showed a pale-faced girl, a haunted look about her eyes, long, dark hair. No one had mentioned a Frenchwoman working as a cleaner for the Fourniers. Having spoken to Susan Fournier, Benedict found out that her parents' cleaner before Alina Zhivkov was not Francine Lenoir but a woman called Diane Hislop. She didn't have Ms Hislop's address at hand but said she'd try and find it and let Benedict know.

Benedict and Jessica made their way to a women's refuge in Hampstead in order to speak to Frida McCleave. From the outside, the refuge was a red brick, newly built block of flats, three storeys high. There were two bicycles chained to the railings outside and a children's toy truck on the small patch of grass near the main entrance. It didn't seem big enough from the outside but, inside, was surprisingly large with several small rooms available to those in need, communal rooms and a kitchen. Not dissimilar, thought Benedict, to his halls of residence when he was a university student. Naturally, men were usually not permitted inside its doors but Benedict's police badge overcame that obstacle. Nonetheless, he felt distinctly unwelcome as the residents eyed him suspiciously. The receptionist rang Frida's mobile, letting her know that she had two detectives needing to speak to her.

Jessica led the way up the stairs to the first floor, passing a couple of women coming downstairs. Frida looked worried on seeing the detectives. 'Has something happened?' she asked as they stepped into her room.

'No, no,' said Jessica. 'It's about that jewellery you found.'

'Oh, OK.'

The room was rather sterile, thought Benedict, but it was functional, clean and warm, painted in a neutral colour. There were a couple of famous prints on the wall – paintings by Van Gogh and one of Degas' ballet dancing paintings. The view wasn't too inspiring, merely the back of the houses opposite.

Frida McCleave looked like a person worried for her safety, she had soft, delicate facial features but a furrowed brow and a tense jaw. She sat with her shoulders hunched, chewing on a thumbnail, her legs tightly crossed.

'How are you, Frida?' asked Jessica.

'Yeah, not too bad. It's decent here. The women here are nice, they've all had the same sort of experience as me, they understand. The manager said I could stay as long as I want. It's the first time in a long where I don't feel as if I'm walking on eggshells. Everyone's so supportive. And it's so nice to feel safe.'

'That's good to hear. These places do good work.'

'Yes, totally.'

'Frida,' said Jessica. 'We spoke to Adrian Burchill.'

Even the mention of the name made her sit up, a look of fear in her eyes. 'Ade? Oh, God.'

'Don't worry, he doesn't know you're here.'

'He has no idea where you are,' added Benedict.

'He'll find me though. I've got to go back to work at some point otherwise I'll lose my job. And he'll come looking for me there. He'll wait for me to finish. I don't know what to do.'

'Ultimately, Frida, you may have to give up your job, however much you enjoy or depend on it. Your safety is paramount, it has to come first.'

'I know.'

'Tell us about this jewellery.'

'Oh, yes, there's not much to say, to be honest. I was cleaning up in the bedroom in our little flat and I just found these boxes under our bed. It's one of those low beds, you know, really close to the floor so I never noticed them before.'

'So, you wouldn't know how long the boxes had been there?'

'No. Sorry.'

'No, don't apologise, it's fine. Mr Burchill never mentioned it?'

She shook her head. 'No.'

'Any idea at all where it might have come from?'

'Not a clue. I'm sorry, I'm not much use, am I?'

'Don't worry, it's fine. You did the right thing by handing it into the police station.'

Benedict spoke: 'We should get confirmation today whether the fingerprints our Hampstead colleagues took from your bank card match any of the ones we found on the jewellery boxes.'

'Frida,' said Jessica. 'Ade suggested you might have stolen the jewellery.'

'Well, he's stupid then, why would I hand it in if I stole it?'

'We didn't tell him you handed it in. We thought it best not to.'

'Yeah but he'll put two and two together.'

'Unfortunately, yes. He said, Frida, that you suffer from kleptomania.'

'Ha! Did he? That's ridiculous.'

'Frida,' said Benedict. 'The woman who owned this jewellery you found under your bed was murdered on Tuesday night.'

'Oh. I didn't know that.'

'Her husband was murdered last night. We don't know for sure but, as you can imagine, we think the killings were linked.'

'God, you don't think Ade did it?'

'We're looking at all angles for now. Ade said you and he were together Tuesday night. Can you confirm that?'

'Erm, no. I met a friend on Tuesday night but I got home about nine and he was still out.'

'Really? OK. Interesting. We're talking specifically around ten o'clock.'

'Ade often goes out with his mates, watching football and that in the pubs. I don't know where he was on Tuesday night though but he definitely wasn't home at ten o'clock.'

'What time did he get home on Tuesday night?' asked Jessica.

'Erm…' She bit her lip. 'I don't know. Late. Maybe around midnight.'

'And last night?'

'Yeah, he was out drinking with his mates.'

'And how did he seem when he came back on both these occasions?'

'He came back pissed last night. Tuesday, actually, now that I think about it, he looked a bit... I don't know. Distracted?'

'Can you explain what you mean by that?'

She scratched her neck and scrunched up her eyes. 'It was like he was upset about something. He wasn't pissed that time. So I asked him if he was OK but he told me to mind my own business.'

'OK. Tell us about your relationship with Ade.'

She did. Frida described how they met, how they started living together and how Ade changed from what she called a 'normal bloke' to someone who used his fists. 'It's what happens now that scares me. The women here are so nice and so helpful, they understand, but I can't stay here forever and I know he'll find me and, like I said, I don't want to give up work.' She rubbed her eyes. 'I never thought a man could make my life so shit. It's always a man, isn't it?

Benedict and Jessica thanked the manager of the refuge and headed out. The day had clouded over and felt positively cold for a late July day.

'So much for Adrian's Burchill's alibi,' said Jessica.

'Indeed.'

'Did you believe her?'

'I'm not sure. I *think* so.'

Benedict's mobile rang. 'Susan Fournier,' he said to Jessica. 'Miss Fournier?'

Looking through her father's things, Susan found an address and a telephone number for the woman who used to clean for her parents before Alina. Benedict thanked her, then rang DC Prowse, instructing him to pay Diane Hislop a visit and ask about her experience of working for Eric and Tamsin Fournier, and if there were any issues between them.

Benedict didn't expect much.

But the next phone call raised his hopes no end. As he expected, Ade Burchill's fingerprints were found on Tamsin Fournier's jewellery box.

Chapter 42: Francine
Annecy, France, nine years ago

Six months passed, winter turned into spring which turned into summer. Uncle Jacques was still missing. Aunt Violette lost so much weight, she had to buy a whole new wardrobe, she'd aged terribly, her once rosy cheeks now lined and grey. She rarely spoke, only ever about practical matters. Francine, meanwhile, was counting the days until she finished with school. Although she was enjoying school now, she couldn't wait until she could escape Violette. She had friends at school now, especially the girl, Ines. Ines and Francine were making plans – as soon as they could, they were going to leave this place that 'time forgot' and move to Lyon, find an apartment together and get jobs. Francine couldn't wait – her future beckoned. She'd got herself a twelve-hour-a-week job in the supermarket in the village and spent most of it on her monthly repayments on her new phone plus a small amount Violette demanded for board and lodging.

Occasionally, Francine had nightmares in which she remembered slicing that axe into Jacques's shoulder, the torrents of blood, his frantic screams. She'd wake up, shaking, but after a while, her heartbeat would slow and she'd find herself smiling.

The police had conducted what seemed to Francine a half-hearted enquiry into Jacques Philipe's whereabouts. They borrowed a photograph from Violette, blew it up and printed it out both in poster size and as a leaflet. They knocked on every door, spoke to everyone in the village, and put posters up in the surrounding villages. All the time, they kept reassuring Violette that he'd probably just turn up one day with a simple explanation. They checked all the hospitals within a thirty-kilometre range and sent posters to the nearest border crossings. On the fourth day, on coming home from school, Francine listened at the top of the stairs as a detective called Lescot spoke to Violette. They ran Jacques's name through their databases and found something. Twenty years ago, when Jacques was thirty and, at the time, a church governor, the mother of a fifteen-year-old girl complained about him. He'd acted 'inappropriately', according to the report but nothing was done. 'You were married at the time,' said Detective Lescot. 'I'm sure you remember the case.'

'Of course. It was all a load of nonsense. Jacques was entirely innocent.'

'But the church did promptly relieve Monsieur Philipe of his duties.'

'Well, they would, wouldn't they? I remember the girl, a right little flirt; she loved the attention. She would hit upon Jacques, and when he didn't respond, she made up lies against him. There wasn't a shred of proof.'

'Yes, I know.'

'So, what are you saying? Because of some unfounded accusation twenty years ago, you're not interested in finding my husband any more?'

'No, no, not at all, madam. It is an ongoing investigation.'

But it soon became apparent that it wasn't. After a fortnight, and not a single lead, the police had to tell Violette they were de-prioritising the search until new information came to light.

One Saturday morning in early June, a fine, warm day, Aunt Violette mentioned in passing that she was expecting the 'well men'.

'The what?'

'I want that well fixed. These men are going to have a look to see what's wrong with it?'

Francine felt faint. 'Today?'

'Yes. They'll be here soon.'

Francine rushed to her room. She knew this day had to come but she'd hoped she'd be long gone by then. She calmed herself with deep breaths; there was nothing to be afraid of. 'Just stick to the story,' she said aloud. 'It'll be fine.' So, why, she wondered, did she feel so sick?

Sure enough, she heard a vehicle parking up outside the house. Checking from the bathroom window at the front of the house, she saw a red transit van drawing up, two men jumping out, one carrying a large canvas bag over his shoulder. Violette welcomed them and led them around the house to the yard. Francine then watched them from her bedroom window. She could hear them talking to Aunt Violette about checking water pressure, the depth of the pump and the fact that the area suffered from a low water table. They asked about her water pressure within the house and scratched their chins as they considered Violette's answer. One of them, the one who seemed in charge, came into the house to check the gauge on Violette's pressure tank.

Violette remained indoors as the man rejoined his colleague outside. Francine heard Violette shout, asking if the men would like a coffee. They did.

The two men talked but Francine couldn't hear them. The second man returned to the van while the first man pulled up his jeans and removed a large torch from his canvas bag. Switching it on, he approached the well and leaned over. This was it, thought Francine, quietly opening the window a touch. Sure enough, he looked puzzled, peering deeper into the well. He suddenly stepped back, his hand over his mouth. His colleague returned. He laughed. 'What's up, Laurent?' Then, on receiving no response, said in a more considered tone, 'Are you alright, mate?'

'Have a look down there, Claude, and tell me I'm imagining things,' said Laurent, handing Claude his torch.

'What are you talking about?'

'Just do it.'

Claude took the torch and, throwing Laurent a puzzled expression, looked down the well. 'Nope, can't see nothing,' he said after a moment.

'You can't? Look harder.'

'What am I looking for? Oh, hang on… it looks like…' He sprang back. 'Oh fuck, what is that? Someone's down there.'

The two men looked at each other, unable to speak. 'How long do you think it's been down there?' said Claude.

'How in the hell should I know? I don't bloody know. Long enough for…' He didn't finish the sentence.

'We should call the cops. Should we tell the woman?'

'Tell me what?' said Aunt Violette, appearing with two mugs of coffee.

'Madam,' said Laurent. 'I'm afraid we've got a situation on our hands.'

'What do you mean?'

'There's a...'

'A what? Spit it out, man.'

Laurent glanced at Claude. 'There's a skeleton in your well.'

Violette screamed, dropping both mugs of coffee. She charged to the well. Claude tried to stop her but she pushed him aside. But of course, without a torch, she couldn't see anything. 'Give me your torch.'

'I don't think that's a good idea, madam,' said Laurent.

'Give me the goddamn torch,' she yelled.

Claude passed her the torch. This time, Violette saw it, saw whatever remained of her husband deep down at the bottom of the well. She stepped away, the torch slipping from her fingers, her legs buckling. Laurent scooped her up before she fell. He urged Violette indoors while Claude rang the police.

As Laurent led her away, Violette glanced up at Francine's window. Francine slipped away but too late; she knew Violette had seen her.

Chapter 43: Frida
Today

Frida lay on her bed, her hands behind her head and realised she was smiling. She hadn't smiled for a long time. For once, life had taken on a brighter dimension and it felt good. It was so wonderful to feel safe for once. Ade would never find her here. But she wasn't out of the woods yet, not by a long chalk. Like she'd said to the detectives, she was worried about her job, and not just because of the money – she enjoyed it, it gave her a sense of self-worth. If she had to leave, she'd miss sweet Stan, even if she did cringe whenever she thought of him now, and she'd miss her boss, Sheila, and all the volunteers, why, she'd even miss grumpy Mary. She had images of Ade hanging around outside waiting until she finished work, of her hiding indoors, too terrified of stepping out.

But what was pleasing Frida the most was the thought she'd dropped Ade fair and squarely into the shit. She remembered Tuesday night perfectly well. She'd met Diane at the Red Lion but she'd got home before Ade had returned from watching the football or wherever he was. The detectives had asked specifically for ten o'clock, which, presumably, was the time the murder took place. Frida knew full well that by ten o'clock, Ade had got back from his evening out, hit her after realising, from her wet hair, that she'd been out without his permission, and was sitting next to her on the settee watching the news on ITV. There was a report about women and girls in Iran and Ade had made a derogatory remark about Muslim women which once upon a time she would have called out but she wouldn't dare now. Would not dare. But she told the detectives that Ade was out at that time. So, when they interviewed him, he'd say, 'I was at home, I have my alibi, Frida will vouch for me'. *No, I bloody won't, lover boy.* She didn't care if she lied to the police if it destroyed Ade's alibi.

She'd spoken to many of the women here. Frida reckoned she might be the youngest but whatever their age, they all had a similar tale. It wasn't really talked about, just something they all accepted, that in some capacity or other, they were all victims of male violence. They all focused on the present and dreamed of a happier future; no one wanted to dwell on the past.

Her phone rang. It was Ade. She ignored it. Checking her call history, she counted them up. That was Ade's eleventh call. She suspected there'd be many more. There was no way she was going to speak to him.

Two minutes later, her mobile rang again. But this time it wasn't Ade; it was Diane. Now, she hadn't expected that. She answered.

Diane spoke to her like an old friend, upbeat and cheerful. Frida felt the sharp humiliation of asking Diane for money. *Shit, are you begging me now? God, have some respect, girl.* She'd never forgive her for that. Yeah, it was true, she didn't have any self-respect. But then, who would, when your so-called boyfriend punches you on a regular basis? How would you cope, dear Diane?

'So, listen, how about meeting up for a drink?'

Frida wasn't sure but for some reason said, 'Yeah, fine, great.'

'The Red Lion again?'

'Erm...' No, too close to home, too dangerous. She could invite her to the refuge but was that too risky? The staff wouldn't like it. These places had to be kept secret. She tried to think. 'Can I give you a ring back?'

'Sure. OK.'

Frida googled local cafés and on finding something nearby that looked nice enough, rang Diane back and agreed on a time.

Frida arrived at Café Fantastic first, a small café that, despite its photos online, looked far from fantastic, rather drab and past its best, the tablecloths needed replacing, the plastic flowers looked *too* fake and the pictures on the wall all faded. Still, it was not the sort of place Ade would ever step into and that, as far as Frida was concerned, was the main thing.

Diane arrived, looking flustered, not her usual calm self. They ordered coffee. Diane paid. When Frida tried to protest, Diane said it wasn't a problem. They exchanged pleasantries and celebrity gossip.

'Look, Frida,' said Diane. 'I want to say sorry to you.'

'What for?'

'The other day, when you asked me for a loan, and I told you to eff off.' She took a sachet of sugar from a little pot and twisted it around her fingers.

'Oh, don't worry about it.'

'No, but... Look, I've been thinking. Like I said, I've got a bit stashed away. You can have it.'

'What?'

'Yeah, I can give you about two grand.'

'But I'd never be able to pay you back.'

'You're not listening, Frida. I said I'd *give* it to you.'

Frida stared at the woman. Was she being serious? Why would she want to give her two thousand pounds? Something wasn't right about this. 'Why?'

'I need a favour.'

'Ah, OK. What sort of favour?'

'If anyone asks, I want you to say that after we met in the pub on Tuesday night, you came around to my place.'

'What sort of time?'

'Say, we got to mine around nine and you left at about eleven.'

'Not at nine or half nine then?'

'No. Eleven.'

Something cold crept up Frida's back. She glanced around and realised that apart from one gentleman behind the counter, the café was deserted. She wanted to leave. 'When you say *if anyone asks*, who do you mean exactly?'

Diane focused on the man behind the counter. 'The police.'

'Right.' Although Frida knew she was going to say the police, it still shocked her. 'So, er, why would–'

'They want to speak to me. This morning some point. I'm gonna tell them I was with you on Tuesday. If they ask, you need to tell them the same.'

'But why?'

'It's just a misunderstanding, right? Nothing more. Don't read anything into it.'

Even Diane's voice sounded different somehow as if it'd gone down a register or two.

'I'm not sure about this.'

'We're mates, aren't we?'

'No, we're not. Not really.'

'You'll do as I ask though. Two grand, Frida. It's a lot of money to you.'

It was true; it *was* a lot of money. Add that to the amount her mother had given her, she could move, start all over somewhere new. Somewhere far away. Oxfam was a national institution with branches everywhere. She'd get a transfer. She could do this. After all, she couldn't stay at the refuge forever. And the irony wasn't lost on her here – she could, in one fell stroke, save Diane and, at the same time, condemn Ade. Diane was on the ropes; she needed her. Could she push this further?

'Well?' said Diane.

'Two grand isn't that much. There's no way I'm lying to the police for that. It's not worth the risk.'

Diane didn't say anything but she looked rattled; she hadn't expected meek, mild Frida to haggle, to up the game. 'Three grand,' she offered.

'Five.'

'I haven't got that much.'

'Fine. I'll tell the police that I never saw you.'

'You wouldn't do that.'

Frida stood, the metallic chair scraping on the floor behind her. 'Thanks for the coffee.'

Diane reached for her hand, knocking over her mug of coffee, the liquid spilling over the tablecloth. 'OK, five.'

Frida sat down again.

'I'll pay you tomorrow.'

'I'll be here at twelve.'

'No, not here. Too public.'

'Where then?'

Diane thought for a few seconds. 'Greenfield Park. So, you'll vouch for me?'

'Yes.'

'Good. Listen, I'm out all day tomorrow–'

'Anywhere nice?'

'It doesn't matter. After that, I'll be gone for a week or two.'

'I can't wait that long.'

'Meet me at the entrance of Greenfield Park at ten.'

'Ten? At night?'

'In fact, make it half ten.'

'No.'

'You want your money, don't you? I can't do any earlier.'

Frida sighed. OK, it was late but it'd be worth it for five grand. She couldn't risk waiting; the police might have released Ade by then. 'Alright, half ten, Greenfield Park, at the entrance.'

'Good. I'll pay you and then we'll never see each other again.'

Frida stood again and gathered her coat. 'Fine by me.'

Chapter 44: Benedict
Today

Benedict was at his desk preparing to interview Ade Burchill when DC Prowse approached. 'So, I spoke to Diane Hislop, boss,' he said. 'Like you asked me to.'

'And?'

'She's got an alibi for Tuesday night. She says she was out with that woman you spoke to, Frida McCleave.'

'Frida?'

'So, I rang Frida too and she confirmed it. Frida and Diane met in the Red Lion pub and then returned to Diane's. Frida left about eleven.'

'Really? But when DS Gardiner and I spoke to Frida, she didn't say anything about this.'

'I know. She said. She said she forgot and that she was sorry she didn't mention it before.'

'Oh, OK. Interesting. Thanks for all that, DC Prowse.'

Ade Burchill sat in interview room 1, leaning back, his arms folded across his chest. His hair was so short to be almost non-existent, a buzzcut, and dyed blond. Next to him, Mr

Newman, the duty solicitor, who'd reluctantly, it seemed, agreed to sit with him. Jessica was already seated, sipping from a glass of water. Benedict rushed in, apologising for keeping everyone waiting. He nodded a hello at Jessica. 'Right, for the benefit of the tape, let me make the introductions.' Burchill sniffed.

Once done, Benedict started. 'OK, so Mr Burchill, just to recap, yesterday morning, we were made aware that four jewellery boxes were found in your residence—'

'How did you find them?' asked Mr Newman. 'Did you enter the residence?'

'No. We never stepped inside your client's flat. The boxes were brought to our West Hampstead station.'

'By whom?'

'I cannot say at this juncture,' said Benedict, although he knew everyone knew. 'These boxes of jewellery were stolen on or around last Tuesday evening from the residence belonging to the recently deceased Mr and Mrs Fournier. We've identified your fingerprints on all those boxes, Mr Burchill. Did you steal the jewellery from the Fourniers?'

'No comment.' Burchill glanced at Newman. Obviously, 'no comment' was what the solicitor had advised.

'OK, it is your right not to comment but you are going to have to explain at some point why your fingerprints are clearly on the stolen items and why they were found *under your bed*, Mr Burchill.'

'No comment.'

'Mm. The fact is, Mrs Fournier was murdered on Tuesday night. So, it's not too much of a stretch to link the two crimes.'

'Bollocks.' Burchill sat up; he didn't know about Mrs Fournier's murder and this obviously worried him.

'Why did you kill her?' asked Benedict, merely to test the man.

'Me?' shouted Burchill, pointing at himself.

'Hang on, Paige,' said Newman. 'I wasn't aware of this. I need to speak to my client about this. We need a recess.'

Benedict had expected it and had no option but to agree.

Benedict and Jessica left Newman to speak to his client.

Outside the interview room, Jessica said, 'You don't really think Burchill killed Mrs Fournier. Do you, boss?'

'No, not at all. It's not as if the woman was capable of fighting off a burglar; sadly, she probably wasn't aware of what was happening.'

Ten minutes later, Newman was ready.

Benedict and Jessica returned to their seats. 'Where were you Tuesday night around ten o'clock, Mr Burchill?'

'I was at home with my girlfriend.'

'Her name?'

'Frida McCleave.'

'We've spoken to Frida McCleave and she states she was out Tuesday evening, meeting a friend.'

Burchill leaned forward. 'Like bollocks she was, she's lying.'

'Is she? Really?'

'Yes, she is. She was with me. We were at home, watching some shit on TV.'

'Did you tell her to provide you with an alibi?'

'No.'

'From what I gather, you have a habit of intimidating her.'

'Do not.'

'What are you saying here, Inspector?' asked Newman.

'Frida McCleave is frightened of Mr Burchill,' said Jessica. 'And we reckon with good reason.'

'She's lying,' said Burchill. 'She's a liar.'

'And a kleptomaniac?' said Jessica.

'Exactly.'

'Mr Burchill, following this interview you'll have to provide a DNA sample. Will this be a cause of concern for you?'

'Look...' He glanced at Newman who nodded. 'OK, I admit, I stole the jewellery but I promise I did not kill anyone. Why would I do that? I wouldn't, honest to God.'

'We think you did. You stole the jewellery and you were worried in case she described you.'

'No, no.'

'She may have looked helpless but you weren't to know her mind wasn't sharp. You killed her to silence her.'

'No, you've got it all wrong.' Burchill was sweating now.

Benedict was fairly certain he was telling the truth, that he didn't kill Tamsin Fournier, but he needed to turn the screws on the man. 'There was no sign of a break-in. How did you get into the house?'

'I had a key.'

'You had a key? How?'

Burchill glanced at Newman. He ran his hand over his lips. 'My ex used to work there. She gave me a copy.'

'When was this?'

He shrugged. 'I don't know. A few months ago.'

'Exactly when?' said Jessica. 'Try and remember.'

'I suppose six months.'

'You can't expect my client to remember the exact date,' said Mr Newman.

'The Fourniers suffered a break-in just over six months ago. They had their silver service stolen. Again, there was no sign of a break-in. That was you, wasn't it, Mr Burchill?'

He didn't answer at first and it was obvious, thought Benedict, that he was weighing up whether to admit it. He decided to help his thought process. 'Better a thief than a murderer.'

'I may have helped myself to a bit of silver.'

'Did your ex persuade you into robbing the Fourniers?'

He nodded.

'Why didn't she just steal the stuff herself?'

'Cos, I suppose, she knew she'd be the obvious suspect.'

'And why would that be?'

He didn't answer.

'What was the name of your ex-girlfriend, Mr Burchill.'

'Diane.'

'Diane? Diane Hislop? She was a cleaner at the Fourniers' house.'

'Yeah, exactly. That's why she got me to steal the stuff.'

'An inside job then, as was the theft of the jewellery on Tuesday. How did Diane get on with the Fourniers?'

'Surely,' said Newman, 'you'd have to ask her that.'

'You're right, Mr Newman, but I'm still interested in whether Mr Burchill had an impression. Well, Mr Burchill?'

'She didn't like working as a cleaner but who would? I think she thought them a bit snooty.'

'Why did she leave? Do you know?'

'I don't know.'

'Hmm. Frida McCleave, your current girlfriend, states she was out Tuesday evening, meeting a friend. That friend, Mr Burchill, was Diane. You see, one of our detective constables spoke to Diane Hislop and Diane collaborates that version of events.'

Burchill almost leapt out of his chair. 'That's not possible. They don't know each other.'

'They do.'

He wiped his brow. This news was a worrying development

for him. Whom could he trust? 'They're lying, both of them. I told you, *I* was with Frida Tuesday night.' He jabbed himself in the chest. 'I bloody was.'

'So, let's say we believe you didn't kill Tamsin Fournier but you did steal her jewellery. Why Tuesday of all days?'

'Because...' He ran his hand around the back of his neck. 'Because Diane suggested it.'

'Oh? You keep in contact?'

'No but she texted me out of the blue.'

'Saying...'

'Saying nothing, just to ring her. So I did and she said Eric goes out every Tuesday and his daughter always came over to look after Mrs Fournier but she always had her boyfriend around and they'd be too busy shagging if I wanted to help myself.'

'So you did.'

'Yeah. I'm sorry. I bloody wish I hadn't now.' Looking more animated, he added, 'Hey, maybe Diane snuffed her out.'

'No, because she was with Frida, remember?'

'Yeah, and I'm telling you, they're lying. They both are.'

'OK, so let's take the scenario that Diane did kill Mrs Fournier, then I can understand why she'd lie. But Frida? Why would she lie, Mr Burchill?'

'Are you expecting my client to do your job for you now, Inspector?'

Benedict managed to contain his laughter. 'Hypothetical questions, Mr Newman. You never know where they might take you.'

As it was, Benedict knew exactly why Frida lied about not being with Ade Burchill. She was so frightened of him that if there was any possibility of him being locked up, she'd happily take it. Looking at the scrawny thug opposite him, he didn't blame her.

Chapter 45: Francine
Annecy, France, nine years ago

Today was the day of Jacques Philipe's funeral. It was also Francine's penultimate day living with her aunt for tomorrow, she and her friend, Ines, were packing their bags and moving to Lyon. They had somewhere to stay for the first few weeks, a distant relative of Ines's. Francine couldn't wait.

Aunt Violette had thought about hosting a wake and had made a list of everything she needed to buy. She even asked Francine for advice, which, in itself, was a first. 'How many do you think I should cater for?' she asked, her pen poised.

Why was she asking – she knew Jacques had zero friends. Even the church had disowned him after his *alleged* inappropriate behaviour with that girl all those years ago. 'I wouldn't bother if I was you.'

Aunt Violette dropped her pen on the table. 'You're probably right.'

The house had swarmed with police and men in white suits following the discovery of Jacques's skeleton at the bottom of the well. Removing him had been a Herculean effort. The police interviewed Violette and Francine at length about that morning in February. They readily admitted that any evidence that may have been would have disappeared in the intervening four months. There wasn't much Francine could tell them but they asked her nonetheless, several times over – she'd been helping her uncle chop wood in the rain. At one point, he suggested she go in and have a bath while he was going to take a walk. No, he didn't say where he was going nor for how long. She had a long bath, during which time her aunt returned from the shops and Jacques was nowhere to be seen.

Five days later, Detective Lescot informed Aunt Violette that the results of the post-mortem had come back. Again, Francine positioned herself at the top of the stairs in order to hear. Jacques Philipe, the detective said, had died from multiple fractures he sustained while falling a hundred and twenty metres to the bottom of the well and hitting the dry bed at the bottom. But he'd also suffered a blow to his shoulder, so deep that it had penetrated the clavicle bone near the neck. It was a brutal blow that could only have been inflicted from behind using considerable force. 'Given the dimensions of the wound, we think it could have been an axe.'

Francine heard her aunt gasp in shock.

'I'm sorry to have to tell you this,' said the detective.

'How awful. Poor Jacques.'

'We think his assailant attacked him with the axe but didn't kill him outright. It was the fall down the well and the subsequent loss of blood that killed your husband, madam.'

'My God, how he must have suffered.'

'I'm afraid so. I'm sorry. So, of course, we are now looking for a murderer. The impact of the blow implies it was an intentional blow. We shall keep you informed of any developments, madam. Now, we know where you were that morning, enough people saw you, but your niece was here and we need to talk to her again.'

'I want to sit in with you.'

'No, she's recently turned eighteen, hasn't she? We can talk to her as an adult.'

Two detectives interviewed Francine, and she knew they considered her their prime suspect but what did they have to go on? The main detective introduced himself as Pierre Lescot, a gangly man with sallow skin and dark, bushy eyebrows.

'Describe your relationship with your uncle,' said Lescot.

Francine shrugged. 'It was fine. We got on well, he was nice.'

'He never did anything to annoy you?'

'No. Like I said, he was nice. I liked him.'

'Did he ever... how shall I put this... make you feel uncomfortable?'

'I don't know what you mean.'

Lescot cleared his throat. 'Did he ever touch you in a way that might be construed as sexual?'

'God no, not ever, He wasn't like that. He was a good man, my uncle.'

'OK. And you're sure of this? He never touched you or said anything that made you feel awkward?'

'I think I would have remembered.'

'Sure, yes, of course. That morning in February, did you chop any wood yourself?'

'No. I just carried the logs to and fro.'

'So, you didn't touch the axe.'

'Uhuh.'

'It must have been a difficult time for you following the unfortunate and tragic death of your mother.'

'Yes, it was but Uncle Jacques and Aunt Violette looked after me and they were both so kind, especially Uncle Jacques. I never wanted for anything.'

They asked her the questions they'd already asked her about their movements that morning, whether Jacques seemed agitated or upset, whether she saw anyone, and whether she saw what direction he went. 'No, I was in the bathroom by then. I didn't see anyone and I didn't see him leave.' Then, after a pause, she added, 'I do miss him. He was like a father to me.'

Lescot smiled sympathetically. 'Yes, of course.'

They had no further questions.

It was a hot, summer's day for Uncle Jacques's funeral. Early that morning, Aunt Violette knocked on Francine's bedroom door. Francine was in the midst of packing, two suitcases open on her bed, half full of clothing. 'Will you be wanting to attend the funeral?' asked her aunt.

'No.' She folded a pair of jeans and placed them in the suitcase.

Aunt Violette stiffened. 'As you wish. By the way, you owe me for next week's board and lodging.'

'I'm leaving tomorrow so you can sing for it.'

'Tomorrow?' She cast her eyes on the suitcases. 'Where are you going?'

'Getting out of this shithole.'

'Oh. I see. If that's what you wish. Probably for the best.'

'Telling me.'

Violette sauntered over to the window and looked out. 'Does the name Eric Fournier mean anything to you?'

'No. Why?'

'I think your mother had a fling with him. I've just found out. It doesn't surprise me, your mother liked her men, she always liked being the centre of attention.'

'Yeah, well, she was an attractive woman.' Francine picked out a shirt from her wardrobe and, placing it on the bed, started folding it.

'Hmm.' Violette sniffed the air. 'I'd better get dressed and ready.' She made to leave but paused at the bedroom door. 'You're very much like your mother, you know, Francine. Vain and self-centred, full of yourself, thinking you're better than other people but... at least your mother wasn't a murderess.'

Francine stopped what she was doing. 'What do you mean?'

'I heard what you said to those detectives. All that stuff about how much you liked Jacques, that he was a father figure to you. I heard you say he never touched you but we both know that's not true, don't we? You told me once, didn't you? Remember?'

'Yeah and you didn't believe me.'

'Oh, I believed you all right. Jacques had his... let's say, he had his weaknesses. All men have their weaknesses. It's in their nature. But you didn't tell Detective Lescot, did you? Why was that, Francine? Because you didn't want them thinking you had a motive.' She stepped towards her, pointing two fingers at Francine's eyes. Francine edged back. 'I have no proof but I know what I know. I can feel it in my gut. He made a pass at you that morning, didn't he? And you, panicking, killed him. I can't prove a thing but I promise you this, one day, *one day*, God will make you pay...'

Chapter 46: Benedict
Today

Benedict knew it was imperative to speak to Diane Hislop. She'd worked as the Fourniers' cleaner, she knew Ade Burchill and, according to Mr Burchill, she supplied him with a key to the Fourniers' house. But, according to Frida McCleave, the two women spent Tuesday evening together, therefore Hislop had an alibi. Benedict reckoned, however, that Frida was lying about Tuesday evening, wanting to incriminate Burchill. Susan Fournier had provided Benedict with Diane Hislop's mobile number and address but the number was dead. But he knew she was still at the address because DC Prowse had been there and spoken to her. They needed to speak to her again – and in far greater detail.

Together with DS Gardiner, Benedict made his way to Hislop's address in Kentish Town. She lived in the top flat of a red-brick terraced house. Someone, not Ms Hislop, buzzed them in. A woman in her twenties with long, tightly woven braids answered the door. Her name, she said, was Brenda. 'We're looking for Diane,' said Jessica. 'Is she in?'

'No, you've just missed her.'

'Can we come in a minute?'

'Sure.' Brenda showed the detectives through to a cramped living room. It had a small sofa, a couple of chairs, a compact dining table and a fold-out desk against one wall. There were several framed photos of Paris and the bookshelves were full of recent novels, including several in French.

'A bit of a Francophile, are you, Brenda?'

'Me? No. I mean, I'm not anti or anything but this is all Diane's stuff. I only moved in a few weeks ago.'

'So, where is Diane? Do you know?'

'She went jogging.'

'At this time?'

'She likes to go out every day, otherwise she says she feels pent up, you know?'

'Where does she go?'

'Greenfield Park. Do you know it?'

'We know it well. Did she say whether she was meeting anyone?'

'No, she didn't say anything.'

'OK, we'll see if we can find her. If she comes back, tell her we called. I'll leave you my card. We do need to speak to Diane as a matter of urgency.'

'Sure. I'll tell her.'

'Have you any photos of Diane on your phone?' asked Benedict.

'I think so, yes.'

They didn't have time to wait while Brenda scrolled through her phone. Time was of the essence here. 'Can you do me a favour? Can you find a couple of the clearest shots and send them to my email on that card?'

'Yes. When?'

'Now. As soon as you can. Can you do that, Brenda? I wouldn't ask if it wasn't important.'

'OK. Give me five and I'll send something over.'

*

Frida was excited. Five thousand pounds. She'd never had so much cash. She had so many ideas of what to do with it, so many she couldn't focus on any one in particular. But whatever, she was going to leave London and get away as far as possible. She'd get a flat in Manchester perhaps, or Leeds or Newcastle, anywhere where Ade could never find her.

But first, she had to meet Diane. She had her coat on, about to leave the refuge, when one of her fellow residents asked her whether it was wise to be going out so late. Frida had felt fine about it until this woman cast doubt in her mind. What if Ade was out there waiting for her? He'd kill her, she wouldn't stand a chance. The evening was warm, she didn't need her coat but it made her feel a little more secure.

She had to catch two buses to get to Greenfield Park, taking almost forty minutes. By the time she got to the park, it was dark. She hovered near the entrance before stepping inside. She didn't like it. The park was bathed in a faint, ghostly illumination. Dimly lit lamp posts spaced at irregular intervals cast pools of weak, flickering light along the winding pathways, their feeble glow barely reaching the overgrown foliage, leaving vast areas shrouded in impenetrable darkness. The usual sounds of the city were muted here, replaced by an eerie hush. The sound of sirens and car horns seemed distant. The grass was wet with dew.

As she stepped deeper into the park, Frida had an unshakeable feeling of being watched.

So, where was Diane? She could see a couple jogging at the

far end of the park, both wearing fluorescent yellow tops.

She heard a rustle behind her. Her heart thundered. What was that? 'H-hello?' A sudden, alarming rush of footsteps. She half-turned. A hazy figure. A screech. The sharp and shooting pain on the back of the head. The pain shot through her. The need to be sick. She tottered, aware she was losing her balance. And then she fell.

*

Jessica drove fast through the largely deserted streets of Camden Town. Benedict's phone pinged – Brenda, true to her word, had sent him two shots of Diane Hislop. Benedict gasped – yes, she'd aged a bit, a little fuller around the face but this was a photo of Francine Lenoir. He turned to Jessica. 'Diane Hislop and Francine Lenoir are one and the same.'

'Really?'

'Yep.'

'So, Eric Fournier was once cautioned in France for hitting a woman, a woman who subsequently took her own life. Several years later the woman's daughter comes to London and works as a cleaner for the Fourniers.'

Jessica drew up near the entrance to Greenfield Park, bringing the car to a screeching halt. She killed the headlamps. She and Benedict rushed out of the car, charging into the park. Jessica called Diane's name. Benedict scanned the park, his eyes adjusting to the darkness. Suddenly, a jogger appeared, a female, running along the path to the side of the park, next to the foliage. Jessica saw her too. They both started sprinting after her. 'Diane Hislop,' shouted Jessica. 'Police. Stop.' The woman glanced back, her expression momentarily caught by the dim glare of a lamp.

'That's her,' said Benedict, stepping up his pace.

Jessica shouted after her again but to no avail. Hislop was fast, too fast for either of them; they had no chance of catching her. But then a figure from nowhere hurled themselves at her, someone, a man, in a fluorescent yellow vest, bringing Hislop to the ground. Benedict and Jessica picked up their pace while the man held onto the struggling Hislop. Hislop kicked out at him, yelling at him to let her go but the man managed to hold on.

The detectives caught up. Jessica gripped Hislop by her left arm, yanking her up. Benedict could hardly breathe.

'She hit someone,' said the jogger breathlessly. 'I saw it, over there…' He pointed in the direction the detectives had just come from. 'Follow me.'

'Get off me,' shouted Hislop at Jessica.

'Diane Hislop, I'm arresting you on the suspicion of murdering Tamsin and Eric Fournier. You do not have to say anything but…' She read Hislop her rights as Benedict followed the jogger, struggling to keep up.

'Over here,' he heard a woman's voice call out from within the trees.

The man led Benedict into the canopy. 'You alright, Debbie?' he called.

'I've called for an ambulance. She's not looking good.'

Benedict could see a woman, also in a fluorescent yellow top, on her knees, cradling a woman's head in her lap, holding her hand. 'That woman hit her on the head,' said the woman called Debbie. 'We saw it all.'

Benedict crouched down and realised he was looking at Frida McCleave. The hair on the top of her head was matted in blood, her eyes were closed but she was breathing.

'Look,' said Debbie, pointing to something.

Benedict stepped over and there, lying in the grass, was a baseball bat. In the distance came the sound of a siren.

'That'll be the ambulance,' said the man. 'Do you want me to go flag it down?'

'Please,' said Benedict.

The man ran off.

Frida opened her eyes.

'Hello, Frida,' said Benedict. 'You're safe now, OK? She can't harm you any more.'

Tears seeped down Frida's face. 'I lied to you. I'm sorry.'

'Don't worry about that. Let's just get you to a hospital.'

'I was only with Diane early on Tuesday night. I lied.' She clenched her eyes shut. 'I'm sorry.'

'It's OK, it's fine.'

Debbie squeezed her hand. 'Shush now, darling. Don't talk. Everything's going to be OK…'

Chapter 47: Benedict
Today

'Diane Hislop, last night you hit Frida McCleave on the back of the head with a baseball bat. Why was that?'

'I didn't,' she said, her eyes blazing with anger. Sitting next to her in interview room 2, a duty solicitor, a young man Benedict hadn't seen before, a sleek-looking, dark-haired man called Reynolds.

'Someone did.'

'Not me.'

'Diane, your hoodie was splattered with blood, as was your shirt. Was it Frida's blood?'

'No, it was my own.' Her face twisted with indignation. 'I bumped into a lamppost earlier.'

'I'm sorry to hear that,' said Benedict, his tone laced with sarcasm. 'But I don't see any visible wounds on you.'

Diane shrugged, her icy demeanour infuriating Benedict.

'Diane, you can deny it until you're blue in the face. But we'll have the results of the blood at some point today and when, as I expect, it shows that the blood on your hoodie belongs to Frida McCleave, you will be charged with attempted murder.'

She didn't respond but maintained her icy stare. Silence hung in the room, heavy and oppressive. Diane met Benedict's gaze with a fierce determination that bordered on insolence.

'The baseball bat has got a logo of the manufacturer on it – Barnett.'

'That's hardly going to be enough, Inspector,' said Mr Reynolds.

'One of my detective constables spoke to your flatmate, Diane. Brenda, isn't it? He showed Brenda a photo of the bat we found next to Frida last night and Brenda recognised it as yours. She also confirmed that your baseball bat wasn't anywhere to be found in the flat. The bat, I'm sure, will have your fingerprints on it. Is there anything you'd like to say at this point?'

'You don't have to say anything,' said Reynolds.

Diane's nostrils flared as she considered Benedict. 'No, I'm alright, thanks.'

Benedict leaned in. 'So, the question is, why? You'd managed to persuade Frida McCleave to provide you with an alibi for Tuesday late evening, the point you killed Tamsin Fournier. She told us. She also told us you were going to pay her five thousand pounds for her trouble. You went to Greenfield Park armed with that baseball bat, Diane, and you made sure your meeting was late, not too many people about. Why? Did she ask for more money? Did you decide you couldn't afford to pay her that much and so needed to silence her?'

'You work it out,' she said, her voice laced with venom.

'I will. We shall speak to Frida in a lot more detail once

she's recovered a little. It's too soon for that now. But I do know she's keen to speak to us.' He paused for a while. Then, softening his voice as a deliberate ploy to provoke her, he said, 'I was sorry to hear about your mother, Diane.'

Diane's face flushed crimson. 'My mother?'

'Or should I call you Francine?' said Benedict, his voice dropping further.

Diane's face flushed. Her calm exterior seemed to collapse on her. She hadn't expected that, hadn't prepared for it.

'Hang on,' said Reynolds. 'I don't know about this.'

Turning to the solicitor, Benedict said, 'Diane's real name is Francine Lenoir. Ten years ago, her mother sadly took her own life, didn't she, Francine? Olivia Lenoir. She left a note saying *Blame Eric*, Eric Fournier, your former boss, her lover, the man who Olivia Lenoir accused of assaulting her.'

Diane's eyes reddened. Benedict always knew that there was usually a key that would unlock a suspect's armour – and he'd just found it. He needed to press home his advantage. 'You were still only seventeen. Your father had just left your mother for another woman and I imagine that must have been difficult for you, Francine. But then to find your mother in the bath with her wrists cut like that. Well, that I can't imagine. It must have been awful.'

'You don't know nothing,' she yelled. 'Fournier may as well have killed her with his own bare hands, the bastard.'

Reynolds made the mistake of placing his hand over Diane's in an apparent attempt to calm her. 'Get your hand off me, you perv.' Reynolds moved his hand away in a shot.

'You moved to England, changed your name and got yourself a job in Norwich. But all the time you were keeping tabs on the Fourniers. So when you heard they were looking for a cleaner, you handed in your notice, and with the help of

Mrs Cleverly's reference, got the job in London. So, why kill Tamsin Fournier?' asked Benedict. 'She was an innocent in all this. Surely, it was a senseless killing?'

'I wanted to make him suffer as he'd made *me* suffer,' she said, jabbing herself in the chest. 'The death of a loved one. But I underestimated him. He wasn't bothered about Tammy. I watched him. It was like I'd done him a favour. I'd done them both a favour. A mercy killing. He was still happy-go-lucky, carrying on with that stupid bitch, what's her name?'

'Angela Wheeler?'

'Yes, her,' Diane spat.

'You followed Mr Fournier on Thursday night.'

'No.'

'You attacked him not far from where Ms Wheeler lives–'

'No!'

'You stabbed him with a knife and left him to die. This is a full-on premeditated murder, Diane.'

'I keep telling you – no. That wasn't me. I wanted to kill him but I didn't.'

'I struggle with how you will come up with any accentuating circumstances for killing Mrs Fournier, a woman suffering from dementia.'

'I told you, he killed my mother,' she screamed.

Benedict's eyes locked onto Diane's. 'He did not kill her. He upset her, finishing with her may have been the straw that broke the camel's back but he did *not* kill your mother. She died by her own hand, as you know.'

Diane's fists clenched. 'No. If he'd have treated her right, she'd still be here today.'

'Your father left your mother. Don't you think that might have had more of an impact?'

'Don't mention my father.'

Benedict paused, letting the silence linger. He knew silence was often an effective means to get someone to talk even when they'd rather not.

After almost thirty seconds, she talked, her voice trembling. 'I loved my father but he... he deserted my mother and he deserted *me*. I used to beg him, let me come live with you. But he never allowed it. Not enough space, demanding new girlfriend, difficult stepsons, yada, yada, yada. He never had any room in his life for me, his only daughter.' She looked sideways, biting her lip.

'Can I ask–'

'What?'

'Your mother's affair–'

'Affair? You make it sound sordid.'

'I apologise.' He pressed on. 'Your mother's relationship with Eric Fournier. Were your parents still together at this point?'

Diane's eyes bore into Benedict's. 'No, my mother would never have been unfaithful.'

Maybe not, thought Benedict, but she had a relationship with a married man. 'How did you get on with your uncle and aunt?'

Diane considered him for a while, her eyes narrowing. Benedict held her gaze, refusing to back down. 'They were fucking retards,' Diane hissed. 'I couldn't stand it there.'

'Did they like you?'

Her laugh sounded bitter and scornful. 'Dear Uncle Jacques liked me very much.' A flicker of a smile, devoid of any warmth. 'A little too much, if you catch my drift.'

'Is that why you killed him?'

'I don't want to talk about that toerag.'

Toerag. An odd word, thought Benedict. 'You will have to one day, Diane. A woman died, still grieving her husband.'

'Huh. Aunt Violette. Mad bitch.'

'Returning to more recent events, why did you get your ex-boyfriend to steal the jewellery from the Fournier's house?'

'He was never my boyfriend.'

'Your associate then.'

'Easy money, wasn't it? We were going to go halves once I'd got rid of it. Also, I thought if she saw him taking it, it might kill her off.'

'You mean a heart attack?'

Diane laughed, a horrible raucous laugh that sent a shiver down Benedict's spine. 'Something like that.'

'But that's putting a lot of faith into an uncertainty and it's not as if you needed the money. I don't think so. I'd suggest you were trying to frame him.'

'Well, if I did, it didn't work, did it?'

'No, it didn't. Did you also set him up to steal various things from the Fournier's house earlier this year?'

Before she could respond, Mr Reynolds leaned in, his voice calm but firm, 'Diane, please remember you have the right to remain silent. You don't have to answer any questions that may incriminate you.'

Ignoring the advice, Diane said, 'I needed to test him.'

Benedict shook his head. Her attitude was astonishing. There was no sign of remorse here. She could justify everything in her mind, in her warped view of the world and the wrongs that she had suffered. 'You do appreciate, Diane, that if a jury finds you guilty of all three murders, you are unlikely to see the light of day again for several decades.'

But Diane's defiance remained unbroken. She didn't answer. She folded her arms, her head tilted to one side and stared at him. She may have only been twenty-seven, she may be slight, but Benedict couldn't remember the last time he'd felt so unnerved by a person.

Epilogue
Today

The double funeral was over and thank the Lord for that, thought Susan as she paused at the church gates and looked up at the sky – it was a beautiful day, not a single cloud. It was an astonishingly hot day. An hour earlier, she'd been pleased to go inside the church and escape the heat of the day. She saw the two coffins at the far end. She and Lizzie hadn't expected many people to turn up and sure enough, the church was almost empty. Not much of a turnout for two people who'd lived in the area for a whole decade. She spied Lizzie in the front pew. A few people turned and mouthed a hello to her as she made her way down the aisle. Susan saw one of the MacMillan nurses who occasionally visited Mum. She thanked her for coming.

She joined Lizzie. Her sister gripped her hand. 'I would have thought the funeral directors could have given us a two-for-one offer,' Lizzie said.

Susan smiled. How many people, she wondered, buried both their parents on the same day? It had to be a rare occurrence. Diane had killed them both. According to the tall detective and his blonde-haired sidekick, Diane's intention had been to pin Tammy's murder on Eric. When that didn't work out, she killed him as well. And now, apparently, the police authorities in Annecy had re-opened a case of a man found dead at the bottom of a well ten years ago. It seems Diane had been responsible for that too. Susan had never met Francine, as Diane was really called. But she had met Francine's mother, Olivia. She and her husband had been friends with her parents. And that was the problem. Olivia and Dad had an affair and when Dad finished it, Olivia killed herself.

So, now, the funeral was over and she could return to her flat and think about what the hell she was going to do with her life. She and Lizzie had decided against a wake. No one seemed to mind. Or care.

'Will you be OK, Susie?' asked Lizzie.

'Sure.' She tried to smile. 'You heading back to Bournemouth then?'

'Not straight away. Got a business meeting with a fella in Knightsbridge.'

'Sounds good.'

'Oh, you know, just floating a few ideas around. We'll see where it goes. Onwards and upwards and all that. Oh, I say, Susie, isn't that…'

Susan followed her sister's eyes and her stomach flipped. Yes, standing about seventy yards away on the other side of the street was none other than Robbie.

'Do you want me to go over there and tell him to sling his hook?' asked Lizzie.

'No, it's fine,' said Susan, her eyes still on Robbie.

He was wearing a lightweight, black coat and shiny white trainers. He looked smart in a casual way, his hair neatly combed.

Lizzie put her hand on Susan's sleeve. 'I'll see you back at the house. You sure you'll be OK?'

'It's OK.'

Lizzie put her arm around her and gave her a little squeeze.

On seeing Lizzie leave, Robbie crossed the road, checking both ways. He jogged up to her. He stopped a couple of feet away from her. 'Susan.'

'Robbie.'

He motioned at the church behind her. 'How did it go?'

'As well as can be expected.'

'Good.' He put his hands in his pockets. 'That's good. Is everything OK with…' This time he motioned at her belly.

'Yeah. I had a twenty-week scan yesterday. Everything's fine. As it should be.'

'That's good to hear. Listen…' Having said *listen*, he didn't say anything.

'What is it you want to say, Robbie?'

'Me and Margot, we've, er, we're not together any more.'

Susan hadn't expected that. 'Oh? Chuck you out, did she?'

'No, no,' he said, too quickly. 'Mutual agreement and all that.'

'So, where are you staying?'

'Sofa surfing, you know.'

'Nice. Look, I'm sorry, Robbie, but it's been a draining day for me and I need to rest up.' She patted her belly to emphasise the point. 'I'll let you know if there's anything you need to know but until then, I'll see you around.'

'Wait. Susie, wait.'

'What? What is it, Robbie?'

'Well, you know, I thought now that… you know. You and me.'

'You and me?' She took a step closer to him. 'There is no

you and me. There never was a you and me, Robbie, and there never will be. There's just me, me and the baby.'

'But, Susie, we could be a couple now.'

'No. My mother was married to a philanderer. I saw the pain it caused her. I'm not going to be like my mother. I don't need you in my life, Robbie. And nor does the baby. Now, if you'll excuse me…'

She strode away from him, her head held high, knowing he was watching her. She hadn't expected Robbie to break up with Margot, hadn't expected him to come to her cap in hand. But she'd done the right thing; she knew that with utmost certainty. No regrets. Nonetheless, her eyes welled up with tears but she was determined not to wipe them away, not while Robbie could see her. She didn't want to give him the satisfaction. She was bound to cry; it was to be expected. She'd been through a lot. Her hormones were everywhere, she was adjusting to a life as a would-be single mum, and she'd lost not one but both her parents. She turned the corner and let out a sigh of relief. She could breathe easy now. What a momentous day – she'd buried both her parents and she'd freed herself from her wastrel of a boyfriend. The future looked bright; she and Lizzie would sell the parental house and she'd have more than enough in the bank to see her through.

And, best of all, she'd gotten away with it. She'd acted on impulse, grabbed a knife from the kitchen, chased after her father and killed him in the street. She never thought she'd get away with it but she had; she'd gotten away with murder, and it felt bloody fantastic.

THE END

Novels by Joshua Black:

The DI Benedict Paige Novels

Book 1: And Then She Came Back
Book2: The Poison In His Veins
Book 3: Requiem for a Whistleblower
Book 4: The Forget-Me-Not Killer
Book 5: The Canal Boat Killer
Book 6: A Senseless Killing

To obtain Joshua's short story, *The Death of The Listening Man*, and join his Mailing List and be the first to know of future releases, etc, please go to:

rupertcolley.com/joshua-black/

Rathbone Publishing

Printed in Great Britain
by Amazon